CW00500196

THIRD COLONY

Samuel Best

This book and parts thereof may not be reproduced in any form, stored in a retrieval system, or transmitted in any form by any means—electronic, mechanical, photocopying, or otherwise—without prior written permission of the author. This is a work of fiction. Names, characters, places, and incidents are products of the author's imagination or are used fictitiously. Any similarities to actual persons, organizations, and/or events is purely coincidental.

Get Free SciFi Stories!

Copyright © 2022 Samuel Best

All rights reserved.

ISBN: 9798354379002

DEDICATION

For Rowan

GALENA

Twelve Years Ago

Farah set down the last of the crates and wiped sweat from her brow. She tilted her head up toward the bright disc of Phobis, at its zenith in the crystal blue summer sky, soaking in the warmth with closed eyes and a broad, easy grin.

Her six-month journey from Earth had been spent moving from one coldness to another: cold metal ship, cold metal floors, even colder hypergel tank for the long sleep.

We could all do with a little more sweat, she thought. No one ever atrophied in the gel, but you climbed out feeling stiff and unused.

A blast of wind and heat swayed her on her feet. She opened her eyes as the drop shuttle accelerated skyward, having just delivered its last load of supplies to the colonists. The smaller craft would dock with the Starliner *Myriad* in orbit before the mile-long ship returned to Earth. The *Myriad* was an older vessel, but it was one of the few capable of surviving the extreme conditions of Rip travel. After it shed the soaked-up radiation from its initial passage to Galena, it would pass back through the wormhole into Earth's solar system, where it would linger in orbit around Mars while the most recent bombardment of radiation dissipated from its many layered hulls.

Farah's gaze slowly dropped to the meager camp she and the other colonists had constructed.

Four squat, prefabricated structures sat in a wide circle on a low hill. They were bone white and seemed like light sources unto themselves in the harsh midday sun. Next to each sat a pile of long black crates containing supplies for the coming year — long enough for the twenty colonists to survive until the next batch of arrivals.

Kellan said it would be two hundred, at least, Farah thought. *My crew is just the advance team laying the foundation.*

She didn't mind at all. How else would she ever get the chance to be among the first on a new planet?

Hal stepped out of the nearest prefab with a sealed medical crate in his hands. Sweat shined on his bald head, streaming down his red cheeks and into his bushy, silver-streaked brown beard.

"Just gonna stand there with your mouth open?" he asked with a grin as he walked to the dedicated medical prefab. He ducked through the low doorway and popped back out a moment later, wiping his hands on his dark blue coverall, still smiling.

"I was just thinking all this exercise will do us good," Farah replied casually. "Especially you."

He let out a loud, "*Haw!*" and slapped his stomach, which pushed modestly against the fabric of his snug coverall.

"Careful you don't get sunburned," he warned

half-jokingly as he walked away, down the hill. "This isn't—"

"—Mars," she finished at the same time, rolling her eyes. She'd heard it from him and half a dozen others twice as many times since they passed through the Rip.

Hal laughed again as he trudged away, making another trip to the drop site for more crates.

Farah stepped into the relative coolness of the medical prefab to begin organizing equipment. She pulled damp auburn hair back in a ponytail and went through the inventory lists, checking off a year's worth of supplies for twenty people.

Moses delivered more crates while she worked, then came Daria, Jakob, Arshan, and Hal once more, all sweating as they lugged the heavy containers. He spared her the jests on his second trip, instead telling her they were cooking lunch at the drop site and it would be ready soon.

Farah sighed, in no hurry to endure overdone soy steak. She was not alone in her desperate hope that Galena would yield some savory local fruit or vegetable that would replace the bland and chalky soyflower derivatives most of Earth had been stuck with for decades.

Even a medical professional like her — with two doctorates — couldn't sustainably afford more than a few heads of lettuce from a Mars hydroponics facility each month. The rest of the time she ate processed soyflower that was supposed to look like meatballs or pasta or — and this was a *true* abomination — ice cream.

Farah set down her workpad and went back

outside, unable to keep herself from the fresh air of a new planet.

The heart of their future colony at the top of the hill offered a panoramic view of the surrounding forest. Ashen trunks without bark stood ramrod straight, like sentinels spaced at near-precise seven-meter intervals. They reached toward the sky with three thick branches, naked as their trunks. Between the trees, dark silver-gray boulders dotted the landscape, stuck into the soft, moist ground at odd angles. Far to the east, two large mountains loomed high, their peaks seeming to fade into the atmosphere.

Galena wasn't just unlike Earth, Farah realized. It was diametrically opposed to it: blue instead of gray; light instead of dark; filled with hope instead of despair. Water still ran freely here. There was *life*. That was part of the reason she had left Earth for Mars nearly a decade before. It had meant living in artificial environments while she finished her second doctorate, but Farah preferred recycled canned air to thick blankets of daily smog. Mars boasted living arboretums with plants now extinct on Earth, as well as pedestrian promenades where she could visit a bookstore or buy groceries without worrying about getting mugged on the walk home.

She was just beginning to feel the first pangs of restlessness on the red planet when her application to take part in the first Galena mission was accepted. Kellan McEwan, one of the key project managers, had made the trip to Mars personally to offer her the job as lead medical officer. What else could she say but yes?

Two years later, her dream had become reality.

Despite her reluctance to chew on yet another soy patty, Farah followed her nose (at the behest of her growling stomach) to the small field where the shuttle had dropped off an impressive pyramid of supply crates. Next to the pyramid, most of the other colonists sat or stood in a wide circle talking to those they had most connected with before arriving on this new world.

Smoke rose from a solar grill as Devan slapped at the charred soy steaks with his spatula and worked what magic he could to make them palatable. He wore a dirty white apron and a limp chef's hat, and loudly sang an off-key song in French while flames danced around his spatula.

"I'm starting to have second thoughts about our choice of chef," said Martine as she walked over to Farah.

"To his credit, he does try *very* hard," Farah replied.

Martine's short, raven-black hair was slicked back with sweat. She was a member of the security detail, and her crew had been trudging through the woods since the first shuttle landed, scouting their surroundings.

"Find anything out there?" asked Farah.

"Trees and rocks," Martine answered. "Freshwater springs, though I don't know how it's not tainted with all this lead sulfide." She gestured to a nearby silver-gray boulder. "We tested it."

"I'd forgotten what fresh water tasted like. No beasties?"

"Seems like Kellan told the truth, so long as we

stay out of the oceans."

"Jeff says we can't trust him."

Martine squeezed Farah's shoulder. "I'm glad you have such a good friend to look out for you, but I hope he's wrong." She walked over to talk to Hassan, another member of the security team.

Devan belted out a verse and flipped a soy steak in the air. It bounced off the side of his spatula and spun to the ground. Without missing a beat, he scooped it up and bit into it, letting it hang from his mouth while he continued humming and cooking.

Hal and his tall, thin wife Elaine climbed to the top of the pyramid, using the stacked boxes like wide steps, and hoisted the top-most crate between them. The other colonists gathered round as husband and wife descended and dropped the crate on the soft ground. Hal opened it to a chorus of appreciation. Three bottles of whiskey appeared, along with cups, which were quickly filled and distributed.

Farah was handed a cup half-full. She joined the others in a toast to their new home, and sat on the warm ground to sip the whiskey and await her soy steak.

The sky had been dark for hours by the time she finally crawled into her canvas tent. Proper housing structures would arrive on the next shipment in a year's time. Until then, the colonists were roughing it.

Farah closed her eyes, and sleep enveloped her quickly.

She awoke in the middle of the night. Someone snored softly from a neighboring tent. Farah emerged from her own slowly, stretching her back and looking up at the stars.

The air had cooled only slightly after Phobis dropped below the horizon. Standing next to her tent in shorts and thin t-shirt, she wasn't the least bit cold.

Twin nebulae painted the western night sky, stretching long purplish fingers across the glittering firmament. The moon wasn't up, but the landscape glowed in the starlight all the same. Nearby, she heard the trickling of a stream — but no insects. There had been none on Mars, either, but she would often fall asleep to a recording of Earth's extinct rainforests and all of their noisy inhabitants.

Permanent electricity would eventually come to the colony, she knew, yet it wasn't something that was promised in the beginning. Once more colonists arrived, hydroelectric dams would be installed.

Farah's tent was huddled near the others on the side of the low hill. She climbed the short distance to the top and stood beside the medical prefab. On an impulse, she scrambled up the side of the squat building to stand on its roof as a warm, gentle breeze played with her hair.

A stone clacked softly nearby. Beyond a flat patch of mossy ground at the base of the hill, she spotted Jarod near a tree, kicking at the dirt. His dark blue coverall blended into the night, but his pale white hands and bald head glowed in the starlight. He was on sentry duty that night, and he was always turning over stones in a seemingly futile hunt for insects. None had been seen since their arrival.

Jarod kicked another stone and continued on, following a wide circuit around the hill. A few moments later, he thought better of it, sat with his back against a tree, crossed his arms over his chest, and closed his eyes.

Farah sighed. She would wake him with the tip of her boot just as soon as she was done enjoying the peace and quiet.

She spied the stream she had heard near her tent, babbling calmly over mossy rocks as it wove a thin path into the forest. The stream seemed to end at a low cliff rising no more than a meter off the ground. Extending into the foreseeable distance beyond the short cliff wall, the ground had changed while Farah slept. It was supposed to be soft and moist — organic, like what surrounded the prefabricated building on which she stood.

Now it was an endless plateau of hard geometric facets that reflected the starlight in small, flat hexagons depending on how they were angled.

Farah's brow knit in confusion when the shin-high cliff wall *moved,* as if the plateau of land behind it were sliding like a rigid sheet across Galena's surface. The cliff wall crept closer to the hill, swallowing up a few more inches of the stream.

An animal the size of her lunch plate separated itself from the mass and skittered sideways like a crab across the stream on a blur of segmented legs. The six edges of its shell formed a perfect hexagon. It rejoined the moving cliff wall a few meters down, locking into place, linking its geometric top shell with the others that formed the unbroken landmass steadily crawling toward the camp.

"Martine," Farah whispered, her voice catching in her throat. "Hal. Jarod."

She strained to cry out, but her windpipe seemed no wider than a pin.

A crack split the approaching cliff wall, extending back like a fissure. The landmass parted as thousands upon thousands of hexagon-shelled organisms flowed around the low hill as if they were water moving past a river boulder...

...except this was happening in slow motion. Farah could see their chitinous legs churning under their great linked shell as they surrounded the meager colony.

"*MARTINE!*" Farah shrieked, finding her voice at last.

A scream pierced the night air in response. She turned in time to catch a glimpse of Jarod's pale white hand before he was pulled beneath the dark edge of the moving landmass.

Hal fell out of his tent blindly onto the wet ground, canvas flapping behind him. He stumbled up the hill at the sound of her voice, rubbing sleep from his eyes. Others were not so quick, but they emerged from their tents one by one to squint into the night.

Martine and Devan emerged half-dressed from another prefab.

"What?" she asked breathlessly. "What is it?"

Farah could only point down the hill. Martine climbed atop the medical prefab with her while Devan and Hal spoke quietly below.

"I don't see—" Martine said before stopping short. She spun in place to look behind her. "It's surrounding the hill."

Farah turned slowly. The mass of oversized crabs had come back together on the opposite side of the hill, isolating the colonists on an island surrounded by an ocean of alien organisms.

"What is it?!" Hal shouted. Elaine ran to him and they held each other tightly.

The mass of crabs slowly crawled up the hill, shrinking the area of uncovered land inch by inch.

"Get everyone out of the tents!" Martine yelled as she jumped down and ran into a prefab.

"They're out!" someone called back.

The remaining colonists scrambled up the hill and clustered together between the prefabs. Farah looked down at them helplessly, unable to think of what to say.

Martine reappeared with a weapon in her hands — a blend of metal rifle and grappling hook. An electric hum filled the air as she marched down the hill, toward the approaching line of hexagonal crabs.

She braced the weapon against her waist. An arc of electricity exploded from the grappling hook and scoured the conjoined shells like a lightning whip. The arc split into several electric snakes that crawled and leapt across the shells, frying the organisms beneath and sending up swirls of black smoke.

The ones with blackened shells sank lower and were trampled over by their neighbors as the mass moved to fill in the gaps.

Martine let loose another arc to a similar result. On her third squeeze of the trigger, the weapon fizzled. She hurled it onto the continent of hard shells with a curse and retreated to join the others.

"On top!" Hal yelled as he charged the approaching line.

Elaine screamed at him to come back as he leaped into the air. Hal cleared the edge of the shells and landed firmly on two feet, running like he was on solid ground. There was a brief moment when he turned back to look at Elaine, and he opened his mouth to speak — and then the shells separated beneath him. His legs kicked briefly in midair as he fell into the pit. Elaine's screams cut off abruptly as the shells came back together, swallowing the cries of her husband.

Farah was alone atop the medical prefab. Between her own quick breaths, the churning movement of the crab legs was a constant whisper. She hugged herself as the open circle of ground crowning the hill shrank, and shrank.

The cliff wall rose around them, up and up and up it went, as if someone was lifting a blanket to smother the hill — only the underside of this blanket was covered with a billion scrabbling, clawing segmented limbs, each as long as a human forearm.

"Everyone get inside!" Martine shouted, but Farah barely heard. She was frozen in place like most of the other colonists, staring at the rising curtain of long crustacean legs that surrounded them.

The crabs came together overhead, their shells interlocking seamlessly to blot out the stars. As the solid blanket of whispering legs lowered slowly onto Farah and the others, someone screamed — but not her.

I won't scream, she promised herself as she stood paralyzed, quaking in the darkness. *I won't I won't I—*

The sharp tip of a leg scratched her shoulder, and she broke her promise.

KELLAN

The six shipyards orbiting Earth were built by Diamond Aerospace under contract with the United States Government in anticipation of a Great Human Expansion throughout the cosmos. Starliners and other massive ships of the void could not be launched from the surface of our little blue-green planet — and one couldn't ferry more than a dozen souls on the smaller freighters — so orbital infrastructure took top priority for "the future". As the top emerging private space company of its age, Diamond Aerospace was granted the contract.

The shipyards were massive, hollow egg-shaped containers, slightly squeezed in the middle.

It was inside these shipyards that the crafts were built which would take humans through the Rip — a hole in the fabric of space that plunked them down a short journey away from a habitable planet: Galena.

Kellan McEwan's eyes swept over the long lines of the *Renata.* The elongated vessel dominated the center of the shipyard. Smaller than a gargantuan starliner, but faster to build, its two bell-shaped engines would provide enough thrust to make the trip to Galena in just under seven months. As long as the ship could handle the stresses of Rip travel and could get him and his cargo to the other world, Kellan didn't care if it was no bigger than a school bus.

He floated weightlessly, keeping a firm grip on the moving handrail as it pulled him along a track toward the boarding station. The long viewing hallway ringed the interior circumference of the shipyard, connecting the many offices, dormitories, and cafeterias inside the thick walls of the shell.

Kellan had been waiting eight years for the completion of the next Rip-capable starship. Ever since the *Halcyon* was lost on Galena, nothing but drones had traveled through the wormhole. Without the anemic yet vital tourist income from rich elites sightseeing through the Rip, there was no hope of building another ship. Kellan had failed to convince his government superiors that Galena was a project worth funneling hundreds of billions of much-needed dollars into — even with rock-solid proof from probe satellite imagery showing that some of the colonists had survived.

Two failed attempts to solidify a human presence on another world, and what did he have to show for it? The first of those colonies was wiped off the map and, on the second attempt, a starliner valued in the hundreds of trillions crashed.

His pet project of seeding humanity to the stars seemed dead in the water...until he had managed to secure the funds for his latest venture.

Just ahead, along the viewing hallway, the boarding station protruded from the inner shell of the shipyard like a tumor. It was a single room inside a transparent bulge that funneled visitors from Earth-launched vessels onto whatever ship carried them away on the next leg of their journey to Mars or the twin luxury cities on the moon. Kellan had carefully chosen his departure time to coincide with shift change, when most workers were already in their sleeping quarters or eating in the mess hall.

Outside of the boarding station bubble, a well-used construction shuttle waited to take him to the *Renata*.

As the moving handrail brought him to the boarding station entrance, Kellan grinned at the pile of storage containers stacked like a pyramid in the middle. He floated through the entrance and waited for the gradual pull from the in-floor GravGens to anchor him to a solid surface.

He landed lightly on the soles of his boots and smoothed down his bright red hair. Two men were inspecting the crates.

"Everything ready, Felix?" he asked the shorter of the two men. Kellan's Scottish accent was high and clipped.

The man had slicked-back hair and a sharp nose. He shared a quick glance with his bald, hulking colleague, Janos, before walking to Kellan — over whom he towered by nearly a full head.

"The rich men are on board, sir, but there's a problem."

Kellan noticed the man was sweating, despite the cold.

"Out with it, Felix," he prompted.

"They've shut us down, sir. I've only just received the notice."

He handed Kellan a digipad and pointed to a block of text on the screen.

"This is a cease and desist order," Kellan

responded calmly. "The government is reappropriating the Renata for a transport mission to Mars. It seems they've had second thoughts about our wild ideations." He offered the digipad back to Felix, who took it with a confused look on his face. Then he glanced around the boarding station, his beady black eyes landing on the pyramid of crates. "What else needs to be loaded?"

Janos shrugged his massive shoulders. "Just these crates, and us."

Kellan thought for a brief moment.

"No Rip-capable vessel can be remotely controlled from the outside, is that correct?" he asked. "The radiation shielding is too thick."

"Yes, sir..."

"And when was this notice sent?"

Felix tapped the screen and swiped to the side. "Just five minutes ago, sir."

Kellan checked his watch, which was synced to Orbital Standard Time.

"The nearest administrative office is about two klicks around the interior shell," he said. "Which means..."

"There!" Felix shouted, pointing.

Far along the perimeter viewing tunnel, half a dozen security personnel approached from the direction of the admin office, armored fists gripping the moving handrail. Kellan estimated they would be to the boarding station in less than five minutes.

He bent down and picked up a storage crate.

"Don't just stand there," he said to the others as he hurried toward the airlock. "Get these on the shuttle!"

The three men loaded the crates into the airlock and sealed the door. As they waited for the cycle to complete, Kellan watched the security guards approaching. They pulled themselves along the moving rail hand-over-hand, speeding toward the boarding station.

The door leading to the shuttle opened behind them. The GravGens in the floor disengaged. Kellan, Felix, and Janos drifted up, weightless, the crates slowly spinning between them.

"Get us out of here," said Kellan.

Felix nodded and pulled himself toward the cockpit while Kellan and Janos pushed the crates into the shuttle. When the last of the containers was accounted for, Kellan and Janos drifted inside.

Kellan sealed the airlock and shouted, "Now, Felix!"

The shuttle detached instantly, pulling away from the boarding station just as the security personnel emerged from the viewing hallway and transitioned to gravity. One of them went immediately to a control desk.

Kellan followed after Felix, leaving Janos alone with the slowly-tumbling storage crates.

"How long before they take control?" he asked.

"They're already trying," said Felix, tapping quickly on his panel. A flood of remote override attempts lit up the screen.

"Pass control to the Renata," said Kellan. "Use autopilot."

Felix smiled wickedly and swiped through several screens, then mashed a large red button. The override attempts instantly cut out, and he whistled appreciatively.

"Good idea...but can we still open the shipyard door?"

Kellan stared in awe at the *Renata* as the small docking shuttle crossed the vast gulf between the boarding station and the awaiting ship.

"They'll open it for us," he said as his eyes traced the contours of the sleek *Renata*. "Either that or we crash a hybrid fusion drive into the wall."

Kellan patted Felix on the shoulder and drifted back to check on the crates. Inside them rested the technology to shape Galena's future — and perhaps all of humanity's as well.

Some eggs would most likely have to be cracked along the way to make the omelet, but Kellan was willing to endure his seemingly never-ending stream of losses in order to achieve his goal.

He only hoped the colonists would feel the same way. *After all,* he thought, *they don't have much choice.*

MERRITT

Eight years since the crash and Merritt still got lost in the forest. Two miles out from the colony was the limit of his geography. He had gone ranging with the hunters once or twice, but nothing about the local forest landscape stuck with him enough to become a permanent map in his mind.

Phobis was low enough on the horizon to remain hidden behind mountains and trees. The soft glow of its yellow morning light seemed to emanate from the pale dawn sky itself. Merritt maintained a general eastern course by knowing where it would pop up on the horizon. Yet without following one of the three irrigation pipes leading to and from the colony, he would've had the near-impossible task of navigating a trackless path through kilometers of identical Galena trees.

They grew no moss on their pale, barkless trunks. Spaced almost without fail at intervals of seven meters, their uniform appearance — smooth gray-white pillars crowned by three heavy taproots jutting out like polished claws — offered no help to wayfinders. The taproots all had the same single joint halfway from the trunk, with the tapered end bent sharply toward the sky. Even to the more observant, the trees were indistinguishable from each other.

One had to hope for a damaged trunk for any kind of landmark, or make the mark themselves.

Merritt tightened the straps on his heavy backpack and checked the charge on his stunner. The staff-like weapon had an oversized tuning fork on one end and a battery pack on the other to balance the weight. The tuning fork looked harmless enough — until he pressed a button and a hundred million volts arced between the prongs.

He slid his calloused palm across the trunk of a tree as he passed, the cool wood rasping like sandpaper. Despite twenty hours of sunlight during Galena's summer, the tree trunks never warmed.

The colonists called it wood, but the hard gray exterior was more akin to hardened sponge. After the colony had been firmly established, the naming of things had become more important to its inhabitants than Merritt expected. Over time, he realized a certain comfort could be derived from the simple act of knowing an object's name. It made the world less alien.

Many enjoyed discovering Earth analogues for plants and animals on Galena, even if the comparisons were less than half-accurate. Rock bats, for example, got their name because they lived in large stone pillars and were slightly larger than giant bats, yet they didn't fly and had long spikes for tails. The resemblance stopped at their dull brown color and thin gliding membrane between each of their four legs.

Behind Merritt, the sound of a boot-sole scraping over stone froze him in place. A moment later, his son, Gavin, stepped beside him gripping his own stunner, silent as he had been before his misstep.

Sorry, Gavin signed reluctantly when Merritt wouldn't stop looking at him. His hands moved rapidly in annoyance as he formed the words, the sleeves of his long, dark green coat swishing. *I'll be more careful. Can we go?*

Merritt looked away when his son's cheeks flushed with embarrassment.

Gavin had lost his ability to speak shortly after his second birthday. Birthrates across Earth had been plummeting for years by then, but even the parents lucky enough to have a baby would soon face a graver concern. A global outbreak of fungal spinal meningitis afflicted one out of every three children, claiming nearly half the lives of those it touched. The doctors had told Merritt that Gavin was lucky to lose nothing more than his voice. Many, many other children and their parents were not so fortunate.

The source of the disease had never been identified. Many suspected it was linked to the meteor shower that tainted Earth's arable land, making new crop growth impossible.

Galena's soil, on the contrary, was so rich it was almost pungent. Plants took root wherever a native seed fell. Merritt and the other farmers had far less luck with seeds brought from Earth — but that was changing.

Merritt turned his attention back to his son.

One wrong move and we die out here, he signed, his hands moving deliberately. Gavin watched them, his jaw muscles working as he clenched his teeth.

A flurry of signing from Gavin: *You don't have to remind me.*

If you want to see your seventeenth birthday, Merritt replied, *you focus. Soft steps, clear mind.*

Gavin rolled his eyes and walked past his father, favoring his right leg. The bones of his left — along with many of his ribs — had been crushed by a falling stack of supply crates not long after the colonists were stranded on Galena. Thanks to the quick actions of Dr. Leera James and the restorative abilities of a native healing moss, Gavin made a miraculous recovery. His ribs and his left femur, tibia, and fibula had healed smoothly, unlike the ligaments in his left knee. As a result, he was stuck with a slight, yet permanent, limp.

The ground of Galena was usually very forgiving to those wishing for silence. Most of it was a blanket of soft, moist plant matter woven together over loose soil like moss. Even with heavy boots, footfalls were muffled.

Father and son were dressed the same: long moss-green coats to keep them warm should they be out past nightfall, with black padded utility pants and long-sleeved gray thermal shirts. At a distance, they even looked the same: jaw-length dark brown hair framed square faces, the brows of which spent more time knit in thought than relaxed. Yet Merritt was broader in the chest and shoulders, with thick legs, while his son was a balanced mix of his father and mother: slender, yet growing stronger by the day.

Several months ago, Gavin started showing the first hints of beard shadow. He scratched at it from time to time, mostly to check if it was still there. Razors were in short supply, so Merritt's beard fluctuated between scruff and wild. Now it was shorn close to his cheeks, which did nothing to prevent the cold sting of the occasional harsh winter winds. He decided he would let it grow over the course of Galena's two-month cold season and cut it back in the spring before the next planting.

Perhaps aware of their resemblance, Gavin usually kept his hair slicked back. For reasons unknown to Merritt (but which he guessed were related to one of Gavin's two peers), his son wouldn't go as far as cutting it off. When he wore it down, as he did now, it often gave his face a dark, brooding cast — especially when he was angry or deep in thought.

Merritt stopped and carefully scuffed the soft ground with the tip of his steel-toed boot until a section of dull gray pipe became visible. He knelt down and put his ear to the pipe that he and others from the colony had buried seven years ago during a hot Galena summer.

Gavin looked back as Merritt stood.

Still no water, Merritt signed. *We haven't hit the breach.*

It was a treefall, Gavin signed confidently. *Or a root has grown into the pipe. Or maybe the spring dried up.*

Merritt nodded. *I hope you're right,* he replied. Then he grinned. *But that wouldn't make a very exciting story to tell Shurri, now would it?*

Gavin's cheeks flushed red and he looked away. Merritt's smile broadened. Ever since his son became a teenager, it was too easy to get a reaction — especially when it came to the only girl his age in the colony.

Still grinning, he softly patted the reinforced

leather shoulder of Gavin's coat as he walked past to take the lead.

The pipe was easier to follow where it hadn't been deeply buried. The job of laying nearly three miles of repurposed irrigation pipe in three diverging runs hadn't elicited zealous enthusiasm. This was before the colonists had fully mapped the hex crab migration patterns or realized how to avoid the ravenous attention of the predatory sky beasts. During the first two years after the colony was established, wandering too far was considered a death sentence.

As a result, the pipes had been buried deep when it was convenient and barely at all when it was not. Merritt was secretly pleased that he and Gavin were following a length of it that had merely been set on the ground and covered with a faint dusting of soil.

Gavin stopped next to him, holding his breath. Merritt did the same, glancing sideways at his son. Gavin's finger pointed slowly to his own ear.

The forest was silent, as usual. To his knowledge, neither insects nor anything resembling small birds called Galena home. Natural sounds in the forest came from seasonal winds or the quiet bubbling of freshwater springs, filtered of their lead sulfide impurities by a dense underground canopy sprouting from the upside-down tops of multitudinous pale-trunked trees.

Merritt cocked his head when he heard something else — something that didn't belong.

From farther along the run of pipe, on the other side of a slight rise, came a wet noise of drinking. Long, deep slurps broke the silence of the forest, paused, then repeated.

Merritt tapped Gavin's stunner as he flicked on his own. It gently vibrated in his hands. The flat tuning fork prongs crackled with electricity.

Gavin swallowed hard and took a moment to find the power button on his own weapon. For a brief moment, all of his boyish bravado evaporated and he seemed to realize that no fallen tree had broken the pipe.

Merritt stepped forward slowly, using the tree trunks between him and the source of the unusual sound for cover. As he moved, he asked himself the same question Gavin had asked before they left the colony: *Why are we going alone?*

Because you and I hardly ever talk anymore, Merritt answered in his mind, playing out an imaginary conversation with his son. *Because we used to do everything together, and now you're always with your two friends.*

Yet, as he drew closer to the noise, he began to feel extremely foolish for turning down Corporal Miles Turner's offer to send along two of his security staff.

"Just in case," Miles had said with an easy grin.

I guess overconfidence runs in the family, thought Merritt.

The wet sounds of drinking stopped abruptly. A soft gurgling of water grew louder.

Merritt stepped around a tree and froze.

A leathery brown beast twice his height and at least three times as long stared directly at him out of silver eyes the size of dinner plates. When Gavin stepped next to his father, the beast's head flicked like a bird's to study the new arrivals. Between its eyes, a blunted pyramidal beak opened to reveal a red mouth, then snapped shut with a loud *CLACK*. Its head was as bald as a vulture's, resting on a wide and powerful neck that connected to a thin, elongated torso. Thick quills on its back — twice as tall as Merritt — lifted up as the beast puffed out its ribbed chest in a threatening posture. Its four massive leathery wings were folded up like bony legs, and it used its razored talons like feet. Veiny flying membranes sprouted from its folded limbs and swept backward like translucent sails.

It's the big flier, Gavin signed with subdued movements, keeping his hands close to his body.

Sky Beast, thought Merritt.

There had been a years-long debate about whether there was more than one. Leera had seen a flash of its eye when it attacked her transport shuttle after the crash. Another colonist had wandered from a scouting mission near the mountains and was never seen again. Others in the group reported they had only heard the beating of enormous wings.

As a general rule, the beast kept to the twin mountains west of the colony and to the skies over the eastern ocean. It seemed to actively avoid the direct route between the two points over colony farmland, save for the extremely rare passage at night on the way to its ocean hunting grounds — yet it was always seen alone.

What do we do? Gavin signed.

Merritt squeezed his stunner with both hands and took a deep breath.

The creature opened its beak wide and snapped

it shut again as a warning, bobbing its head. Its long throat shivered. At its taloned feet, water flowed freely from a jagged hole in the irrigation pipe.

Injured, Gavin signed. *Back wing*.

Merritt noticed the dark wet patch of blood on the creature's back near a hind joint. One of its back wings connected to its torso at an unnatural angle. Merritt's eyes darted over the tops of nearby trees until he saw one with broken taproots on its crown. The creature had probably come down hard during a wounded flight, sensed water flowing through the underground pipe, and cracked it open.

Gavin took a step toward the beast and it screeched an ear-piercing *brrrraAWWK!* Membranes inside its mouth vibrated with the sound and its whole body seemed to swell.

It stumbled from the effort, its injured wing flapping. Its body hit the soft ground with a dull thud.

"*Now!*" Merritt shouted. "Drive it back!"

He ran forward with Gavin close on his heels. A thin film slid over the creature's silvery eyes as they approached. It turned its back, and Merritt thought it would run. Instead, it kept turning, using momentum to swing one of its winged limbs like a club. Gavin ducked but it hit Merritt square in the chest, sending him flying backward.

Gavin rolled forward and shoved the tip of his stunner staff into the creature's underbelly as Merritt slammed into a tree trunk and fell to the ground. Blisteringly bright arcs of white energy crackled from Gavin's stunner against leathery skin.

The beast howled. Merritt was sure the colonists would hear such an alien noise as they worked their farms.

Gavin jumped to his feet and shoved the stunner forward. The tip glanced off the creature's back as it limped out of range.

Groaning, Merritt used his stunner as a crutch to stand. He hobbled forward, barely able to draw a breath. Together, he and Gavin drove the beast back from the broken water pipe with crackling stunners, farther away from the colony. All of its fight was gone. Its pained scream morphed into high-pitched whining, then it fell silent as it limped over a rise and out of sight.

We should kill it, Gavin signed. He stared in the direction of the beast, breathing hard.

It will die on its own, his father replied.

Smarter to do it now, when it's injured, Gavin signed. *What if it gets hungry and comes back to the farms?*

Merritt struggled to catch his breath while he studied his son. Gavin returned his gaze. The boy was neither filled with bloodlust nor being needlessly defiant, which was sometimes the case in recent months.

We have lookouts, Merritt signed weakly. He stumbled and Gavin caught his arm.

With his son's help, Merritt walked back to the broken pipe. He kept one arm firmly over his ribcage, sure that something had snapped, as Gavin eased him down to the ground.

"You know what this means, don't you?" Merritt hissed between clenched teeth, still clutching his chest.

Yeah, Gavin signed, trying to suppress a grin. *It*

means you have an excuse to sleep in on harvest day.

“Not only that,” Merritt said. He didn’t bother hiding his smile as he shrugged off his backpack with a grunt and tipped it toward Gavin. “You get to fix the pipe.”

LEERA

Two continents roughly the size of Australia sat on opposing sides of Galena. Between them were countless rivers, streams, and tributaries delineated by narrow strips of land.

Probe imagery had shown a small ocean in the northern hemisphere, bordered to its north by a polar ice cap and to the south by a mountain range that extended along the northern border of one continent. The colonists named it the Northern Ocean.

Galena's second, and larger, ocean straddled the equator and covered a vast swath of surface east of the colony, beyond the Casmin Sea. Its long fingers reached halfway around the planet before thinning to rivers that fed verdant plains.

Dr. Leera James dipped her bare toes into the cold water of the Casmin, a longitudinally narrow body of water stretching north and east of the colony and surrounded by mossland. Its eastern border — just visible to her on a perfectly clear morning over the tumultuous surface of the Casmin — gave way to the larger of Galena's two oceans, which the colonists had taken to calling the Equatorial.

The pull of Galena's moon — closer to its parent than Earth's own — was so great on the tide that even the smaller seas like the Casmin held unbreaking waves. Four-story triangular walls of water rose from wind-slashed surfaces, trapped in perpetual stasis and unable to crash down into the roiling gray mass below.

As a cold and constant wind whipped her shoulder-length gray hair, Leera shielded her eyes from the piercing morning light of Galena's star, Phobis, on the eastern horizon and squinted toward the ocean. In the distance, static waves appeared as receding pyramid silhouettes against a bright blue sky.

Frigid water sloshed against her ankles. Leera shivered despite her thermal vest, knit undershirt, and padded utility pants, yet didn't retreat. She liked it there, by the water. The rivers, streams, and seas of Galena were safe for swimming (as far as anyone knew), and therefore she relished every opportunity to indulge.

Yet the oceans were another story.

Massive beasts larger than any Earth had ever known rolled in the depths, rising to feed on swarms of fish-like creatures in late afternoon. Their slicked, golden bodies disturbed the surface to feed. Leera's colleagues still told stories of the unfortunate people whose escape pods from the falling ship *Halcyon* had splashed down into the ocean instead of on land. Those would-be colonists had been swallowed mere moments after emerging from their pods.

Three years ago, two colony residents — an aging couple — had ended their own lives by wading into the Equatorial Ocean and being swallowed whole. Witnesses saw a spout of water followed by a great splash. When the water settled, the swimmers were gone.

The leviathans usually fed on fish — but Galena fish only lived in the oceans. The seas and waterways were curiously devoid of anything larger than an Earth minnow.

Willef — the stout foreman from the *Halcyon* — had worked out a way to set trap nets off anchored rafts in shallow seawater just before dawn. As long as he collected the net contents before midday, he never saw so much as a bubble rise from below. One or two rafts had vanished in the four years he'd been fishing, but he claimed no one could prove it was — as he called them — the sea monsters.

Leera's attention was torn from the horizon as a gentle stream of bubbles disturbed the water a meter from her feet. An orange blob appeared from below, and the helmet of a multipurpose Constellation Mark VI space suit broke the surface — one of four suits recently recovered from a new-found debris site at the base of the twin mountains.

Niku Tedani walked out of the Casmin Sea, his boots sinking into black sand as water sloughed from the suit. He slid the lock at the base of his helmet and popped it off. Though the water of the sea was frigid, and the depths he explored were colder still, his straight black hair lay plastered to his forehead with sweat.

Leera remained silent while he unclipped his weight belt and let it fall to the sand. He gladly accepted a bottle of spring water and drank it down in a few seconds.

"I found something," he said at last, still breathing heavily. A genuine grin spread across his broad, tanned face.

Leera crossed her arms to shield her numb hands against a sudden blast of icy wind.

"What?" she asked eagerly, unable to speak her hope aloud for fear of cursing it.

Finding the space suits had been like reaching treasure at the end of a rainbow. Supplies and other oddments would occasionally make their way back to the colony after someone discovered a few scattered crates in the forest, but often they were of little to no practical use — items fit for a space voyage, but not for life on a new planet. Leera had immediately realized that the Constellation suits represented a way to explore Galena's bodies of water. Her scientific profession as a systems biologist had run into a few dead ends since becoming a resident of a new world, but none so great as being unable to take a closer look at life underwater.

"A passage," said Niku.

"A...what?" she asked.

"Tunnel."

He turned and pointed along the eastern shore, several hundred meters from where they stood.

"I'd say it's about there. Smooth, circular entrance, a little taller than me, wide enough for three people. Seems to run in a straight line toward the ocean."

"Straight line?" Leera repeated. "As in unnatural?"

Niku's smile returned as she caught on. His work in microbiology hadn't been stymied by lack of equipment to delve into the depths. He claimed to have enough work for ten lifetimes by doing little more than skimming new samples from the water's surface once a year.

Yet an eight-year sober Niku was a restless one, and Leera hadn't been surprised when he volunteered to wear the Mark VI.

"Suit needs a recharge," he said, "but I'd like to go back in, see where it leads."

"We could follow it from above," Leera offered. "Try to find the exit that way."

"That's not as fun."

"It's also not as dangerous."

He waved her off playfully.

"What would Uda think?" Leera half-scolded.

"She practically shoved me out of the house when I said I was thinking about volunteering."

"And little Toma?"

Niku's smile was unshakeable. "He would come, too, if we had a suit small enough."

Leera stared at the choppy sea, thinking. "I'll ask Miles to loan us a couple of his guards." She held up her hands to stop Niku's protest before it could begin. "There are four suits. We need to be safe."

"It's not the extra company," Niku said, wiping beads of water off his helmet. "It's the delay." He sighed. "But, as you always say, better safe than dead."

"I say that?"

He shrugged. "Maybe not in so many words. Projection through action."

They fell into step together as they turned back toward the colony.

"You mean projection through *in*action," said Leera.

Niku thought about it for a moment. "Uda says that not doing something can be the best choice. It runs counter to my instincts, but those were never a hundred percent reliable in the first place."

Leera smiled. "Smart woman. But you won't tell Toma, will you?"

"That not doing something is a choice? Of course not. He'll figure it out eventually...just not before he starts working the farm."

They carried on in a similar manner during the long walk to the colony. Between her work, his work, and his family, they never lacked for conversation. Their shared adventure on a new world born from a terrifying crash landing and numerable tragic losses had hardened their friendship to the point where their existences were, to each other, as natural a fixture as the rising sun.

The easternmost farms of the colony came into view first, appearing as a distant patchwork quilt sloping down a broad hill. Without the natural sunshield provided by the western hills just before the river, the eastern farms sat exposed to the beating rays of Phobis an extra five hours a day. Eight years of fine-tuned irrigation leveled the playing field, leaving a farmer's skill as the only variable.

As such, the first farms Leera and Niku passed between were lush with tall stands of soyflower stalks and budding vegetables in shades of green and orange and light brown, while those farther up and down the eastern border varied in their shades of sunburnt crop. All of it remained edible, for the time being, but that didn't mean it was preferred.

"The Alders certainly set a fine example," Niku

observed as he crouched down on soft soil. He gently worked his fingers around a leafy green stem and pulled up a skinny carrot with a snap of roots. After a quick dusting, he crunched off the the tip and nodded appreciatively.

"Gavin seems to have the knack," Leera acknowledged, watching Niku bite off more of the carrot. "Should you be doing that?"

He stood and they continued their walk.

"If it wasn't for the seeds Merritt's wife gave him, we'd be eating nothing but soy paste," he told her. "I think it's a source of pride for him."

Leera glanced at him from the corner of her eye, and Niku chuckled.

"I've asked him, and he said it's fine. Besides, the company men are gone, and the farmers' crop debt to pay for the journey has been forgotten."

It had been years since Leera thought of the company wardens that made it down to Galena's surface after the crash. Like more than a few others, they hadn't survived for long — leaving the colonists in charge of their own colony.

A child shouted from within a dense patch of soyflower stalks nearby. Niku clapped his hands and crouched down with a happy shout as a little boy burst from the corn-like stalks and flew into his father's arms. He had the same wide face and near-perpetual smile, coupled with the tight curly hair and deep olive skin of his mother, Uda.

"You've been a good boy?" Niku asked, tickling his son to delighted howls of laughter. "You've been helping?"

"Yes!" Toma finally managed to shout between

laughs.

Niku stood and dropped the boy onto his feet on the soft ground, tousling his hair.

Leera knelt in front of Toma. He watched her with wide, curious eyes as she produced a smooth, dark stone from her pocket and placed it in his small palm.

"This is a Casmin stone," she explained. "Fish use them for pillows."

He looked up sharply, studying her eyes. Then he flashed a grin and bolted into the soyflower stalks, clenching the stone with a tight fist.

"What do you say?!" Niku bellowed at the swaying stalks.

"Thank you!" came the reply, already from a good distance away.

"Fish pillows?" asked Niku, turning back to Leera.

She shrugged good-naturedly. "I'm out of practice. Thank you for letting me indulge him."

"He likes you." They endured a rare awkward pause as she stared after Toma, thinking of her own son and husband on Earth. Niku cleared his throat. "I should check in with Uda. Meet up after you talk to Miles?"

"It's a plan," Leera agreed.

"Don't go without me!" Niku said to her back as she walked away.

She spoke over her shoulder with a mischievous smile. "Wouldn't dream of it."

GAVIN

The first of the crab sticks came into view as Gavin emerged from the sparse forest of ash-colored trees, stuck in the ground like a thrown javelin. It buzzed as if charged with a low-voltage current, and a red light glowed at the top.

His father leaned against him heavily, arm slung over his shoulders. Gavin tried to support the extra weight and simultaneously keep the pressure off his father's broken ribs.

The repurposed radio sticks formed an amoeba-shaped perimeter around the heart of the colony, forsaking only a few of the western farms which the migrating hexagonal creatures avoided regardless. Their two-year migratory pattern brought them to the colony every other summer. The hex crabs traveled in a massive continent of interlocking geometric shells — thousands upon thousands of dinner plate-sized critters following the winding path of the underground canopy. Barbed and jointed legs stabbed the soft top layer, gleaning nutrients while oxidizing the soil.

They also had the nasty habit of picking the flesh from any organic creature caught in their path. The loose ring of crab sticks emitted a negating signal which fooled the hex crabs into thinking there was no canopy under the surface. The critters broke around the perimeter of the colony like water around a boulder while the western farmers sequestered near the colony center for a week until the swarm passed.

Gavin readjusted his grip around his father's ribcage. His injuries had taken their toll shockingly fast. Only an hour ago the two had been laughing and joking. There was a fair amount of wincing on his father's part, but he'd still been able to navigate the forest without help. As they climbed a small rise a mile from camp, he cried out and dropped to his knees. The two had been making their way together since then.

"Straight...to Leera," Merritt groaned between clenched teeth.

Gavin wasn't able to sign, *I know*, so he nodded stiffly, struggling with his father's weight.

He managed to lift a finger to point at one of the crab sticks as they walked past. There was no red light at the top.

"I see it," Merritt whispered. "Need to...charge."

Every few weeks, a pair of colonists made the trek to a nearby crashed lander to charge the sticks from the depleting on board power cells. When that power source ran out...so would the colony's protection against the migrating hex crabs.

The center of the colony was atop a gentle rise in a small clearing. Temporary habitats were converted into permanent structures over the years, creating a downtown area where most of the colony's business and pleasure was conducted.

Makeshift tents were fortified with crash debris after the radiation of travel through the Rip dissipated. Many argued the structures were generously capable of being called *buildings* by that point.

The administrative office — where his father spent too much of his time — dominated the small clearing. A single-story prefabricated hollow shell had been elevated on stilts over the black scar where a lander once scorched the ground. Like the two other prefab buildings in the middle of the colony — the hospital and the cafeteria — doors and windows were cut from the solid shell. Temporary doors and window coverings provided protection from the cold during Galena's brief winter, but, on a planet seemingly devoid of insects, they were forgotten the rest of the year.

The buildings were arranged in a wide circle, facing each other with a well-trodden common area between them.

Gavin set his jaw and grabbed the waistline of his father's pants, pulling him the last few steps across the common area and into the cool interior of the small hospital.

Like the administrative office, it was a single-story hollow shell, except longer than it was wide, with plenty of natural light pouring in through the many cutout windows in the walls. It was very clean and very bright.

At the back of the room, amid the medical equipment salvaged from the crash, Dr. Leera James stuffed a sealed water bottle into her backpack. Various odds and ends were scattered near the pack on her desk. She tossed a roll of gauze pads into the pack before noticing Gavin and Merritt stumble inside.

The four patient beds near the entrance were empty. Gavin funneled his remaining strength into a final effort and hoisted his father up onto the bed. He cried out as he settled onto his back, his eyes sealed tight against the pain. Gavin stripped off his and his father's packs and tossed their stunners to the side.

"What happened?" Leera asked as she hurried over. She grabbed a pair of gloves from a sterilization box and expertly slipped them on.

Gavin breathed hard from exertion while he described the encounter — one of the extremely rare times he was grateful he didn't need to bother with speech.

Leera watched his hands intently, seeming to catch most of his story about their encounter with the sky beast. She bent over Merritt and gently probed his ribcage. He winced and tried to turn away, but she held his shoulder in a surprisingly firm grip while continuing her examination.

"Any other injuries?" she asked. Using gloved fingers, she parted Merritt's hair in several places to check his scalp.

Gavin shook his head, no.

Just ribs, he signed.

Over the years, Leera was one of the few colonists who had picked up more than just a few words of sign language during everyday interactions with Gavin.

"Well, my dear," Leera said with a sigh, her kindly face offering Merritt a sympathetic smile. "It's the moss for you."

Gavin's father groaned in disapproval. "Too much...to do. Hydro dam maintenance."

"You should only be out for a day or so," she told him, already walking over to the moss tanks.

Four gestation tanks gurgled softly beneath a window — squat cylinders sitting upright, with green metal exteriors and plexi windows to reveal their contents. The low-grade current provided by the colony's sole hydroelectric dam was enough to keep them bubbling and provide additional power for the few pieces of medical equipment that required it.

Thick rectangles of sod-like material slightly larger than shoebox lids floated in the tanks, occasionally contracting in slow-motion like the pulsing of a jellyfish.

Leera pulled on a thick nylon glove that went up to her elbow. She popped open one of the tanks and stepped back. A loud hiss and a puff of steam escaped the container, and the water bubbled furiously for a brief moment before calming. Leera gingerly reached her protected hand into the tank and scooped out its contents.

The patch of moss dripped purplish water onto the white floor as she carried it to the front of the long room. Gavin's father watched her approach with wide eyes. Even after eight years on Galena, he hadn't been injured badly enough to fall into unconsciousness while the living moss repaired his wounds.

As Leera placed the wet patch of rectangular living moss on his father's chest, Gavin couldn't help but remember how his own life was saved by the moss. He would have died beneath the fallen storage crate if Leera hadn't carried him to the moss grove.

That was back before she figured out how to cultivate the organism outside of its native environment. Knowing that the moss died during the process of healing others, she made it her mission to discover a sustainable way to harvest it.

Gavin's father let out a long sigh, and he closed his eyes. The moss seemed to flatten over his chest, shifting higher and stretching to cover his entire ribcage.

"He'll be fine," Leera assured him.

Slow day, Gavin signed, nodding toward the empty beds.

Leera smiled. "Thankfully. Now I have less guilt about leaving on my little adventure."

Where? Gavin asked.

Her eyes sparkled with delight.

"Niku's found something in the Casmin Sea. A tunnel he thinks leads out to the ocean. An *unnatural* tunnel. I'm meeting up with him and Miles and one of his rangers to explore."

Gavin perked up at hearing Miles's name.

Room for one more? he signed.

"We only have four suits, I'm afraid. Besides, I can think of one person you'd rather be spending time with."

She'd still be here when I got back, he signed grumpily before pulling on his backpack and grabbing his stunner.

A shadow passed over Leera's face as he turned to walk away.

"Gavin, a bit of advice."

He stopped and met Leera's eye.

"She won't always be."

Outside, the air smelled of wet soil. A cold breeze pulled away the temporary relative warmth of the hospital.

"Everything all right, kid?"

A wiry man with a wispy goatee approached. Despite the cold, he wore only his padded workpants and a loose t-shirt. Slender corded muscles flexed in his thin arms as he nervously ran a rough palm over his newly-shaved scalp.

Cracked ribs, Gavin signed. *Leera gave him the moss. Said it should only take one day.*

Skip sucked his teeth and looked away, shaking his head. He'd made fast friends with Gavin's father on the voyage to Galena.

"I *told* him I should go with you. But he wanted some of that 'father-son time' he's always goin' on about." Skip looked at Gavin, studying him closely. "How 'bout you?"

I'm fine. I'm faster than my old man.

Skip burst out laughing, causing several passing colonists to turn in surprise.

"Ain't that the truth? What was it, a cave worm?"

Sky beast, Gavin signed.

Skip stopped laughing. "And you both made it back alive."

Well, signed Gavin, hesitating. *It was injured.*

Skip clapped him on the back and squeezed his shoulder as they started walking.

"Can I give you some advice?"

Why not? Everyone else is.

"When you tell the story to Shurri, leave out the injury."

Why does everyone care about me and Shurri?! Gavin signed in a petulant flurry.

Skip laughed again.

"It's a small colony, kid. Best way to keep a secret is to not have any."

Is something wrong with the hydro dam? My dad mentioned it in the hospital.

"That thing's always on the fritz," Skip said, waving away Gavin's concern. "Your dad'll take care of it when he's done bein' lazy." He cracked his back and let out a content sigh. "Speakin' of which, time for nap number two." He winked and strolled away whistling.

The Cohen's farm was smack in the middle of the eastern plots, on a long sloping hill that faced the morning sun. Gavin admired healthy stalks of soyflower as he walked the beaten path that led past the other farms. While he couldn't eat it because of his soy intolerance, he took pride in growing it for the other colonists.

The original plan for the farming colonists was to give most of their harvest back to the company that financed the journey. That crop debt was to feed the next wave of colonists until proper infrastructure was established — eventually transforming Galena into a world not too different than Earth.

Those plans crashed along with the *Halcyon*, the ship that brought them to their new home.

Now, the colonists ate what they needed, traded for what they wanted, and stored the rest. There had been a few minor disputes over the years, but Gavin's father and all of the other farmers usually arrived at the same solution. There was no magistrate or mayor. Gavin's father had volunteered to oversee the organization and maintenance of the colony, but his word carried no more weight than Skip's or Leera's.

Gavin turned left at the border of the Cohen's farm, and stopped.

Shurri waited for him next to a stand of soyflower stalks, her straw-colored hair flapping in the cold wind. She wore a light blue, long-sleeved thermal shirt under linen overalls, with a length of black cloth tied around her waist for a belt.

How did you know I was coming? Gavin signed with a crooked grin as he walked to her.

I could smell you, she signed back, then she punched him in the arm.

He mouthed an exaggerated *Ow* and rubbed his bicep.

You were supposed to be here over an hour ago, she signed.

His smile broadened. *My dad and I fought the sky beast.*

Shurri's eyebrows went up skeptically as she crossed her arms. She was a year younger than Gavin, and had long ago mastered the entire repertoire of her emotive mother's facial expressions.

I'm serious! Gavin signed. *My dad's in the hospital!*

Her skeptical eyes narrowed.

And you're not dead? Was the animal already hurt?

Details! he signed with a flourish before putting his arm over her shoulder. *Let's focus on the bravery part.*

"Shurri!" came the shrill voice of her mom from the direction of the Cohen residence.

The two teenagers ducked behind the stand of soyflower stalks as if someone had hurled a stone.

"What's your plan, then, oh brave one?" Shurri

whispered, her eyes sparking with mischief.

Gavin grabbed Shurri's hand and pulled her up with him. For a moment their faces were an inch apart. They lingered there for a long moment, breathing hard with excitement.

"*SHURRI!*" her mom screamed.

This way! Gavin signed.

He took off at a full run. Shurri ran after him, easily catching up with her long strides.

"You're still slow," she said between breaths.

You don't know where we're going, he signed clumsily. The soyflower stalks whispered as they ran past.

She fell in behind him as he led them out of the eastern farms and through the colony's common area. Leera, Niku, Corporal Miles Turner, and a young ranger with black hair named Weston were loading up a handcart with supplies when Gavin and Shurri burst from behind the administrative building like rabbits spooked from a bush.

He waved at a smiling Leera as they ran toward the western farms.

"Gavin!" Shurri called, breathless.

They skirted the northwestern farms until the river came into view. Gavin stopped at the top of a low rise, hands on his knees, panting. Shurri slowed to stop at the bottom of the rise and walked up it slowly, one hand pressed to her side.

What was that about slow? he signed.

She kicked a clump of soil in his direction as she stood next to him and looked at the river.

A short distance away, a small natural waterfall poured over an outcropping of rock. Farther on, the twin mountains loomed high — the source of the river.

Straddled over the rocky outcropping was a low metal bridge, the foundations of which were buried deep on either side of the river. Metal rods lined the underside of the bridge, plunging into the cold, rapid waters. The rods supported the hydroelectric apparatus beneath the surface.

"Doesn't look like it's working," said Shurri, starting to catch her breath.

Gavin walked at a slow pace down the hill, trying to ignore the stitch in his side for Shurri's sake. She walked beside him, her cheeks flushed.

My dad said it's broken, Gavin signed.

"And we're going to fix it?"

He shrugged. Shurri glanced at him from the corner of her eye.

"Or was this just an excuse to get me alone, away from my farm?" She laughed easily when he blushed. "It's too easy with you."

They stood at the edge of the three-meter-tall dam on the eastern bank of the river. Gavin was much younger when the salvaged dam had been repaired and installed. He had little reason to visit the site over the years, having come back only once with his father for a bit of routine maintenance the year before.

The dam had been a humming, churning thing, turning the water below into a boiling white cauldron. Now the machine was silent, and river water flowed between the rods undisturbed.

"What are we supposed to do with this?" Shurri asked.

Gavin used handholds on the side of the dam to

climb up. When he got to the top, he turned back and looked questioningly at Shurri. She crossed her arms and walked toward the edge of the river, then plopped down cross-legged and plucked at a blade of grass.

Gavin scrambled on all fours to the middle of the dam, then dropped to his stomach and turned so he could access the main control panel on the downstream side.

"You don't even know what you're looking at," Shurri said. She threw a small stone into the river.

Gavin popped open the control panel and stared at its contents.

There was no official school on Galena. His father said it was in the works, but with only three sixteen year olds and a handful of toddlers, there was no reason to rush.

Gavin, Shurri, and her twin brother, Arthur, worked alongside skilled colonists, learning agriculture, mechanics, solar engineering, and medicine, among others. If they had questions about Earth's history, they asked and were eagerly answered.

The control panel was a deep box filled with wires and buttons. Gavin rubbed his hands together and blew against his fingers to warm them up.

He tried the easy options first: primer, fuses, and humidity sensors. The controls were dry. He activated the main pump and heard a single chug as the dam burped a white cloud of water from below.

With a knowing grin, he sat up and waved his arms to get Shurri's attention.

Kick the side for me, he signed.

She rolled her eyes.

Do you want to be a hero and fix it or not? he asked, still smiling.

Shurri got to her feet with exaggerated slowness and walked back to the dam. She tapped its metal foundation with the tip of her dirty white shoe.

"Like that?" she teased.

A little harder, Gavin signed.

She tapped it again.

Harder!

As she pulled her foot back to kick, he reached deep into the control panel and twisted a cube-shaped relay.

Shurri kicked the dam hard and the river water beneath it exploded upward, soaking Gavin.

As he wiped icy cold water from his eyes, he saw Shurri on the soft ground, curled up laughing.

He slowly climbed down the side of the dam and flicked his hands free of water.

How's your foot? he signed as he plopped down wetly beside her.

"It hurts," she said, her laughter tapering off. "But it was worth it. And now I can tell everyone I fixed the dam."

Like they'd believe you.

"Oh, and they'll believe *you* about the sky beast?"

A cold wind chilled Gavin to the bone. He watched the dam as it came back to life. The waters below roiled steadily and the machinery hummed.

So, he signed, turning toward Shurri. *Now that we're alone...*

He didn't have her attention. It was laser-focused on the bright blue sky.

“Gavin...” she whispered, her eyes welling with tears.

He jumped to his feet and shielded his eyes from the pale yellow glare of Phobis.

Stuck like a dart in the sky, in low enough orbit to see its hazy outline, was a starship.

MERRITT

Merritt awoke alone in the hospital. The light was fading through the windows, meaning he'd been unconscious most of the day — or the better part of the next.

He groaned and swung his legs off the side of the table. He wore a clean, loose linen shirt and his padded utility pants. On the floor next to the table was his backpack and the dried-out husk of the living moss that healed his wounds.

Merritt carefully rotated his arms in their sockets, probing the soreness of his chest. It had nearly vanished. He lifted his shirt. Only a faint purple bruise clouded the right side of his ribcage.

"Hello?" he croaked, his throat dry.

A bottle of water had been set out for him. He drank it down quickly, wincing at the soreness in his chest. Moving slowly, he shouldered his backpack and headed out into the cold evening air.

The common area was empty. Usually, at that time of day, it was bustling with colonists trading for their evening meals or sharing stories over mugs of Skip's homemade potato vodka.

A brief shock of panic coursed through his mind as he thought of the crab sticks. Had their batteries failed? Did the migration come early?

Then he heard laughter, and a shout of joy in the

distance — and music.

He followed the sounds past a few lonely tree trunks to find nearly two dozen of his fellow colonists at the edge of the western farms. An orange and blue bonfire roared in a hastily-dug fire pit while Skip stumbled with a jug of his vodka, pouring more of it on the ground than into the eager mugs of his friends. Two of them strummed homemade guitars while others half-sang, half-shouted to the heavens.

Merritt felt a smile growing on his face despite knowing why they were celebrating. It seemed like years since the last real gathering of this kind.

Skip noticed him. His eyes sparked with firelight as he howled to the sky and beat his chest. He shoved his liquor jug into someone's startled hands and beelined for Merritt. Tears took the place of the firelight in his eyes as he smiled bigger than Merritt had ever seen.

"What?" Merritt asked at last, half-laughing.

Skip looked up at the darkening sky. One star shone brighter than all the others. Except it wasn't a star.

It was a starship.

Merritt's backpack slid off his shoulder and hit the soft ground with a thud. His knees weakened and buckled. Skip caught him halfway to the soil and eased him down.

Merritt couldn't take his eyes off the ship.

"They..." he said weakly.

"They're here," Skip whispered, his voice tremulous with excitement. He sat next to Merritt and looked skyward. "Maybe now we can finally get some hot water in our tanks!"

Merritt smiled, but a weight grew in his belly as he watched the other colonists celebrate.

"Do you think they want to leave?" he asked.

Skip's gaze slowly dropped from the firmament. "Some do. Some have had their fill of the frontier life. More than a couple got it in their heads that Earth improved after we left."

Merritt nodded. "That was always going to be a possibility, even with the resupply missions. What about you? Would you go back?"

Skip put his arm around Merritt's shoulders and pulled his friend close. "You know the answer to that, partner."

Merritt looked up at the ship. At that distance, it was no longer than his fingernail. Sunlight gleamed off its hull.

"You think Janey's up there?" he asked.

Skip's wife and his six children were meant to follow him on the next Rip voyage after the *Halcyon*. Instead, they had been stuck on Earth for eight years.

His eyes followed Merritt's to the orbiting ship.

"No way they could keep her off," he said proudly. "I been gettin' the place ready. Last month I finally finished the kids' bedrooms. Almost like I knew they'd be comin' soon." He hesitated a long moment. "You know, there's company men on that ship."

"I know."

"We all signed contracts sayin' we'd give them most of our harvest. I don't think they forgot. Payin' back eight years of crop debt is more than any of us can handle."

"I know, Skip."

"In my mind, that contract broke when they

didn't send anyone else after our ship crashed."

Merritt glanced up at the ship. Eight years had been a long time without any message from Earth. He could have gone the rest of his life without contact, but there were colonists with strong ties back home—some with families they were supposed to see after a two-year tour.

"What do you think they want?" Skip asked.

Merritt patted his friend on the back as he stood. "We'll find out soon enough."

The glow of the fire bloomed as Shurri's brother, Arthur, tossed a dried-out taproot into the blaze. A blue tongue of fire licked out at him and he fell back laughing onto Gavin, who was seated near the fire. Gavin pushed Arthur off to the side, a big smile on his face. Next to Gavin, Shurri held her knees to her chest and stared into the fire, seemingly content. Gavin looked at her with flushed cheeks, silently laughing, then inched closer.

Merritt's smile turned melancholy as he watched his son. There were moments when he doubted his decision to bring them to Galena. It was no easy life to scrape your living from the soil; to be responsible not just for yourself, but for your fellow colonists. Each person was a thread of the same tapestry, woven together. He consoled himself in those rare moments of doubt by remembering how unsuitable a place Earth had become for raising children.

A jug of vodka was offered to him, which he politely declined before retreating from the radius of the fire's glow.

Night had officially fallen on the colony, leaving a blanket of stars above. The twin nebulae peeked above the western horizon. At that time of year, they would crawl slowly east, never fully rising, before ducking back down just before sunrise.

Merritt leaned against a cool tree trunk far from the bonfire, watching the celebration without truly seeing it — his thoughts many miles above the planet, focused on the ship.

"We need to talk," came a soft but powerful voice from nearby.

Merritt turned to find Henry Tolbard standing next to him. The man was a head shorter than Merritt but broader in the shoulders. He wore his ranging gear: padded utility pants and a vest with many pockets over a knit gray thermal shirt. Henry's newest pair of boots showed almost no signs of wear — but the previous pairs were little more than paper-thin husks. They had carried him farther on his rangings, and over far more rigorous terrain, than anyone else had traveled in the colony. His short white hair had thinned somewhat over eight years, and his snowy beard was yellowing on his cheeks, but his eyes still held the same fire Merritt had seen when they first met on the initial voyage to Galena.

"Yes, we do need to talk," Merritt agreed. "Can you find Willef and meet me at my house?"

Henry raised a bushy eyebrow. "Willef? Why?"

Merritt looked near the bonfire, at Gavin. "Just a feeling."

The night was moonless. Merritt navigated between the eastern farms without thinking, letting his feet find the way while his mind was elsewhere. Out of habit, his hands brushed against the long leaves of soyflower stalks that crowded the narrow path between farms. He closed his eyes because he could always hear his wife, Emily, whispering to him in the rustle of leaves — but he could never understand what she was trying to say.

The outline of Merritt's home appeared ahead in the darkness. At a distance, it was a smooth dome. Up close, it became apparent that the rough, corrugated metal repurposed from the top of an old grain silo had been bent and beaten into shape, leaving a rough exterior of overlapping sheets with two cut windows and a doorway.

In preparation for winter, Merritt swapped the cloth flap of a door for a solid slab of rigid insulation peeled from the inner hull of the fallen *Halcyon*. Such insulation lined the walls of most colonists' homes after their first Galena winter proved to be colder than expected. Those colonists with prefabricated lodges they had purchased before the voyage needed little to no modifications, but for those like Merritt and Uda who made their homes from salvaged materials, there was always room for more comfort.

Merritt's breath puffed out in the cold night air as he shouldered open his sticky front door. It cut an arc in the hard-packed dirt floor. Merritt studied it, frowning, realizing he would have to re-cut the insulation for a better fit.

The dome was as wide as a large garage. The roof peaked at four meters, leaving Merritt and Gavin hunched over near the walls. Five years ago, Merritt constructed a partition out of plastic sheeting, giving Gavin his own room. The rest of the space inside the dome was occupied by a long work table — an area used just as much by the son as by the father — and littered with half-finished projects. A solar-powered generator collected dust under a tarp. Several broken crab sticks lay in various states of repair. A four-wheel rover vehicle rested amidst a circle of its own parts.

Merritt's bed was a hammock near the entrance. He flipped on the electric lamp next to it and angled the light toward the work table. After rummaging through a stack of paper maps that Henry Tolbard had painstakingly drawn during each of his rangings, Merritt found the one he wanted.

He had just opened it on the table when Henry appeared in the doorway, his weathered face lit ominously from the lamp he carried. He nodded his greeting and joined Merritt standing at the table. Willef walked in a moment later.

The short man was nearly neckless, with a face lined like a stack of pancakes that gave one the impression he was always squinting out at the world.

"Was drinking," he said simply, his voice a dry cascade of gravel.

He half-walked, half-waddled to the others as they stood around the table. His injuries from the crash had left him with a permanent pinch in his lower spine which restricted full range of motion in his legs.

"Thanks for coming," Merritt said to him.

Willef grunted, then squinted down at the open map. Merritt suppressed a grin. Despite Willef's demeanor, he could sense the man's interest.

Henry placed a thick finger on the map and spun it around to get a better look.

"This is one of my first maps," he muttered,

leaning in closer. "I thought we lost it."

"I kept them all," said Merritt.

"I haven't been that far south since I drew it," Henry told him.

"No one has. Tell me what you remember about the land."

"Forests. Boulder fields. Some rock bat pillars, but easily avoidable. Nothing too exotic. Also nothing very interesting. Why?"

"That's exactly what I'm looking for," said Merritt. "Willef, I have a favor to ask you."

Willef's dark, squinting eyes studied Merritt for a long moment. "Let's hear it."

"I don't know what to expect with that ship in orbit," said Merritt. "I don't know if they plan to come down to the surface. If they do, we have no way of guessing their intentions."

Willef shrugged. "What can we do?"

Merritt slid the map across the table. "I'd like you to take the children on a field trip."

Willef glanced from Merritt to Henry, perhaps sensing he was being teased.

"What's a field trip?"

"A school expedition," Henry clarified, catching Merritt's meaning. "Teach the kids some survival skills out in the wild."

Willef pointed a stubby finger at Henry. "But you're the great explorer. Built two colonies on the moon, remember?"

"Henry and I need to stay at the colony," said Merritt. "He knows the continent better than anyone."

"You think we might have to leave the colony,"

Willef realized.

"I don't know anything yet," Merritt said. "I just want to be ready, and this colony is my only priority."

"And you trust me with Gavin? Even after my failure on the Halcyon?"

"Willef, I'd trust you with anything. Especially my son."

Willef clenched his jaw and nodded, but he couldn't seem to meet Merritt's eye.

"I'll do it."

"Can you be ready to go in the morning?"

"I am ready now."

"What about the younger ones?" Henry asked. "Toma and the rest?"

"We'll send those families to the first colony," said Merritt, "along with anyone else who's of the same mind."

Henry smoothed down his white beard and frowned. "The people on the ship might know where that is. There's a cave at the base of the twin mountains. It's warm and dry. I could take them there in the morning."

"What about the cave worm?"

"That cave has no connection to the underground tunnels."

Merritt nodded. "We'll send a couple of the rangers. Miles can stay back with us."

"He's with Leera, Niku, and Weston at the Casmin Sea."

"Well then, we work with what we have," said Merritt, folding up the map.

Henry caught his eye. "Do you really think these precautions are necessary? They have no reason to be aggressive."

Merritt paused while he thought about how to answer.

"I think this colony is ours," he said at last, "and I think others might not see it that way. They never told us about the first failed colony. Trust is a luxury, and there's no telling what else they're hiding."

KELLAN

The shadow of night slipped off the surface of Galena like a sheet pulled from a bed. The *Renata*'s massive viewscreen on the observation deck showcased a full view of the planet from low orbit, and Kellan's eyes took in every detail.

A continent the size of Australia bordered a shimmering equatorial ocean. Long rivers cut across the land, flowing from a massive western mountain range. Lead sulfide deposits the size of small countries dotted the northern and southern edges of the continent, their grayish, dulled silver surfaces muting the brilliant light of Phobis.

Kellan was alone on the observation deck. The underfloor GravGens sent a gentle vibration through the bones of his feet. He stood with his hands clasped behind his back, admiring the view of Galena as a child does the bounty under a Christmas tree. The other passengers had little interest in the view from above. Like Kellan, most of them were eager to get down to the surface — but for a different reason. While they prepared the shuttles for descent, Kellan allowed himself time to observe the planet he had been dreaming about for years.

Some of Earth's scars were visible no matter how

far one traveled. The brown and barren continents faded behind a bluish atmospheric haze from a high orbit, yet the gray smog of industry that swallowed half the planet remained. Kellan had watched his homeworld shrink into the black while the *Renata* sped toward the Rip. Earth was a tainted marble, half blue and half gray.

Galena remained pure — would *remain* pure, if he could gain control over passage through the Rip.

When scientists back on Earth had detonated Ceres to trigger the opening of the Rip and cement a link to a similar anomaly near Galena, everyone expected a new-age gold rush — yet the troubles of Earth proved too heavy for the dreams of another world. Travel through the Rip was left to the only agencies that could occasionally afford it: governments and, much later, tourism.

Kellan's wristpad buzzed. A short message from Felix flashed on the small screen: *Shuttles ready*.

After a final look at Galena spinning slowly on the viewscreen, Kellan left the observation deck.

The *Renata* was brand new. Eight years ago, before the last mission to Galena, the starliner *Halcyon* had been patched up where patches were needed in order to get the massive vessel through the Rip — but the interior had been largely ignored. There were so few tourists on the journey that the company hadn't bothered opening more than two lounges on the promenade. Entire sections of the ship that had fallen into disrepair were simply avoided.

Every surface of the *Renata* sparkled. Kellan slid his palm over a silver handrail that ran the length of the crew corridor. Even on Earth it was getting harder to find good metal. Most of what he'd seen were dull alloys which cost several hundred times their true worth. His own apartments boasted only small metallic accents set in faux hardwood surfaces — still far more luxury than what most could afford.

After the soil of Earth had become too acidic for crops, lumber was the next commodity to wither.

One of the many reasons Galena is so important, Kellan told himself as he walked toward the shuttle dock.

He followed the gentle curve of the crew corridor, the soles of his shoes padding softly on thin carpet. Janos awaited him outside the shuttle dock — a muscular, rough-hewn man massively incongruent to the sharp gleam of his surroundings. At Kellan's insistence, Janos had donned the long-sleeved white uniform of a field medic, harking back to his post-graduate years. A decorative quilted seam over the left breast of his shirt showcased three shining buttons, each bearing the tri-leaf insignia of the New Europa Medical Corp.

He tugged at his tight collar, seemingly uncomfortable outside his more traditional attire. Kellan craned his neck to meet the man's eye.

"Let's take a walk," he said as he passed the door to the shuttle dock.

Janos arched an eyebrow and glanced behind him at the door, then fell into step next to Kellan.

They walked in silence as they followed the corridor, passing no one. At a junction, Kellan used a keycard to open an inconspicuous door next to an elevator. Beyond the door was a narrow vertical shaft with a simple metal ladder leading down.

Kellan descended first. Janos — whose bulk nearly filled the utility shaft — moved silently above him, and Kellan looked up more than once to make sure the man was following.

At the bottom of the ladder was another door, which Kellan opened with a different keycard. The door swished open and there was an immediate tugging sensation, as if an invisible force attempted to draw him forward.

He walked onto a gantry suspended above a cavernous, egg-shaped room at the heart of the ship. Next to the door, Felix stood before a stack of monitoring equipment, checking the displays against information on his wristpad.

"Down here already?" Kellan asked as he walked to the handrail. Janos stood by the door, arms crossed.

"Had a blip from the grid," Felix told him. "Tower One fluxed out of sync for a millisecond."

"Everything back to normal?"

Felix nodded. "Like it never happened."

Tower One was the first of sixteen hypermass objects floating in the center of the vast room, aligned in a four-by-four grid. Each was thirty meters tall, and had a surface like pitted black stone. They had been constructed as elongated rectangular prisms — monoliths — their edges sharp enough to cut glass. After they were transported to the *Renata* and aligned within the repulsion grid at the center of the ovoid room, their unnaturally dense compositions had transformed their solid exteriors, morphing their shape as if they were made of liquid. The "natural resting state" of the hypermass objects resembled a cupped hand. Despite their curved appearance, they were still referred to as towers.

Kellan gripped the handrail as he looked down at sixteen of the densest objects ever crafted by humanity. The pull was stronger at the edge of the gantry. He imagined falling over — pulled toward and then pulled apart by the sheer power of gravity concentrated between the hypermass towers in the center of the egg-shaped room.

Janos stood next to him, frowning at the objects. Kellan noticed the look on his face and grinned. He slapped him on the back and Janos grabbed for the handrail, temporarily thrown off-balance. Kellan barked laughter and patted his friend on the shoulder. Janos shook his head and breathed a sigh of relief, then retreated from the handrail.

Felix handed Kellan a tablet, pointing to a scrolling stream of data.

"It will take six hours to power down the repulsion field when it's time."

Kellan studied the flowing text on the screen.

"I thought you said two hours."

"That was before the towers changed their shapes. Something about their new forms negates more than fifty percent of the field. We had to boost the output to keep them separated."

Kellan smiled. "Which means they contain more mass."

"Somehow," said Felix, glancing down at the towers.

Kellan handed the tablet back to him. "Will they be ready to launch?"

"They're ready now."

"Excellent. Wait for my signal." He turned to Janos. "Let's get down to the surface. I'm sure the colonists have a few questions for us."

THE ENVOY

Earth stank.

Cities were never a solid bet if one wanted a semblance of fresh air. They were too clogged with people, too buzzing with vehicles, and, like the rest of the planet, completely devoid of vegetation. Massive air recycling complexes built on acres of defunct farmland weren't enough to keep the ripe bouquet of organic civilization at bay.

A few city centers boasted hydroponic displays — usually a quad-array of bulbous glass showcases, each containing a single tree or bush. There was no practicality to them, and local citizens treated them accordingly. Practicality meant mass-produced soy matter in all shapes and sizes: steaks, cereal, desserts — all flavored and fried to fool the tastebuds. Anything natural worth eating was grown in the orbital gardens — products that were far beyond the means of most people.

Major population centers weren't generally known for their clean air even before Earth's soil took a turn for the worse and became acidic to the point of poisonous nearly four hundred years ago. Some cities were naturally blessed with a strong breeze, like Chicago — but even Chicago, without any green, soured in the end.

On a galactic scale, four hundred years is a short

time for a planet to begin to repair itself — yet Earth took up the challenge. The first evidence of new plant growth — from the flower pot of a little girl in the English countryside — was greeted with worldwide enthusiasm. The event turned the poor girl into a saint, ensuring she would never be left alone for the rest of her life.

Despite the slow crawl that was the reintroduction of vegetation to the world, Seattle remained as gray and clogged as ever.

The Envoy pulled the collar of his long black coat up a little higher to cover the back of his neck against a light rain as he navigated the streets. Water dribbled from the brim of his black fedora when he tilted his head down to avoid eye contact with the people passing by.

Skyscrapers loomed over stopped traffic. Sidewalks brimmed with people in rain coats holding umbrellas, maneuvering into and around each other during the morning rush to work.

They flowed past The Envoy like a fast-moving current around a drifting log. He had somewhere to be, just like them. Unlike them, The Envoy approached the concept of time from a different angle. His deadlines were usually measured in years or decades instead of weeks and months — a practice decidedly antithetical to the most progressive societal framework.

A gap between two skyscrapers revealed the distant Space Needle, somehow glimmering in the morning gloom. Behind it, Mount Rainier remained cloaked in gray, as was the case most mornings, regardless of season.

The Envoy paused to stare at the Space Needle, and at the bustling spaceport behind it. On the vast runway, three rocket sleds full of passengers dropped down their J-shaped launch shoots in unison. After dipping into the curve and starting up the shorter side, the sled engines ignited in explosions of blue-orange flame. They were little more than specks to The Envoy at such a distance, but in his mind he could still hear the metallic *TING* as the sled-rails popped off the vehicle.

Most sleds those days were bound for either Sunrise or Tensu Station, depending on the time of day. Anyone working a three-month shift on the orbital shipyards would hitch a ride to Sunrise before hopping a shuttle to one of the egg-shaped production facilities.

The Envoy glanced skyward past the wet brim of his hat, searching for a break in the low gray sheet of clouds through which he might glimpse one of the six ovoid shipyards.

His memories of driving bolts through insulation and running electrical wires in the shell of the first shipyard were as fresh as they were when he began the project all those years ago. By the end, it was a team of thousands that completed the sixth and final contracted shipyard — long after The Envoy had been given his current assignment.

A gentle tug pulled at his chest as he watched the dark sky, as if an invisible string connected it to something beyond the clouds. He knew in that moment that at least one of the orbital shipyards drifted overhead. The pull — the *connection* — was stronger than usual, and The Envoy looked down at the dirty sidewalk, frowning.

Something's happened, he realized. *That's why I've been called in.*

The crowds thinned as he walked the last few blocks to his destination. It was a quieter part of the city — old brick buildings jammed against each other, stacked with shoebox tenements and the working-class families that had occupied them for generations. Rain spattered against faded and paint-curled billboards rotting on the sides of buildings, most of them warning about the ever-present children snatchers that plagued city streets. Ever-declining birthrates had opened a new black market for those low enough to kidnap and those rich enough to convince themselves they were offering someone else's child a better life.

The Envoy stood between two of those billboards for a long moment, his gaze sweeping the street. Satisfied that he was not being ostensibly observed, he turned to face a blank concrete door at the base of a tall but narrow concrete building sandwiched between two run-down brick apartment buildings. He waved the palm of his left hand over the middle of the door and it swung silently inward.

The man known as The Envoy stepped inside, out of the rain.

He was in a small room the size of a broom closet. After the heavy concrete door closed behind him, the room was completely dark except for a small glowing yellow button on the side wall. He pushed it in with his thumb and waited with the button depressed, allowing the system to scan his thumbprint. The people inside already knew who he was, of course —

entry would have been impossible otherwise. Although a casual passerby on the street wouldn't notice any surveillance equipment on the exterior of the building, cameras and sensor instruments running a wide gamut of scanning capabilities monitored every square inch surrounding that building in a five block radius.

The glowing button blinked off, leaving The Envoy in utter darkness. A moment later, a vertical slice of light appeared in the wall opposite the front door. The slice widened to reveal a well-lit elevator, which The Envoy stepped inside with a heavy sigh.

He did not relish his visits to the main office. In truth, requests for his presence had grown more infrequent over the last two years — a fact which, he now realized, he only truly appreciated whenever he received a summons.

The elevator rose steadily, passing the empty floors that comprise most of the building. He was deposited on the top floor, and upon stepping out of the elevator was greeted by two heavily armed security guards who proceeded to subject him to a thorough body search. Beyond them was the gauntlet of body scans and biometric verifying equipment that The Envoy walked through to get to the central offices.

Several employees he didn't recognize from his last visit stared at him openly as he passed. He tilted down the brim of his fedora to hide his face and headed for a long hallway on the far side of the room, navigating between cubicles staffed by young government workers wearing immersive headsets and typing on invisible keyboards. Their workstations registered the movement of their fingers and streams of words spilled onto their screens.

A long hallway stood between him and the room he wanted. He ignored more than one attempt to engage in conversation as he passed open office doors, keeping his head down and pretending he hadn't heard anything.

The door at the end of the hall was open. The Envoy closed it behind him after he entered the small conference room. A round table sat in the middle, surrounded by rolling chairs. All were empty save for two, occupied by a man and a woman. A visual screen made to look like a floor-to-ceiling picture window showed a digital view of a downtown Seattle which did not exist — a view teeming with vegetation under a perpetually sunny sky.

The Envoy didn't wait for an invitation. He plopped down in a chair opposite the other two occupants and dropped his fedora on the table in front of him with a wet splat.

The two government agents glanced at the long, pink-brown scar that cut a canyon through his short salt-and-pepper hair, then quickly looked away, as people always did — even those who were used to the sight. It ran in a straight line from his empty left eye socket up his forehead and to the back of his skull. The place where his left eye used to be was covered with a black teflon patch bolted in three places to the bone of his eye socket.

"Wet out there today," said the government man. He was older and slightly overweight. Unkempt gray hair ran a half-ring around his bald scalp. The front of his shirt was only half-tucked in. A flower-shaped coffee stain decorated his left breast pocket.

"Wet out there every day," added the woman. She was trimmed and manicured in every way that her partner was not. With her ramrod straight posture and her habit of sitting perfectly still with her fingers interlaced on the table in front of her, she could easily be mistaken for a statue if one never noticed the deep intellect swimming behind her eyes.

The Envoy knew them both from previous meetings. Reynolds, the man, was essentially along for the ride. He blustered and frothed easier than most, but when push came to shove, he deferred to his partner, Caroline Diona.

"Took you longer than usual to get here," said Diona, studying The Envoy closely. She glanced down at his wet hat, then slowly back up to his eye. "You should have let your new handler pick you up."

"I haven't *met* my new handler," The Envoy replied. "You're always changing them."

Reynolds grunted, his paunch doing a jump behind his loose shirt. "We're not always changing them," he said. "They request transfers. Seems like working with the glorious Envoy ain't all it's cracked up to be."

"I know you like to keep a low profile," said Diona to The Envoy, calming her partner down with a nearly-imperceptible wave of her hand, "and nothing screams 'look at me' like a convoy of government cars stuck in mid-morning traffic. It's not just about you, though. Anything could happen while you're walking those streets. We don't need to see your face on the evening news as another mugging statistic."

The Envoy studied his wet fingertips, then brushed them off on his wet pants.

"Should I stay inside forever?"

"You should let us escort you to these meetings," Diona replied with a hard stare. "At the very least."

After a very long moment, The Envoy nodded.

"I'll let your handler know," said Diona.

"She'll be *thrilled*," Reynolds added sarcastically.

Diona ignored her partner and tapped on the table in front of her. A rectangular screen faded in and glowed brightly. It showed a government-issued identification card for a man with short, bright red hair and a matching mustache.

"This is Kellan McEwan," said Diona. "Our liaison to the World Space Association."

"*Former* liaison," Reynolds corrected.

The Envoy stared at the ID. His hands closed into fists when he recognized the smug look on the man's face.

Kellan had sent a group of colonists to their doom more than a decade ago — a group that included The Envoy's friend of nineteen years. After what Kellan did to Farah and the other colonists, The Envoy had spent no small amount of time the past twelve years dwelling on what he would do should he meet the liar again. Most of those daydreams ended quite grimly.

The two agents shared an uncomfortable glance.

"Have you met him?" Diona asked.

The Envoy's skin grew hot under his collar. Yes, he recognized Kellan...but he wondered if the agents were aware of their history. Judging by their reactions, probably not.

"The WSA is a joke," he said through clenched

teeth, still staring at the glowing picture.

"Maybe to you," said Reynolds.

"Not just me. To everyone who thinks we should be sending that money to the cities instead of funneling it into the black hole of government spending."

A warning glinted in Diona's eyes.

"You're part of that government," she said. "You became part of it when you agreed to your current assignment."

The Envoy peeled his malignant gaze away from the ID screen and took a deep breath to calm his raging mind.

"Like they would have let me do anything else," he mused, forcing a half-grin.

"You could have said no," Reynolds offered with a smirk.

"I'm sure. What's the story with McEwan? Did he get more people killed?"

Diona swiped the tabletop and the ID was replaced with security footage of McEwan and several other men in the launch bay of an orbital shipyard.

"That's number three," said The Envoy, recognizing the grid pattern on the wall of the bay which distinguished the shipyard from the others.

He watched as the men in the footage hurriedly loaded cargo through the open hatch of a docking shuttle.

"McEwan stole government property," said Diona.

"Is that the Renata? It's a beautiful ship."

"This isn't just about the ship." Diona paused to

let him think about it.

"What's in the crates?" The Envoy asked.

"Cloning equipment," said Reynolds, "and a whole lot of DNA. Private citizens, mostly. They paid a pretty penny for the privilege to be cloned on a new planet. Also a few unscrupulous government types not afraid to break the law, but I'm sure it's no one from the Seattle office."

"Who wouldn't want to get out of *here?*" joked The Envoy.

Reynolds chuckled. Diona frowned.

"Can we take this a little more seriously, please?" she asked.

"Sorry," said The Envoy. "It's a side effect of being around for so many years. I should say, though, that theft of spacecraft and grow-your-own-human kits falls outside my jurisdiction."

"There's more," Diona told him. "McEwan hacked into classified files before he stole the ship."

"According to his ID," said The Envoy, "he already had access to almost everything." *I could have warned you against that, if you'd asked,* he wanted to add.

"Almost. The more sensitive files regarding the guest in Shipyard 6 remain classified to all but the most relevant employees. Neither of us has access."

"Prisoner," said The Envoy.

"Excuse me?"

"You called the Weaver a 'guest'. It's a prisoner."

He held her stare.

"Be that as it may," she continued, "we believe McEwan got his hands on sensitive data that represents not just a threat to Earth, but to the Weaver as well."

The Envoy nodded slowly as realization sank in. "You and your friends aren't finished poking and prodding it yet, so you need me to make sure it's safe."

"Per your agreement," said Diona, "anything and everything related to the Weaver also involves you."

The Envoy watched the security footage on the tabletop screen. After the last crate of cargo was pushed past the hatch, Kellan McEwan disappeared inside the ship and the hatch closed.

"Where's he going?"

"Galena," said Reynolds.

The Envoy couldn't hide his surprise. "Through the Rip? Why?"

"McEwan has designs on the colony," Diona explained.

"He's obsessed with it," Reynolds added. "Cuckoo-bonkers obsessed."

The door opened behind The Envoy. Reynolds and Diona rose quickly to their feet and saluted.

"At ease," said a deep voice. "Agents, could we have the room?"

"Yes, sir," they said in unison.

Without another glance at The Envoy, they departed.

"Hello, General," The Envoy said with a resigned sigh.

"Hello, Jeffrey." General Trager walked around the table and sat in Diona's seat. "I know you think that seeing me is never good news."

"Whatever do you mean?"

Trager chuckled easily. He was in his mid-sixties, with a weathered face that boasted more smile lines next to his eyes than wrinkles elsewhere. He ran a hand with prominent knuckles through his short white hair.

"I'm here to tell you the rest of it," said the general.

"I figured there was more."

Trager took a deep breath before continuing.

"Yes, McEwan stole a ship and some cloning equipment. If he ever returns, we'll arrest him, but I'm not going to expend the resources needed just to bring him back. He's been a thorn in this agency's side for too long. Good riddance to him and good luck to the people in that colony. Now, about your mission. Our system will show that we're sending you to Galena to find out what kind of information McEwan obtained from our files before he left."

"You really want me to go through the Rip?"

"You've been before."

"I thought I was done with it."

"The need arises. You *are* The Envoy. You're the only one who can talk to the Weaver, find out what it wants."

"The Weaver is here, on *this* side of Rip...and I already *know* what it wants. It wants to be free. Beyond that, I have no control over what it decides to show me."

"Still," said Trager, "your connection to it as a result of the Titan missions makes you our most valued asset. Speaking of which, what's this I hear about you walking the streets instead of taking an escort?"

The Envoy waved him off. "No more strolls. Diona twisted my arm."

"Good," said the general. "Listen close. We've identified a signal originating on Galena which several of my superiors have convinced themselves shares more than a passing resemblance to one of the Weaver's emanations."

"There's only one Weaver left. It's told me that much...and you have it trapped inside an orbital cage."

General Trager stood.

"Nevertheless, you will go to Galena. You will attempt contact with this organism and discover if there's any truth to this belief. And *if* the opportunity arises after you fulfill your primary mission, you will track down Kellan McEwan and find out what he's planning to do with the information he stole from our system." He cleared his throat. "I trust your personal feelings toward McEwan won't cloud your judgment."

"I only have one feeling when it comes to him."

"Then bottle it up until your mission is over. I'm not sending you on a vendetta. I need information."

The Envoy regarded his wet fedora thoughtfully.

"If I'm your most valued asset, why send me?"

Trager walked to the door.

"No one else can do what you do, Jeffrey. Believe me, I'd keep you here if I could, in much more secure accommodations than you've negotiated for yourself. As for your trip, you won't be alone. Your handler will be your shadow."

"One bodyguard I've never met on an alien world?"

"Believe me when I say that if you're not safe with this handler on Galena, you're not safe anywhere."

Jeffrey Dolan, the man known as The Envoy,

leaned back in his chair after the general left and put his legs up on the table. He stared up at the ceiling with his right eye and imagined he could see through the top of the building, through the cloud cover, and all the way up to Shipyard 6.

Inside, the Weaver floated, held captive by an electrified, net-like tensor array and a steady flow of sedatives that would paralyze a continent full of elephants. It floated there under constant observation — the first extraterrestrial encountered by humankind.

Slightly curled up in its dormant state, the alien creature roughly resembled a charred croissant the size of an aircraft carrier. Its outer skin had the same texture as broken, craggy rock. Deep fissures in the stony skin glowed with warm red light. A mouth-like pool of shifting red light swirled over one of its tapered ends.

All around the dormant giant buzzed probes and cameras; scientists wearing bright orange Constellation space suits wielding syringes and sampling tubes.

Jeff closed his remaining eye, and the image grew stronger. He actually *was* seeing the Weaver inside the orbital shipyard. His connection to the creature after its machines brought Jeff back from the dead on Titan had granted him this ability. That connection had also revealed the biggest secret that his own government had yet to discover.

The Weaver wasn't sleeping.

It was waiting.

LEERA

Phobis peeked above the horizon just after six o'clock, its pale yellow rays glimmering across the Casmin Sea. The rays hit four small dome tents arranged in an arc on the black sand of the western shore.

Leera had been waiting for Galena's sun, sitting before her tent while listening to the lapping of gentle waves and the rustling of tent fabric in the cold morning wind. She tugged her knit cap down over her ears and sipped scalding tea from a dented thermos.

Tea brewed from the roots of a bitterbell plant packed a strong punch — perfect for opening one's eyes in the morning. Bitterbell grew in brambles at the base of Galena's towering bare-trunked trees. It produced small bell-shaped flowers in the hotter months and bulbous fruit just after winter — both extremely deadly if ingested by humans. Several unfortunate colonists discovered this shortly after crash-landing on Galena.

Boiling its roots removed the toxins yet left the water more bitter than burnt coffee. The plant seemed altogether useless until Willef discovered the root sap could be fermented to create an extremely sweet and concentrated honey-like substance. Without a hint of irony, he dubbed the sticky substance "bittersweet" and was hailed as a hero.

Soyflower sugar didn't deserve the name and artificial sweeteners that survived the crash had been among the first supplies to run out. Since its discovery, many colonists added a small shed to their main domiciles specifically for the fermentation of bittersweet.

Leera took another sip of her tea and grimaced, wishing she had added more of the dark brown sap.

Niku stirred in his tent and went still. His snores could be heard over the constant wind. Miles Turner and his ranger, Weston, had gone to sleep after Leera the night before but had awoken before dawn to scout the area on the eastern shore of the Casmin above the underwater tunnel.

Beside her, in the large hand cart, four multipurpose bright orange Constellation Mark VI space suits waited in their storage crates.

Leera looked up at the brightening sky, but couldn't see a ship. If it hadn't been for the fact that others had also seen it, she could have written it off as a hallucination. It wouldn't have been the first time a heat glimmer presented her subconscious with an excuse to imagine a rescue ship approaching on the horizon.

Shockingly to her, the appearance of a real spacecraft was at first entirely rejected by her rational brain. It seemed so far outside the realm of possibility after eight long years that she found it easier to believe the ship's hazy outline was just another optical illusion.

Niku coughed inside his tent. His sleeping bag swished and he zipped open the front flap just enough to poke his head out into the cold.

"Tea?" he croaked.

Leera showed him the thermos and he squinted at it with bleary eyes. He grunted and vanished back inside his tent. A moment later, he emerged wearing padded utility pants and a thermal undershirt, then hurried toward the nearest tree.

After his morning business was concluded, he plopped down next to Leera on the black sand, his breath puffing out in a cloud. She handed him the thermos and he took a generous swig, his face twisting in disgust.

"You don't have to say it," she admitted.

Niku took a smaller swig and handed the dented thermos back to Leera. He glanced at the sky, then quickly at her before turning his gaze toward the opposite shore.

"We can still go back to the colony," he said.

Leera shook her head. "I thought about it last night. Paul and Micah wouldn't be on the ship. Even if Micah had his kidney transplant, he'd be too weak to travel."

"They could have sent a message."

"It will be waiting for me when we get back." She nodded toward the eastern shore. "This is important."

"It might be nothing."

"It's important to *me*. Are you sure *you* don't want to go back to Earth?"

"Everything I have is on this planet. As you say, it can wait. What about the rangers? Did they change their minds about our little adventure?"

"No," said Leera. "They'll stay until after the dive."

Niku looked at the sky again. "Micah is ten now?"

"Eleven."

"He'll be so excited to see you when you get home."

"Assuming the ship is here for that."

Niku frowned. "What do you mean?"

"It might not be here for us."

"Why *else* would it be here? I only signed a two-year contract."

"I thought you were staying."

"Well of *course* I'm staying, but others want to leave."

Leera's gaze followed Niku's to the sky.

"I just don't want to set my hopes too high," she said. "It's fear, I think. All these years of longing for rescue, and when it comes down to it, I'm terrified of finding out they're not here for us. It's more comfortable to prolong the mystery than to risk hearing the answer I dread."

They sat in silence, sharing the thermos. To take her mind off the ship, she studied the four-story-tall unbreaking waves in the Casmin Sea — triangular walls of water rising from the choppy surface.

"The waves should go down after the moon passes," Niku commented.

Leera nodded absentmindedly as she watched the water. The perennial waves which appeared on every large body of water remained a mystery — one most colonists had given up trying to solve years ago. She was sure the moon played a role, but there had to be additional elements contributing to the phenomenon — powerful undersea vents or a unique topography coupled with obscenely strong currents.

The oceans couldn't be explored because anyone taking a swim would be consumed by a massive sea creature within minutes. Smaller seas like the Casmin seemed to be devoid of such predators, yet there was no equipment for deeper dives — until the space suits were found.

Niku used a pair of binoculars to scan the eastern shore.

"I see Miles and Weston," he said.

Leera stowed her thermos in her backpack and zipped up her tent. She and Niku each grabbed a handle of the cart and pulled it behind them down the black sand beach, following the shoreline.

It took them several hours to round the southern tip of the Casmin and work their way north to the area of beach positioned above the tunnel entrance. They paused often given the weight of their load. Four multipurpose space suits did not make for light cargo.

Phobis was high in the sky when Leera and Niku finally reached their destination. Miles and Weston were asleep, using their packs for pillows. Niku grinned mischievously and kicked the soles of their boots to wake them up.

They shared a lunch of thick-cut soy jerky and cold potato fries. Weston told them how the advanced engineering degree he'd earned while in the U.S. Army wasn't enough to land him a job after his contract was over. He had wanted to go into city planning.

After a year of searching for employment in an economy that had too many people and not enough jobs, he used his savings and a bequest from his late uncle to buy a ticket to Galena, hoping to make better use of his skills on another world.

Leera was thankful he had, because his irrigation system design and implementation kept the colony's crops alive during two dry summers. At the same time, she was taken aback by the fact it had taken her eight years to hear Weston's story. With just shy of fifty colonists, she would have guessed she knew them all. Thinking back on her time in the hospital, Leera couldn't remember ever seeing Weston as a patient. Admittedly, most of her personal knowledge of the other colonists came from her conversations while treating them.

With lunch out of the way, they began the detailed process of helping each other into their bright orange space suits. They secured their weight belts, shouldered their air and power packs, and clicked the slide locks of their helmets into place.

Four spare oxygen tanks clanked against each other on a loop harness secured to Weston's pack. Each held an extra hour of breathable air, and had been filled using the compressor found alongside the recovered space suits.

Miles tapped the comms button on the glowing screen of his wristpad. His voice came through clear inside Leera's helmet.

"Can everyone hear me?"

Leera, Niku, and Weston all gave him verbal confirmation.

"We'll take it nice and slow," he said as he walked toward the water's edge. "Not that we have much choice in these suits."

Leera moved like an automaton. She slowly lifted

her weighted boots and stomped down into black sand while she held out her arms for balance. Already she felt the physical strain of moving in such a heavy suit. Sweat beaded on her brow, and her quick breaths fogged the inside of her face shield.

"It gets better in the water," said Niku beside her. "A little."

The fabric of the space suit maintained its form as she walked into the Casmin Sea, the choppy waves slapping her chest. She had expected the suit to cling to her like shrink-wrap, but there was still a small buffer between her skin and the fabric.

Instinctively, she took a deep breath as water sloshed over her helmet. Her footsteps slowed, but it became easier to lift and lower her boots.

"Just like walking on the moon," said Weston.

"I've never been," Leera admitted.

"Don't," said Miles. "It's a money trap. All the slot machines are rigged."

Weston laughed. "Great calamari, though."

"I don't trust seafood that has to travel more than an hour from where it's caught," said Niku.

"Then you'd like it. The aquafarm near Avalon grows them better than anywhere on Earth."

A churning current kicked up black sand, making for poor visibility under the surface near the beach. Leera felt as if she were inside a washing machine on a gentle cycle. She followed Niku, who walked behind Miles. Weston brought up the rear.

It didn't take long for conversation to die off completely, each person focused on the simple yet exhausting task of putting one boot in front of the other.

When they were several meters below the surface, Miles paused and motioned for Niku to take the lead. Niku gave him a thumb's up and slowly angled to the right, walking more or less parallel to the shore. After a few short but laborious minutes of walking, a rocky ridge appeared ahead.

They skirted its left side. The ocean floor descended quickly while the ridge grew taller beside them, becoming a steep cliff.

Niku stopped and pointed at a void in the rock wall. Leera caught up to him, breathing hard.

A circular tunnel ran deep into the rock, roughly three meters in diameter. Miles and Weston stepped inside the tunnel and flicked on their helmet lamps. Leera rubbed the tunnel wall with a gloved hand, marveling at its smoothness compared to the craggy surface of the ridge.

They walked along the darkening tunnel in pairs: Miles and Leera in front, Niku and Weston behind. The harsh beams of their helmet lamps were the only sources of light, illuminating the smooth walls and floating particulates.

Their progress on the hard tunnel floor was quicker than it had been on the sand.

After ten minutes of walking, Miles said, "We should be halfway to the ocean shore by now."

"You think this goes all the way?" Weston asked.

This question was answered a moment later, when they discovered a smooth rock wall at the end of the tunnel.

Leera checked her wristpad: four hours of air remaining.

Their helmet lamps swept over the circular wall

like searchlights.

"Well," said Miles, "this is disappointing."

"That's an understatement," Niku added.

Leera moved to the wall and rested her gloved hand against its surface.

"We know so little about these waters," she said thoughtfully. "Could an animal have made this tunnel?"

"Maybe the cave worm, if it's also aquatic," said Niku. "...which is a horrifying thought. Merritt said the cave worm tunnels were smooth, but also roughly-formed. This tunnel looks like it was machined-drilled. An animal would have to be extremely specialized to bore through solid rock in such a way."

"What about natural water flow between the ocean and the sea?" Weston asked. "Ocean caves are carved out over time by water movement."

Leera's glove slid across the smooth rock. "That doesn't explain the wall..."

She felt a slight indentation in the center of the circle of smooth rock — so slight that she doubted she'd felt anything at all.

"What is it?" Niku asked.

"I'm not sure."

She pressed against the indentation and a square of rock just wider than her fist sank into the wall, leaving a black hollow. Leera reached inside.

"Now wait a minute," said Miles.

Leera barely heard him. "I feel something. I think it's a switch."

Niku squeezed her shoulder and she paused.

"I can't be the only one who's curious," she said,

looking at the others. Images of her husband and son popped into her mind like camera flashes, then faded. "Look," she continued, "this is the turning point. If it works, and we keep going, there's no guarantee we'll have an easy way out. We all talked about it together, but *this* is that moment."

They all shared a glance, but no one objected.

"Here we go," she whispered as she pressed the switch.

The rock door snapped away from her like the hatch of a depressurized sub, violently yanking her and the others past the threshold and into a rushing darkness.

GAVIN

Compass Rock jutted up from Galena's soil in the middle of a wide clearing in the forest just outside the colony. It was a thin, dull silver knife of lead sulfide leaning at an angle to point due north.

Gavin entered the clearing expecting to be the first one to arrive, but Willef was already there. He sat cross-legged next to Compass Rock, his eyes closed. He wore stained gray utility pants and a thick long-sleeved cream-colored shirt. Four bulging backpacks sat in a row beside him.

As Gavin approached the rock, Willef opened his eyes. A tan scalp shone under thinning hair. Everything about him appeared squat to Gavin, from his short neck to his arms and legs. His wide lips seemed to be perpetually frowning, though Gavin's father claimed he had been a different person before the crash — less brooding and quick to laugh.

Gavin smiled and nodded at him, then sat next to one of the backpacks, unsure about what else to do. Willef seemed to be studying him from beneath a heavy brow. Gavin picked up a stone and tossed it aside, keenly aware that Willef didn't know any sign language.

On his father's advice, Gavin wore a pair of dark green workpants with extra padding on the knees and shins. Two months ago they had fit him perfectly, but now the bottom hem of each pant leg didn't quite reach his boot laces. The khaki jacket he wore over a simple white t-shirt had dark brown quilted pads on the elbows and shoulders. It was a comfortable outfit as long as Phobis was in the sky, but he hoped Willef had packed him something heavier for nighttime.

"Where's your friends?" asked Willef.

Gavin looked toward the trees, then shrugged. He noticed Willef's pack for the first time, propped behind the man's back. A serrated machete with a gleaming blade was strapped to the side.

Willef noticed Gavin's interest and arched a thick eyebrow.

"You like it? Made from the Halcyon. We melted down the metal." He frowned. "That was early on. Before we felt safe."

Why do you have it now? Gavin signed on reflex, before remembering Willef wouldn't understand.

The erstwhile ship's foreman seemed to catch his meaning regardless.

"I don't need it at the colony," he said. "But we're going beyond the crab sticks, past rock pillars and more." He flashed Gavin a wide grin. "Who knows what we'll find?"

Gavin thought of the injured sky beast he encountered with his father, wondering if it was nearby. He had wanted to bring his stunner but was told he could only bring what he could fit in his pockets.

"I brought one for you, too, if you want it," said Willef.

Gavin hesitated, sure his father would disapprove — then he nodded, unconsciously puffing out his chest a little.

Willef's booming laugh carried easily, startling Gavin. Surprise gave way to embarrassment and his cheeks flushed red.

"No no," said Willef, still chuckling. "Don't worry. It's a natural feeling. Here, you'll see."

He unstrapped the machete from his backpack and held the blade while offering the hilt to Gavin, who took it slowly.

"Squeeze the hilt," Willef told him, clenching his own fist. "It's okay."

Gavin tightened his grip on the contoured hilt. He studied the shining blade and focused on the weight in his hand.

Willef clapped. "There you go. Confidence." He held up a warning finger. "Just don't chop off your foot."

"Ow, quit it," someone said from the far side of the clearing.

Gavin turned as Arthur Cohen stumbled out from behind a tree. Shurri was right behind him, a crooked smile on her face. They wore matching khaki pants and white knit shirts, though Arthur's was smeared with old grass stains.

Shurri gave her brother a gentle push on the shoulder and he let out an overdramatic yell as he tumbled to the ground. She rolled her eyes as she stepped over him and sat near Gavin. Arthur made a show of brushing himself off as he walked over to sit as far from his sister as possible.

"Long time ago," Willef said without preamble, "on Earth, there was a program for kids called Nature Scouts. You heard of it?"

All three teenagers shook their heads, no.

"Well, they stopped it after a while. Not much nature, and...not much kids. Anyway, this will be similar. We hike, we camp, we hunt. I show you some things. Maybe you learn something."

"Hunt?" said Arthur.

Like his twin sister, he had straw-colored hair and a slender frame, though his had been stretching upward more quickly than hers as of late — making him "all limbs", according to their mother.

"Well, we must eat," Willef said.

"I thought you were bringing food," said Shurri.

"I brought supplies. Think of this like a school trip. All of it is learning."

Gavin signed a question to Shurri. Willef looked at her quizzically.

"He wants to know why you're taking us away from the colony right after the ship arrived."

Willef drew a breath as if to answer, then seemed to think better of it. Gavin signed something again, this time more emphatically.

"We deserve to know," Shurri translated.

"Because nobody knows why they come," Willef said at last. "Maybe they bring supplies. Maybe they don't even come down to the surface. We play it safe until they tell us the why."

"What about the other families with children?" Shurri asked.

"They go to the mountains. If they want."

Arthur's brow wrinkled in confusion. "You can't think the people on that ship would come here to hurt anyone."

Willef grunted as he strained to stand up. He

brushed dirt from his hands and squinted at Arthur. "They don't teach history anymore?"

"Look," said Shurri, pointing at the sky.

Gavin looked up, shading his eyes. The ship was visible as a small, hazy dart high in the atmosphere. A glimmering dot separated from the larger ship, moving away from it in a gentle arc.

"That's probably a shuttle," said Willef as he bent down to pick up his pack. He struggled to settle its heavy weight on his shoulders. "Looks like they come down after all. Everybody take a pack."

Gavin strapped his machete to the side of his pack and slowly lifted it, shocked at the weight.

Shurri pretended she couldn't get hers off the ground. "What's in here, rocks?"

"And jars of sand," Willef said, smiling. "You'll get used to it."

Arthur groaned as the straps of his pack cut into his shoulders. He looked as if the weight would make him tumble backward in a light breeze.

Willef waved for them to follow him. "Come. We have a long way to go."

He patted the side of Compass Rock and walked southward. Grumbling, Arthur followed after him.

Gavin waited as Shurri hoisted her pack from the ground and pulled the straps over her shoulders.

"Arthur's not going to make it a mile with this weight," she said.

How about you? Gavin signed as they walked after the others.

"I give myself two miles. You know my mother said to listen to him no matter what?" She tilted her head toward Willef as he led the way into the sparse forest. "She also didn't want us to bring any food, but we both snuck soy jerky in our pockets. I'm sorry you can't have any."

Gavin shrugged, thinking about his machete. He wondered if he'd have to use it to catch his dinner.

"You know it's not that good, anyway," Shurri continued. "Everyone always complains about it. But what else is there?"

Potatoes and carrots, Gavin signed.

"Yippee." She glanced up at the sky. "Maybe they brought ketchup. I remember liking ketchup."

There's always bittersweet.

Shurri made a disgusted face. "I ate too much of it one time and haven't touched it since. Now it's *too* sweet."

My dad stops the fermentation process halfway through, Gavin signed. *Makes it less sweet.*

"It's not poisonous when you do that?"

I guess not.

"Nice sword, by the way," said Shurri, eyeing his machete. "Is that for the sky beast?"

I thought you could talk it to death, signed Gavin with a huge grin.

She gasped and shoved him sideways. The weight of his pack carried him stumbling into the trunk of a tree and Shurri burst out laughing. Arthur and Willef turned back to see what happened.

"You two keep up," Willef shouted. "Don't get separated."

"Or do," Arthur added.

"No," said Willef. "We need them to help catch dinner."

Shurri helped to steady Gavin after his awkward

embrace with the tree and brushed off his shirt.

"Did you hear that?" she asked, batting her eyes. "You might get to impress me with that big shiny sword."

It's a machete, he signed, staring at the ground, embarrassed.

She surprised him by darting forward and giving him a light kiss on his lips before hurrying after Willef and her brother.

He stared after her for a long moment, then shook his head to clear his thoughts. Suddenly his pack didn't feel as heavy as it did before.

After three interminable hours of walking — and much vocal resistance from Arthur and Shurri — Willef finally stopped at the top of a small rise and let his pack slip from his shoulders. It thudded to the dry ground, sending up a mist of fine black particles.

His charges joined him on the low hill. They looked down on an expanse of dusty ground easily a mile wide and twice that stretching into the distance. The low hill on which they stood was part of a natural wall mound that encircled the flat, sunken area.

Three-sided rocky pillars covered the dusty expanse, thrust upward at odd angles. Each pillar curved as it tapered to a point and was easily four meters tall — one edge as sharp as a knife where two smooth sides met, the other side a broad surface of shallow bowl-shaped grooves.

"They look like teeth," said Shurri.

"With cavities," Arthur added.

He pointed to the nearest pillar, which had a large hole at its base.

This is where the rock bats live, Gavin signed.

Shurri repeated his observation out loud.

Willef nodded. "One of many places that we know about."

"What do they eat during the winter?" Arthur asked. "The hex crabs don't come by for months."

"Teenagers, mostly," Willef answered.

"Ha."

"Nobody knows," said Willef. "Maybe they sleep all the time. We won't be here long enough to find out."

He walked down the low rise, toward the field of rock pillars.

"Where are you going?!" Arthur shouted after him.

"To catch my dinner. You stay here, no matter what happens."

A noise like the hooting of a strange owl grew louder in the distance — *oooWAoooooo*. It was answered by an identical call, only this time it came from a pillar directly in front of Willef. He froze in place and held up his hand, signaling the others to back off.

Gavin, Shurri, and Arthur stood close together, watching him.

ooooWAooooo.

"I thought you said they slept during the day," Arthur whispered, his voice quivering.

Willef looked back. "I will draw one out. Be ready to catch it."

Catch it how? Gavin signed.

He's just showing off, Shurri replied with her hands. *Soy jerky for dinner tonight.*

Willef stood with his heels touching, then slid one

boot across the ground and tapped three times. He put his weight on that foot and slid the other one to meet it, tapping the toe of his boot on the ground again. He repeated this odd slide-walk in a wide circle around the nearest pillar.

When he made his way around the pillar, he stood before the hole in its base, wiping his brow. He turned back to the others and shrugged.

"Tolbard said this worked!" he called to them.

There was an animal shriek and something burst from the hole in the nearest pillar. Gavin only had time to register a muddy brown blur as it smacked into Willef's chest and knocked him to the dusty ground.

The creature shrieked again as it clawed at Willef's shirt. Its beak-like mouth split vertically, and a second beak opened up and down within, stretching the sides of the outer beak. A black band of leathery skin in place of eyes wrapped halfway around its crested head. Thin membranes connected each pair of bony limbs. Its long spike of a tail lifted up and down as the dual beaks snapped at Willef's hands. Fully splayed across his chest, the creature was roughly the size of a giant bat.

Willef managed to grab its thick, corded neck and rip it off his chest. He flung it toward the nearest pillar. The rock bat soared like a sack of potatoes until the last moment, when it flicked its winged limbs just enough to spin and land against the pillar on its belly, shrieking at Willef.

In response, a chorus of shrieks rose from the other pillars.

Willef got to his feet and ran. He sprang up the

low hill with remarkable speed, saying, "*Run!*" as he passed the others.

Gavin, Arthur, and Shurri followed him down the hill, toward the forest. Another chorus of shrieks sounded close behind. Gavin risked a glance over his shoulder as he ran. Rock bats — too many to count — had left their pillars and were not far behind. They leapt from the hill and glided through the air, carried by their wing-like membranes.

Shurri ran next to Gavin. Arthur was next to her. All three of them held the straps of their heavy packs as they pounded for the trees.

A rock bat hit Gavin's pack from behind and fell back with a loud screech. Gavin stumbled forward, arms pinwheeling, then regained his footing.

"They're turning back at the trees!" Shurri shouted between ragged breaths.

The rock bats that were still in mid-flight peeled away from the pale trunks without passing the tree line. They squawked in frustration when Willef ducked behind a wide trunk.

Arthur cried out in pain. One of the rock bats sank its bony claws into his shoulder as it flew past. Its momentum carried him forward too quickly. He lost his footing and tumbled to the ground. His pack slammed down into his back with the rock bat on top, its claws slashing at the fabric.

Gavin and Shurri ran for him, Willef close behind. Shurri reached him first. She interlaced her fingers and swung her fists at the creature like a baseball bat, connecting with the side of its crested skull. It flew off Arthur's pack and rolled across the ground, dazed.

Arthur groaned in pain as Gavin got his pack and

helped him up, half-dragging him toward the tree line. A swarm of rock bats scrambled across the soft ground behind them, beaks open wide.

Shurri appeared on the other side of her brother and helped support his weight. A moment later, Willef shouldered them both out of the way and picked Arthur and his pack off the ground, running into the forest.

The animal shrieking faded as they ran. Willef stopped next to a small bubbling spring, breathing hard, and set Arthur back on his own two feet. Blood trickled from a trio of narrow cuts in his shoulder. Willef peeled back the cloth and poked at the wound. Arthur hissed in pain.

"Clean scar," said Willef, and patted the boy's cheek.

Shurri helped her trembling brother sit next to the spring and gave him some water from his thermos.

Gavin walked back a short distance, until he could see the tree line. Several of the rock bats paced back and forth on clawed hands halfway down the ridge of their wings. There was a distant call from the field of pillars, and they all turned away from the forest. Gavin looked up to the tops of the trees, then down at the soft ground, wondering what kept them away. A foul odor soaked the air and didn't dissipate after the creatures departed. Gavin sniffed, then gagged. It was particularly pungent at the base of a nearby tree.

I don't like it, he signed to Shurri when he rejoined the others.

"You don't like what?" she said aloud.

It's an arbitrary boundary. There's no reason they wouldn't come into the forest.

"No reason you can think of."

"I'm sorry," Willef cut in. He sat cross-legged next to Arthur, staring at him intently. "I should have made you hide. I never tried that before."

Arthur grimaced and rolled his shoulder to test the motion. "It doesn't hurt that bad."

"It was a waste anyway," Shurri declared. She refilled her thermos in the cool spring. "We didn't get anything to eat."

"Would you have eaten one of those things?" Arthur asked.

"I'm hungry enough."

Willef unzipped his pack and pulled out a dead rock bat. Its thick neck was bent at a sharp angle. He tossed it on the ground between the group.

"The one that tickled Arthur," he said. "Who wants to clean it?"

MERRITT

Sunlight glinted off the hull of the shuttle as it approached. Merritt adjusted the brim of his faded gray ball cap — one of a thousand bearing the red-stitched logo of the crashed starliner *Halcyon* that had been found in the wreckage. Also discovered that day were two crates of broken *Halcyon* branded coffee mugs and three crates of plastic hellocard sleeves with a cartoonish depiction of the Rip printed on both sides — relics of a gift shop that hadn't been open during the voyage from Earth. A continuing joke among the colonists was that they would find the entire contents of the gift shop before coming across something as desirable as table salt.

Merritt stood between Uda Jansen and Skip in the middle of a clearing half a mile from the colony. A bonfire raged in a shallow fire pit behind them, belching smoke into the sky.

Skip chewed his bottom lip and occasionally tugged on his wispy goatee while he stared anxiously skyward, hopefully awaiting the arrival of his wife and six children. Merritt had smiled inwardly when he noticed the small bouquet of white soyflower blooms in his friend's hand.

Uda shielded her deep blue eyes from the midday sun with a calloused hand as the shuttle descended.

At fifty one years old, only the slightest hint of gray was beginning to thread itself into her curly brown hair.

A dozen colonists stood or sat near trees at the edge of the clearing. The rest had either departed the colony with Henry Tolbard as their guide to the twin mountains, or were going about their day-to-day business back on their farms. Most who were in the clearing had never expected to make Galena their permanent home or were hoping for the arrival of someone they'd left behind; most back on their farms had no plans on returning to Earth.

Uda had balked at the idea of being anywhere else if visitors arrived. She sent little Toma with a family friend to the mountain cave alongside the other families with small children. No one was expecting them to be gone longer than two days — just until the motives of the visitors could be determined.

Merritt had gone back and forth about the idea to send away some of the colonists. On one hand, it instantly projected distrust to even the most well-intentioned visitor. On the other hand, it sent a message that the Galena colonists were prepared for the worst case scenario.

Most of his fellow colonists agreed. Those that didn't remained on their farms. As they had decided long ago, theirs was not to be a community where one person or a small group of people determined the fates of all. While acknowledging such an arrangement was only possible because of the colony's limited population size, the sentiment was unanimous. There had been hiccups along the way —

disputes between neighbors that required the intervention of a third party and community disagreements over optimal harvest methods being the most common.

Overall, the people enjoyed a life of harmony.

Merritt clenched his jaw as the shuttle drew nearer, hoping its arrival did not signal the end of that paradigm.

The squarish craft spun slowly as it approached the clearing, orienting its hatch toward the waiting colonists. Orange-blue flame from six rotating side-mounted engines scorched the ground as the landing gear sank deep into the soft topsoil.

Merritt held his hand before his eyes to protect from the exhaust blasting out from the shuttle in all directions. The engines slowly died down, leaving the ground beneath sizzling and smoking.

A wide ramp silently lowered until its lip touched the blackened soil. The shuttle cracked and popped as its outer material cooled.

A man appeared at the top of the ramp, smiling. He was short, with freckled cheeks and a small mustache the same coppery red as his hair. For some reason that eluded his understanding, Merritt had been expecting whoever was in the shuttle to be wearing a military uniform or combat gear. This man wore green khaki pants with side pockets and a black puffy vest over a black long sleeved shirt. He looked more like a tourist than anything else.

"I come in peace," he said with a Scottish accent as he walked down the ramp, holding up his hands in mock surrender.

"Welcome," said Uda.

The man approached her and offered his hand.

"Thank you," he said amiably as they shook. "I'm Kellan McEwan. I'm liaison to the World Space Association."

"What does that mean?" Uda asked.

"It means your colony was my idea. Mostly."

"You got anyone else in there with you?" Skip asked, peering up the ramp.

Kellan's smile grew wider. He turned back to the shuttle and called, "Come on down!"

A skinny man in his early thirties wearing his Sunday best walked down the ramp, carrying a small suitcase and looking around nervously.

"Alan!" someone shrieked from the trees.

A woman his age ran forward. The man dropped his suitcase and she jumped into his arms. Merritt recognized her as Xia Shao, a hardworking farmer whose output was among the highest in the colony.

Several shadows appeared at the top of the ramp, one of them noticeably taller than the others. Skip walked toward the shuttle, the bouquet gripped tightly in his hand.

"Janey?"

The tall shadow stepped forward into the light, revealing itself to be a beautiful woman with fair skin and long brown hair. "My Skipper?"

Skip dropped the flowers and his lower lip trembled.

"Papa!" shouted a young child.

A little boy of nine or ten ran down the ramp, his shoes thumping loudly on the metal. He was followed by five others ranging in age up to their late teens who all hurried down the ramp toward their father.

Skip dropped to his knees as the first of his children fell into his arms. The others closed in around him in a group hug. The children relented enough to allow him to stand. He swiped at his wet cheeks as Janey came forward to hold him, both of them sobbing. They moved away from the shuttle as a family, heading toward the colony. Skip glanced back over his shoulder to nod a farewell to Merritt.

"Strong woman," Kellan commented as he watched them leave. "I expect the family will thrive."

He offered his hand to Merritt. "You're Merritt Alder, but I have no idea how you got on the Halcyon."

Merritt squeezed Kellan's hand firmly. "I was a last minute crew hire on Sunrise Station."

"Ah, that explains it. I only have security footage sent back from the Halcyon before it entered the Rip. And you brought your son, Gavin. Where is he?"

"On a field trip."

Kellan smiled knowingly. "Remarkable timing. Is this all that survived the crash?" he asked, nodding toward the dozen colonists who were now slowly approaching the shuttle.

"No. Some are back on their farms."

"And hello to all of you," Kellan said to the waiting colonists, stepping past Merritt. "The shuttle will be departing at midday tomorrow, if any of you are hoping to catch a ride back to Earth. However, I should warn you that my ship, the Renata, will be in orbit another few months until radiation levels are low enough to travel back through the Rip." He looked around the clearing appreciatively. "It's a lot more cramped up there than it is down here. A lot less beautiful, too. The choice is yours."

There were a lot of smiles and happy chatter among the colonists as they began to disperse, most of them discussing the unexpected possibility of leaving Galena the next day.

Merritt noted that more than half were those that had never expected to remain on the planet after the *Halcyon* returned to Earth. He recognized one woman, Layla, who'd been on the maintenance crew with Merritt during the voyage. Nestor was a cook from the ship's galley who was always outspoken about getting back home.

There were also farmers among them. After eight years of close community, Merritt couldn't say he was surprised. Not everyone had adapted easily to their new lives on Galena. Those who seemed to have an in-born gift for growing plants usually liked it more than those who couldn't charm blooms from their soyflower stalks. Many had families they should have returned to years ago.

Kellan watched them leave. His gaze drifted up to the treetops.

"I'd like to talk to my wardens, if that's possible," he said, almost as an afterthought. "Ramirez and Cohen."

Merritt and Uda shared a quick glance.

Kellan smiled sadly. "I take it they didn't survive."

"They were killed shortly after the crash," said Merritt.

"Not *during* the crash?"

"Cohen was poisoned, and Ramirez..." Merritt trailed off, remembering how a man named Tulliver landed a shuttle on top of the warden. "He died in a shuttle accident."

"That is unfortunate. But I'm pleased to see you've managed to get along without them."

"You don't seem too broken up about it."

"To be quite honest, I wasn't expecting to find much. A few empty farms and even fewer hungry survivors, perhaps." Kellan clasped his hands behind his back and studied the ground with a concerned look on his face while he gathered his thoughts. "I don't want to step on anyone's toes, but we have a lot to discuss. I'm going to tell my crew to set up camp here, in this clearing. That way we don't interfere with your daily business. I'm hoping you'll host me back at the colony for a few days so I can get the lay of the land."

"Why are you here?" Merritt asked.

Kellan looked up and met his eye. "I'm not here to take the colony from you. I've seen your farms from the Renata. The colony is in far better shape than my meager expectations led me to believe. You have irrigation, silos for storage, and you've found a way to survive against the native wildlife. You're doing just fine without a change in management."

"You lied to Leera James about a first colony. Those people weren't so lucky with the wildlife."

"Did she survive the crash?" Kellan asked hopefully.

Merritt nodded.

"That's fantastic news." Kellan took a moment to process the information, muttering to himself. "Extraordinary. And yes, I withheld the existence of the first attempt at a colony from Leera and her team. The information was classified at the time as the initial...*event*...was still under investigation."

"Hex crabs swarmed their settlement and ate everyone," said Uda.

Kellan couldn't disguise his interest. "Hex crabs, you say? Are these the organisms that migrate as a group, linked together?" Then he cleared his throat. "Questions for another time, perhaps. Such danger makes your survival all the more impressive."

Merritt stared at him for a long time, as if trying to make a decision.

"Are you hungry?" he asked at last. "I made potato stew last night."

"That sounds wonderful. Lead the way."

Uda caught Merritt's eye as they walked out of the clearing in the direction of the colony. She signed a single word: *Careful.*

LEERA

She tumbled through darkness in a powerful current, her helmet lamp sweeping over silvery bubbles and the rough rock walls of a long tunnel. Someone's bright orange legs flashed in her view and were lost in a fresh wall of bubbles.

After several moments of frozen panic, Leera called out for the others, but there was no response over comms.

The current grew stronger, pulling her along as if she were in free-fall. Leera curled up in a ball and her back slammed against the rock wall. She bounced off and knocked helmets with someone else. Then she slammed against a grate blocking the tunnel and was stuck there like a fly on a windshield as three other bodies smashed into her, knocking the breath from her lungs.

Small strands of green seaweed clung to the metal grate that scraped against her face shield. Leera tried to push away from it, at the very least to try and roll the bodies off her back, but she didn't have the strength. Beyond the grate, all was dark. Deep green water turned to black out of reach of her quavering helmet lamp.

The current lessened. Leera finally drew a breath as the pressure against her back lightened. She jerked back in fright as a thin line descended over her face shield — before realizing the water level in the tunnel was dropping. She floated free of the grate and sank along with the water until her boots hit the smooth rock floor.

Niku stood next to her, doubled over and breathing hard. Miles and Weston slowly got to their feet, gloved hands slipping on the slick metal grate for support.

Leera saw Miles speak behind his face shield, but nothing came over comms. She checked her wristpad and reset the comm circuit.

"Try it now," she said.

"Everyone alright?" Miles asked, out of breath.

"Just winded," said Weston.

Leera put her hand on Niku's back. He nodded with his eyes closed and swallowed hard.

"There's a room ahead," said Miles, turning his attention toward the darkness.

His helmet lamp swept past the grate to reveal a wide, circular room with a low, flat ceiling. A single rock pillar in the middle, like the axle of a wheel, was the only object within.

Leera moved from Niku to the wall, her balance unsteady, leaning against the slippery grate.

"What do you see?" Miles asked.

"Another indentation, like the one in the outer door," she replied.

After a light touch, a square of rock silently slid inward. Leera reached inside the hollow and pressed a switch.

"Remember what happened last time..." Niku warned.

The metal grate slid down from the ceiling and

disappeared into the floor. Miles and Weston took a few hesitant steps into the circular room, followed closely by Leera and Niku.

Their helmet lamps swept the floor and ceiling, sliding over wet rock walls and nothing else.

"Dead end?" Niku mused.

"A lot of effort and nothing to show for it, if that were the case," Leera mumbled as she studied the curving walls.

Weston's helmet lamp played over the crack in the floor where the grate had disappeared. "Could be a safe harbor."

Niku's lamp found Weston in the darkness, illuminating his boyish face. "You mean like a cage for observing sharks?"

Weston shrugged.

"Another door closed farther down the tunnel," said Leera, "or the room would still be filled with water."

"What's that?" Miles asked, facing the central rock pillar.

A faint blue light glowed from a flat section of rock halfway up the pillar, as if it had been painted with a bioluminescent compound.

"A control mechanism of some sort," Leera guessed.

Miles looked at the others. "Should we push it?"

"Well," said Niku, "it's either going to flood the room again, flush us into the ocean, or turn on the lights."

"Among a hundred other possibilities," Leera added. "But the other option is that we go back to the colony."

Miles exchanged a quick glance with Weston, who nodded, then placed the flat of his palm on the glowing rock. The blue light flicked off and he pulled his hand back sharply.

"The room is spinning," Niku whispered.

Leera felt it, too, though very faintly. The floor under her boots vibrated with a minuscule tremor, almost imperceptible.

"And we're descending," said Weston.

Leera placed her gloved hand against the wall. "Descending at an angle, away from the Casmin."

"Are we going to talk about the fact that this was made by things that weren't human?" asked Niku.

"It's an incredible discovery," said Leera softly.

"Hey!" Miles shouted.

He ran as fast as he could in his bulky space suit back toward the tunnel. A smooth rock barrier silently rose from the floor. He reached it just in time for the top of the barrier to meet the ceiling, trapping them all inside the circular room.

"Are we stuck down here?!" Weston asked, his breath coming in sharp gasps.

Leera joined the others in pushing against the rock wall that blocked the tunnel exit. She sighed from the effort and tried to cross her arms. The Constellation-class space suit made the action difficult. Instead, she felt along the walls, searching for a control mechanism.

"There's a way out," she said. "We just need to find it." Then, adding with a smile to keep the mood light, "But who's going to believe us?"

"What do you think they look like?" Niku asked, staring up at the ceiling. "Whoever built this room wouldn't be much taller than us."

"Unless they slither around on the ground," Miles offered. "Or maybe they walk on all fours."

"Or twelves," said Leera.

"Wait a minute," said Weston, an edge of concern to his voice. "You don't think they're still *down* here, do you?"

Niku turned toward him, his helmet lamp illuminating the sheen of sweat on Weston's forehead. "They could be."

"Wouldn't we have seen them by now? We've been here eight years."

Leera shrugged, quickly realizing that lifting the weight of the suit on her shoulders wasn't worth the gesture. "They might never go to the surface. The entryway to this room suggests they can either hold their breath for extended periods of time or they have suits like us."

"Or they can breathe air and underwater," Niku added. "If that's the case, they wouldn't need to go on land."

Leera nodded. "There's probably more food down here anyway."

"What about the sea monsters?" Weston asked.

The room's descent stopped with a gentle shudder, like an elevator reaching the bottom floor. They all rocked on their feet to keep their balance.

They spent several long moments looking around the room expectantly.

"Now what?" Miles asked.

"The ceiling..." Leera whispered, looking up.

Dim light glowed from the rock, as if it were illuminated from within.

"It's dissolving!" Weston shouted in alarm.

The rocky surface of the ceiling faded as the light intensified. Ripples of shadow flowed over the walls and floor, coursing over the space suits like water reflections.

"We're under the ocean," said Niku in disbelief. Then he laughed, startling Leera.

"The ceiling didn't dissolve," she said. "It became transparent. We're looking up toward the surface of the Equatorial Ocean."

"How deep are we?" Miles asked.

"Twenty meters," said Niku. "Maybe a little less."

Particulate matter floated like snow in the clear water. Farther above, orange light from the setting sun danced over the choppy water, casting shadows down to the ocean floor.

A large creature swam slowly into view near the surface, its silhouette eclipsing most of the filtered light.

Leera's voice caught in her throat as she pointed up at it. After a long moment, she was able to whisper, "There's your sea monster, Weston."

From below, the shadowy shape of the creature conjured images of a blue whale swollen in the midsection. Its front end — or, to be pedantic, the end currently moving in a forward direction — tapered to a point in a long cone. The tail-end was blunted, with no discernible fluke. Four massive flippers, two on each side, paddled in slow motion to propel the beast onward.

"It must be fifty meters long," said Niku.

"What does it eat?" asked Miles. "How do you feed something so large?"

"I'm sure there's a lot more up there we haven't seen," said Leera. "We might be in some kind of observation facility, like an aquarium."

"To build something that can withstand the pressure at this depth..." Niku mused, pacing the outer wall of the circular room. "Remarkable."

A deep, hollow *CLUNK* shook the floor. The wall opposite the sealed tunnel entrance split down the middle, the crack growing wider to reveal darkness beyond.

"I have a question," Weston said quietly. "Why didn't we bring the stun sticks? What if whoever built this place isn't friendly?"

The crack in the wall grew wide enough for all four of them to pass side-by-side — but no one moved.

Leera squinted into the darkness. "It's another tunnel."

Light seeped into the black space, slowly illuminating it to reveal what appeared to be an empty tunnel through water on the ocean floor. The walls and ceiling were transparent. It was three meters high and five across, and the end of it vanished out of sight in the distance.

Leera looked behind her. The tunnel which had delivered them into the circular room was still sealed.

"Thoughts?" said Miles.

Weston grinned. "I shouldn't have volunteered."

"We go, obviously," said Niku.

Leera nodded. "Obviously."

"Okay, then," said Miles, taking a deep breath. "Wes and I will go first. That way we'll be the first to kick the bucket if the ceiling collapses."

"Wait, what?" Weston said in shock.

"He's only kidding," said Niku. "We'd all die at the same time."

Weston swallowed hard. "Comforting."

Miles walked into the tunnel, his boots thumping solidly on the rock floor.

Leera put a gloved hand on Weston's shoulder. He was still sweating, even against the steady airflow from the cooling fan in his pack.

"Not a fan of tight spaces?"

He shook his head. "I do fine up there," he told her, his eyes flicking up toward the surface. "Something about being under the water..."

"Whoever built this place did a better job than we ever could," she said. "We're going to be fine."

Weston took a deep breath and nodded, then hustled to catch up with Miles. Niku fell into step beside Leera and they both walked into the long tunnel, leaving the circular room behind. She reached out to touch the side of the tunnel, expecting her glove to dip into water. Instead, it bumped up against a hard, invisible surface.

Miles and Weston walked a few meters ahead, snakes of light from the water above dancing over their space suits. The ocean floor extended into the distance to either side of the tunnel — a barren expanse of fine sand, its surface like a gently wrinkled bedsheet. Circular black pits wide enough to swallow a large truck punctured the ocean floor every thirty meters.

"Sinkholes?" Leera asked, pointing.

"Maybe vents," said Niku. "There could be an entire independent ecosystem inside those holes."

There was a soft click over the comm system and Niku glanced down at his wristpad. “They switched to a private channel.”

“I’m sure they’re just discussing which one of them gets to fight the first alien we see.”

“Do you think we’ll find anything down here?”

Leera thought about it a long moment. “This place feels empty.”

Niku tapped on his wristpad. “The air is breathable.”

She glanced up at the water overhead, seemingly held at bay by an invisible tunnel wall.

“I think I’ll leave my helmet on,” she said. “Just in case.”

They walked in silence for a few paces.

Niku said, “I didn’t bring anything to eat.”

Leera smiled. “It always comes back to food with you.”

“Maybe we’ll find some alien TV dinners.”

“Would you actually eat one if you did find it?”

“If the safety seal wasn’t broken, sure.”

Leera laughed, the sound loud in her helmet. There was another click from the comm system.

“I see something up ahead,” said Miles.

Leera stepped closer to the wall of the tunnel to look past him, but she saw nothing — nothing at all, in fact. The ocean floor, and the tunnel, seemed to come to an abrupt end at the top of a low sand hill roughly fifty paces out.

Miles and Weston were the first to reach the top of the gentle rise.

“Dr. James,” said Weston quietly, “these are pressure suits, right?”

"That's right," she answered, climbing the gradual incline with some effort. "Why?"

Niku reached the top and drew a sharp breath. Leera stopped next to Weston and stood up straight.

The ocean floor fell away from them at a forty-five degree angle. The tunnel, with its invisible walls, plunged deeper to the depths. Some distance down, where the fading sunlight barely touched, the floor flattened out again.

Dark structures rose from the ocean floor in the deep — purposeful structures not crafted by time or tide.

Transparent domes the size of football stadiums — their contents occluded by the darkening waters — punctuated a landscape of black, ovoid skyscrapers and squat circular buildings with rounded roofs.

The tunnel seemingly led straight down into the heart of the alien city.

"A third colony," Leera whispered. She remembered discovering the ruins of the first human settlement shortly after arriving on Galena.

"I would say *ours* is the third colony," Niku offered.

"Unless this was built by natives," said Weston.

Miles checked his wristpad. "We either take off our helmets or we turn back now."

"We don't even know *how* to get back," Weston reminded them.

"What's the range on these comms?" Miles asked, tapping on his wristpad.

"Haven't tested it," said Niku. "Through water...who knows?"

Miles turned to Weston. "How would you feel about going back to that first room to find a way out?"

Weston didn't bother to hide his obvious relief. "You got it, Corporal." He unclipped three of the four spare one-hour oxygen tanks from the harness on his power pack and handed them to Miles.

"You stay here until we reach the bottom of this section of the tunnel," said Miles, pointing down the slope. He accepted the spare oxygen tanks one at a time and clipped them to the side of his own pack, where they dangled like decorations. "Let's make sure the comms work at least that far. We'll go do our thing and check back in two hours from now. You'll have to hike it back to this point from the round room on your own to check in."

"Copy that. Do I have to take off my helmet?"

"Only if we're not back in time. In that case, pop off your helmet and save the spare tank so you have enough to get back."

Weston shifted on his feet, looking uncertain. "How long do I wait?"

Miles shrugged and grinned as he started down the slope. "Until you get hungry."

Niku went next, stepping slowly. Leera followed after him, leaning back against the sharp angle. Her left boot slipped out from under her and she fell hard on her tailbone. The still-wet fabric of the space suit slid easily on the smooth rock floor.

"Watch out!" she yelled as she barreled into Niku.

She knocked his legs out from beneath him and he hit the floor on his shoulder with a loud *Oomph!* Both slid into Miles, knocking him down on top of them. They slid down the tunnel in a mass of flailing limbs, picking up speed.

"Corporal!" Weston shouted from above.

Leera managed to push Miles off to her side with a grunt. Her boot heels scraped against the floor, but it didn't even slow her down.

After twenty seconds of steady sliding, Leera stopped trying to fight it and watched the deep water overhead. Far above, at the surface, the light of Phobis was almost gone. Only a faint, wavering orange glow remained.

Niku put his gloved hands behind his helmet in a mock attempt to appear relaxed. "Guess it's better than walking."

"Are you okay?!" Weston's loud voice blasted over comms.

The smooth floor began to flatten out. Leera, Niku, and Miles slid to a slow stop.

"We're fine," Miles grunted as he climbed to his feet against the weight of the bulky space suit. He offered a helping hand to Leera and Niku. "Seems like comms work from here." He stretched out his left arm, grimacing as he squeezed his elbow. "See you in two hours, Wes."

Leera looked up the long tunnel they had slid down. At the very top, the small, bright orange figure of Weston waved, then turned back and disappeared from sight.

"Doesn't look like too far of a walk," said Niku.

Leera joined him in the middle of the darkening tunnel. In the not-too-far distance, the first of the black structures loomed high.

The water surrounding them was turning to murk as night descended. She flicked on her helmet lamp and shined it upward. Something like a thick silver ribbon shot across the light and vanished.

As Leera walked behind Niku and Miles, she clicked off her lamp. It was one thing to admire sea monsters from a distance — it was another thing entirely to advertise her presence to the whole ocean.

Niku and Miles soon followed her lead. Their helmet lamps flicked off, plunging the tunnel into a deep gloom. Soon Leera found herself walking with her arms outstretched, only barely able to see the dim outlines of the others' space suits.

"Something is out there," said Niku, looking up. He slowly raised his arm to point at the invisible tunnel wall. As he did so, a faint blue light glowed in the dark water.

The light emanated from a cucumber-shaped ocean animal with cactus-like spines. Dark blue light bloomed in thin stripes down its length. Leera's breath caught in her throat as the stripes of light elongated, tracing the true outline of the creature's shape. It wasn't short like a cucumber. It was instead a bioluminescent raft of long rope drifting in the lower currents, loosely tangled in a large rectangle.

"Is that one animal?" Miles asked. His orange suit was purplish-blue in the bright glow.

"Could be," said Niku. "Might be a group of them in a colony, like a siphonophore." The bioluminescence flicked from deep blue to bright green, bathing the tunnel in vibrant light. "Oh wow," Niku whispered, his voice thick with fascination.

Leera smiled. "That should fill a couple of diary pages for you."

"A couple?" he joked.

"There's a door up ahead," said Miles.

Electric green light from the ocean organism dimmed slightly near the end of the tunnel, which terminated in a smooth rock surface. Overhead, above the invisible tunnel ceiling, a towering structure of dark stone rose into murky water.

Miles ran a glove over the rock surface and found a slight indentation. He turned to the others. "Ready to see if anyone's home?"

Niku and Leera both nodded. Miles pushed the indentation until a small square of rock sank inward. Then he reached in and pressed a switch. The door slid silently upward, revealing a black void beyond.

Leera flicked on her helmet lamp and followed after the others.

THE ENVOY

Jeff awoke suspended in a tank of thick, pinkish hypergel. His black neoprene body suit protected his core from the natural icy temperature of the viscous substance, but his hands and face tingled from the cold. Knowing what happened next, he worked the breathing tube out of his mouth and sealed his numb lips. It had only taken him four stints in a hypergel tank and four instances of choking on a mouthful of numbing gel before realizing it was a bad idea to allow the tube to be yanked out on its own when the door automatically opened.

There was a deep rumble from below as the gel was rapidly sucked down through the floor, leaving him like a puppet with cut strings. He slumped against the tank door just as it popped open to the side, dumping him onto the cold metal floor which vibrated from the GravGen unit underneath.

Jeff stood up slowly and cracked his back, groaning. He watched the hypergel on his body suit slide off the slick material and plop to the floor in a puddle. The steady vibration from the GravGen unit caused the puddle of goop to shiver.

The company he worked for before he went to Titan all those years ago — Diamond Aerospace — had been instrumental in pioneering GravGen technology. Without it, humans probably would have been less inclined to spend more time in space — which was a good or a bad thing, depending on the current political climate.

Jeff took a towel from a cabinet next to the hypergel tank and wiped the remaining gel from his face and hair.

He couldn't help but think of the Weaver, trapped in its orbital prison near Earth. Like the advent of GravGen technology, most modern advances in the scientific field were born less from direct study of that alien creature than from its creations — the ring-shaped machines that brought their creator back from extinction.

A broken torus had been recovered off the Florida Escarpment in the Gulf of Mexico not long after Jeff's final trip to Titan. Another was found half-buried under the Ross Ice Shelf in Antarctica. Fragments of others had filtered to the government over the decades, but none as intact as the Two Primaries, as they came to be known.

Jeff began the tedious process of peeling off his body suit to take a shower. His limbs moved stiffly after being in the hypergel for five months, and his joints creaked.

Well, he thought, *I can't blame creaky joints on the stasis. Not entirely.*

He turned on the shower and winced as the ceiling lights automatically bloomed to full brightness. Pins and needles danced over his skin and he sucked in a sharp breath as he stepped into the water stream, which felt ice cold even though the temperature gauge was reading hot.

Most of the side effects of spending a few months

in hypergel on long voyages were easy to ignore, especially when Jeff weighed them against the torment of consciousness — but the light sensitivity that slowly pressed against his remaining eye like a heavy weight lingered the longest and hurt the most.

After his shower, Jeff located his belongings in a drawer under his crew bunk and donned his tailor-made Envoy uniform: white slacks made of thick cloth and a thick white long-sleeved shirt. The shoulders of the shirt were gray, and gray stripes ran down his arms over his elbows, terminating at gray wrist cuffs. A nondescript patch above his left collarbone identified him as a special liaison of the North American Government. It did not specify his name and rank.

Gravity dissipated outside the crew quarters and Jeff's feet left the ground. He floated past a metal plaque on the wall showing a profile of his ship, the *Celerity*.

Vessels were often designed with a purpose, and this one was built to impress. A pitch-black hull revealed no seams or fasteners, as if the entire ship had been molded from one solid piece of material. Its flat underside and two flat side hulls formed a triangle when viewed nose-on. The nose narrowed to so fine a point it seemed to vanish. Three bell-shaped Hydra engines sat in a triangular configuration at the back of the ship. In profile, the ship looked like an arrowhead with engines.

It was, in the most literal sense, *Jeff's* ship — The Envoy's ship, assigned to whomever held his position. He'd only needed to use it a handful of times since he started working with — working *for* — the government. Other than the infrequent yet unavoidable order to visit Shipyard 6 and attempt communication with the Weaver, the *Celerity* remained in its docking bay at Tensu Station.

Every time he drifted past the metal plaque, Jeff felt a tugging in his chest. He wanted to give the ship a proper spin some day, without oversight, just to see what it could do.

Gravity returned as Jeff drifted into the cockpit from the passage connecting it to the crew quarters mid-ship. He pointed his feet toward the floor as he sank slowly, waiting for the GravGen unit to take hold. The lights in the ceiling made his skull ache, so he put on a pair of tinted glasses that he kept for just such occasions. They were an awkward fit over his eye patch, but did the trick.

A woman sat with her back to him in the pilot seat. The cockpit was narrow, with only a single seat at the front which faced the curved viewscreen and the glossy control panel.

"They wheeled you onto the ship in a hypergel tank," said the woman. "I've seen a lot, but that's a first."

Jeff would have mistaken its smooth and perfectly enunciated qualities for the ship's meticulously-crafted onboard computer had it not been for the fact that he'd permanently disabled that feature on a previous voyage.

The viewscreen showed nothing but black, except for a faint yellow glow leaking in from the left side.

Phobis, Jeff thought. *Galena's star.*

He unfolded a small seat buttoned to the inner

hull at the back of the cockpit and sat down with a sigh.

"Did you sleep?" he asked.

She nodded. Long, brown hair shined from the glare of the ceiling lamps. "Until just after the Rip." She pressed a small button on the control panel and her chair slowly spun around. "I'm Ayani Varma, your new handler." Her brown eyes studied him as if she couldn't understand how all his pieces fit together. "Is it true you're over five-hundred years old?" she asked.

He rubbed his right eye under his glasses, then readjusted them on the bridge of his nose.

"Most people usually don't open a conversation with that kind of question."

Ayani crossed her arms over her dark blue flight suit, yet there was no hint of confrontation in her eyes — only curiosity. "I'm not most people."

"A question for a question, then," said Jeff. "Is it true you saved eight of your classmates from a lab fire at the academy?"

A shadow passed over her face. Her eyes flicked away for the briefest of moments, then found Jeff's again. "No. It was only five. You read my file?"

"I like to know the people assigned to watch my back."

"My direct superior inflated the number to make the academy look better in the press," Ayani explained. "It happened right after the training accident."

"The port crash," said Jeff, nodding. "I remember."

"Image rehabilitation, he called it. All I did was

pull them out into the hallway."

"And saved their lives in the process."

"It still landed me in front of the tribunal. I was on academic probation until I graduated."

"Why?"

"I wasn't supposed to be there. It wasn't even my class."

"What does that matter?"

Ayani looked away, embarrassed. "I was...I was there to sabotage someone else's lab project. A roommate who stole my research paper."

Jeff smiled. "So, you're a hero to some and a thorn in the administration's side behind the curtain?"

"What about you?" she asked. "According to public record, you don't exist. You've *never* existed."

"No one at the Seattle office told you anything?"

"They know you *exist*, but that's it."

Jeff looked at the viewscreen. A small, blue-green dot had appeared in the center. He'd seen surface scans of Galena and thumbed through a few of the Farming Initiative brochures. It had been pitched to potential colonists as a new Earth — a frontier world ripe for the shaping. All it would take was a little elbow grease and a can-do attitude. Jeff often found himself wondering if there was more to it than that.

Ayani eventually filled the long silence with her previous question. "Are you really five hundred years old?"

He broke from his reverie and met her eyes. "That's another case of rumor running away from itself."

A frown tugged at the corners of her mouth. She looked down, slightly disappointed, but nodded and moved to turn back around to face the front of the ship.

"I'm only four-hundred and forty one," said Jeff.

She shot him a glance to see if he was joking.

"Born 2029," he added. Her eyes narrowed, and he shrugged. "Hey, you asked."

"How is that possible?"

"What's your clearance level?" She opened her mouth to answer but he waved her off. "It doesn't matter. I don't really care. The short version is that I died on a mission to Titan and was brought back to life by a machine called a torus. One of the interesting side effects of my resurrection is, apparently, immortality."

Ayani spent a few moments digesting the information, staring at nothing in particular — then she looked at him.

"This feels like *really* classified information."

Jeff grinned without humor. "I'm a little sore about being made to go to another world, so they can sue me."

"Your designation," said Ayani. "The 'Envoy'. Envoy to whom?"

"To *what,*" he corrected. "I'm guessing you also weren't told about the Weaver. It's an alien the government has locked up in Shipyard 6."

Ayani's eyes widened. "Can't say I've heard of it."

"Before its kind went extinct, they built the tori to resurrect them later. When a torus brought me back to life, it was simply fulfilling its base programming. I washed up on the east coast of Florida. No scars. No birthmark. I looked ten years younger."

"You look sixty," Ayani interjected. "A *good* sixty, but definitely not forty-one. No offense."

Jeff sighed. "Four hundred years of kicking around will do that to a guy. My hair is going gray, finally," he added, running a hand over his head. "Thought it'd be dark forever."

"So you can talk to this Weaver? That's why you're The Envoy?"

"Not so much talk as listen," Jeff admitted. "I think Trager and the others expect it to tell me if there's ever an invasion coming."

"What would invade?"

"Who knows?" said Jeff. "Ask Trager."

"You don't seem to like what you do very much," Ayani observed, "and you don't agree with keeping the alien in captivity. Why don't you just leave? You don't have to be The Envoy."

He stared at her a moment, then said, "It's a prisoner, and it's alone."

"It's not human."

"Neither am I, really."

"Don't you have family?" asked Ayani.

Jeff didn't expect to answer, but found himself saying, very distantly, "Long ago." He cleared his throat. "The Weaver was building a new home for itself on Venus when the government snatched it up."

"You think they should have let it occupy Venus."

"*We're* not doing anything with it," said Jeff.

"Four hundred years," Ayani muttered. "Does the Weaver have anything to do with the meteor shower that changed Earth's soil?"

"Well, that's the thing," Jeff replied, nodding. "The Weaver was...maybe just a *little* bit...trying to terraform the three inner planets by bombarding them with blue goop that mutated or destroyed all organic life."

"Right," said Ayani. "Yeah. Just a little thing."

"But hey, Earth's getting better," Jeff said. "I heard some kid grew a flower in Ireland."

"England."

He waved his hand dismissively. "Time. Geography. Everything kind of loses its meaning after the first couple hundred years."

Ayani suddenly grew serious and looked down at her hands.

"Why are you telling me all of this?" she asked quietly.

Jeff shrugged. "Like I said, you asked."

"Yeah, but you didn't have to *tell* me."

"You didn't have to tell me why you were in the classroom before the fire, but you did. Seems only fair to reciprocate."

"They are *not* equivalent," Ayani said, her eyebrows rising. After a moment, she shook her head and pushed a button on the side of her chair. It slowly spun around to face the viewscreen.

Jeff watched the back of her head while she ran diagnostics on her control panel.

"Why'd you agree to be my handler?" he asked.

"No one else wanted the job," she replied.

"That can't be the only reason."

Her hands paused over the controls. "I wanted to know if the rumors about you were true." An alert flashed on the control panel. "Ionizing shield has shed all the rads we picked up in the Rip. We'll land on Galena in less than an hour."

Jeff stood up from his small seat at the back of the cockpit and approached the viewscreen. A tingling sensation tickled him between his shoulder blades.

"Can you make the image bigger?" he asked.

Ayani swiped the side of the control panel and Galena filled the viewscreen. Green fingers of land stretched across the surface. Brilliant blue water filled the spaces between.

Jeff sucked in a breath and his back went rigid. General Trager had been right about a signal. Whatever was sending it out from the surface of Galena felt a lot like what Jeff experienced whenever he entered the Weaver's chamber in Shipyard 6. It started by paralyzing him with an iron grip on his spine. Eventually, the grip loosened enough for him to regain control of his body.

There was more to this new sensation, however.

The Weaver was a singular organism, and every signal it released across any discernible spectrum was indicative of that fact — it was one voice singing a solo. Jeff felt a choir of voices as he approached Galena, each individual as strong or stronger than anything he'd felt in the Weaver's presence.

"What is it?" asked Ayani.

Jeff's voice was barely above a whisper.

"Trager's superiors found a signal coming from Galena that matched output from the Weaver. I can feel it."

She looked up at him. "What do you feel?"

"*Something* is down there," Jeff told her, "but it's not what they think."

GAVIN

Roasted rock bat, much to the contrary of Gavin's expectations, had a delicious smoky flavor unlike anything he'd ever tasted. There had been no flavor variety on Earth, not for him. His father provided him with a brand of soy protein paste he squeezed from a tube, despite the pain it caused his stomach. Occasionally, there would be an exotic vegetable from one of the orbital farms, or a bag of crisps his father had traded. The vast majority of the working class consumed a diet consisting primarily of bioengineered soy product, and Gavin was no different. Despite his soy intolerance, he had been forced to endure stabbing stomach pains for hours after every meal.

He sat with Willef, Shurri, and Arthur around a small fire near the freshwater spring, gnawing at a crispy bat limb. Juvenile rectangular-shaped patches of red living moss crawled slowly over flat stones near the bubbling spring, leaving behind translucent pink smears.

Food was much better on Galena. The soy crop hurt his stomach, but not as much as whatever was grown on Earth. He had only needed to resort to eating it several times since the first potato harvest came in. Between those and the carrots — and soon, hopefully, onions — he had learned a dozen different ways to make a satisfying stew. Baked potatoes smeared with bittersweet were a particular favorite.

Gavin and his peers had been hesitant to try the meat at first. Watching Willef skin and clean the alien creature made them go pale. Yet as soon as Willef turned the carcass on a spit over the flame, and the fat began to drip and hiss in the fire, Gavin's mouth watered.

"Why don't we eat this at the colony?" Arthur asked, tearing off another piece from the spit.

Willef picked the last bit of meat off a bone and tossed it over his shoulder. "Soyflower was engineered to give us all the proteins we need," he said, licking his fingers. "Hunting rock bats isn't worth the risk."

"But it's really good."

Willef chuckled as he pulled out one of Henry Tolbard's hand-drawn maps. "Then you do the dance next time."

Gavin looked at Shurri, and she smiled at him, her mouth shiny with grease. He laughed silently.

"And also," said Arthur, "Gavin can't eat the soyflower. He's not getting any protein."

"He can eat it," Shurri clarified, "but he shouldn't."

"I think his mother put protein in the potatoes," Willef said thoughtfully. "Otherwise he'd have no muscle."

My dad said she changed the seeds to grow in Galena soil, Gavin signed.

Shurri translated for Willef, who nodded.

"Then she could have added nutrients."

"Do you remember her?" asked Arthur.

Gavin thought a moment, then signed, *Some things very clearly. Her hair and laugh. But her face is blurry.*

"It's the same with me and my dad," Arthur said. His and Shurri's father was one of the two wardens left in charge of the colony eight years earlier, but he died shortly after arrival.

"Mom doesn't even have a picture of him," Shurri added. She tossed a bare bone into the fire.

After the last of the rock bat had been consumed, Willef stamped down the fire and spread the ashes to cool. He pulled on his heavy pack with a grunt and looked at the sky between the treetops.

"A couple hours of daylight left," he said. "We can make it to the river."

Arthur groaned as he stood, keeping a pale hand on his injured shoulder. Shurri complained as she pulled on her pack. Gavin winced as the straps of his pack pressed into his aching shoulders.

"Everyone have water?" Willef asked, looking them over. He tucked his map into the side pouch of his pack.

They nodded.

Besides the one field of rock pillars, the landscape south of the colony was mostly sparse forest, occasionally intersected by a stream. Much of it was flat, making for steady progress. After an hour of walking, the ground began to rise and fall in a series of wide hills, and the forest thinned. Phobis was now a hand's width above the horizon, its pale yellow light cooling as the blue sky deepened toward dusk.

"You have science lessons?" Willef called out

from the head of the line.

"You mean classes?" Shurri asked.

"Different kinds," said Arthur. "Ecology, microbiology, meteorology, which is boring."

Gavin signed a quick sentence to Shurri.

"Depends on how busy the teachers are," she translated.

"Dr. James says you need to teach us how to fish," Arthur told him.

Willef grunted. "No one goes in the ocean but me."

"But you stay close to the shore."

"And still some of the nets go missing. Safer at dawn and dusk. Still not safe. If I ever get eaten, one of you will learn how to fish quick enough."

"Our mom says the ocean animals are sea monsters," said Shurri.

Willef nodded. "She scares you to keep you away."

"Have you ever seen one?"

"Not a whole one. Deep in the water, I see a back, a fin, maybe one time an eye. Something big washed up on the shore last year, but it was too mangled to tell the shape. Horrible smell. I tried to cook a steak." He spat on the ground. "No good. But I found a tooth."

"Can we see it?" Arthur asked.

Willef laughed. "It's too big to wear as a necklace. It's at the colony. Half as tall as you, and about as wide. You can see it later."

"What does it look like?"

Willef turned back and grinned. "Like the tooth of a sea monster."

The terrain climbed steadily, and Willef told

them they were approaching the river. A sound of rushing water grew louder as they left the open hills behind and entered a forest. Jagged boulders and sheets of razor-edged stone had been strewn about as if a mountain of rock had exploded.

Ahead, the ground dipped away, out of sight. A cold mist rolled up from below.

"The river," Willef shouted over the noise of the water. He pointed to his left.

A wide river cut through the forest, flowing in their direction, gaining speed as it approached a drop-off. Gavin walked forward to stand near the edge of a tall cliff. The river spilled over the cliff in a frothing waterfall and pounded into a deep pool below. A narrower, gentler river continued on from the pool at the base of the cliff, wending slowly along the bottom of a canyon cut by the water.

"Don't get close to the edge," Willef shouted. "We go this way." He indicated a path upstream of the waterfall, where the river looked shallow enough to cross.

Gavin brought up the rear as Arthur and Shurri followed after Willef. The air surrounding the rushing water was pleasantly cooler than it had been walking over the exposed hills. Gavin inhaled deeply, until a foul odor bombarded his nostrils. It was the same pungent stink he'd encountered after their flight from the rock bats.

"Do you *smell* that?" Shurri asked, wrinkling her nose. "Something is *rotten*."

Willef sniffed the air, then walked to a nearby tree. A coating of gray slime had been smeared across the base of its trunk. He crouched down next to it, frowning and mumbling to himself.

"Never seen this before."

More over there, Gavin signed, pointing to another tree.

"Look at this," said Arthur. He slid his hand down a deep groove in the tree — a yellow gash in the spongy material beneath the grayish outer layer. "They're all over the tree."

Gavin placed his hand inside a groove and looked up, tracing the pattern of deep slashes to a trio of thick taproots angled toward the sky like talons.

The sky beast perched between them, its large bulk spilling over the top of the tree. Two silver eyes as big as dinner plates gleamed in the light of the setting sun as the creature stared down the length of the tree.

Willef stood up slowly, waving the others back.

"Run now," he said.

Gavin looked at Arthur and Shurri. They were frozen in place, staring up at the creature. He grabbed Shurri's hand, startling her, then he motioned for them to leave.

"Arthur!" she hissed as she followed Gavin away from the tree. Arthur snapped out of his trance and hurried to catch up.

The sky beast shifted on its perch. It flicked its head to the side and watched Willef with one eye, then it raised its two winged forelimbs and loosed a piercing shriek that vibrated its throat. The tree swayed as the beast spun in a circle, clawing at the taproots.

Willef slid off his pack and unzipped it in one smooth motion. He pulled out a machete with one hand. With the other, he withdrew something Gavin had only seen on television before leaving Earth: a pistol. It was constructed of white material and had a wide barrel with red slashes painted down the side.

Gavin stopped and turned to Shurri.

We can't leave him, he signed.

"We can't stay here!" she cried.

She pushed against his chest but he wouldn't budge. Arthur ran past him, back the way they had come.

"Go!" Willef shouted.

The sky beast let out another shriek and lurched over the side of its perch. Talons scored the tree trunk as the creature slid down toward the ground, its eyes locked on Willef.

He planted his feet in a wide stance as he raised the pistol, cursing the sky beast in a language Gavin didn't recognize. The gun belched fire when he pulled the trigger. A section of the tree exploded beneath the sky beast, bursting outward in splinters. Willef cursed and threw the empty gun aside. He turned and ran, machete blade glinting. Gavin unstrapped his own machete from his pack as he ran behind Arthur and Shurri.

Thick connective fibers snapped as the top half of the tree fell slowly. The sky beast jumped to the bottom half and slid down with a squawk, carving fresh gashes in the trunk. It hit the ground with an earth-shaking thud.

"Packs off!" Willef yelled.

The four of them dropped their backpacks as they burst from the tree line, running for the nearby hills.

Willef grabbed Gavin's jacket collar and pulled him close.

"You take them that way," he said, nodding to the left. "If they die now, it's your fault."

He shoved Gavin away and turned back, waving his machete. The sky beast emerged from the trees, limping on an injured limb. Its leathery folded wings flapped like broken sails as it ran without obvious skill toward Willef with the same motion as a horse's gallop. Even though it was inexperienced at chasing down prey on the ground, it ran faster than any of them could manage at a sprint.

"Ya-*ha!*" Willef shouted as the creature, more than twice his height, bore down on him. He swung his machete as if he meant to slice off its bald head.

At the last second, he rolled out of the way. The sky beast lunged past him, screeching in frustration. It tried to turn but tripped over its own bony legs. Dark soil erupted from the ground as it rolled over, claws scraping for purchase.

Willef jumped to his feet and ran toward the trees. After regaining its footing, the sky beast hobbled after him.

Gavin stopped, breathing hard.

"What are you doing?!" Shurri yelled, running past him with Arthur.

There's no place to hide, he signed with shaking hands. *Better chance in the trees.*

"It can *climb* trees!"

The water, Gavin signed as he ran toward the forest.

"Arthur!" Shurri yelled from behind.

Gavin glanced back to see them following after

him. Willef shouted from somewhere nearby, closer to the river, but still out of sight. There was a loud thud and Willef laughed triumphantly. The laugh turned into a sharp scream and cut off abruptly.

Gavin, Shurri, and Arthur skidded to a stop, their ragged breaths conspicuously loud in the sudden silence.

Shurri pointed to a red smear on the trunk of a tree. The three of them ran over to find Willef seated with his back to the trunk, pressing his red-slicked hands to a deep gash that ran from his right shoulder to the left side of his ribcage.

The sky beast squawked and Gavin spun around. The creature shook its bald head as if it were dizzy. Black blood trickled from a cut behind one of its eyes.

Willef tried to speak, but only managed a thin wheeze.

Gavin signaled to Shurri.

"What are we doing?!" Arthur pleaded as he stood next to them, watching the sky beast helplessly.

The creature regained its senses and spotted them.

Willef screamed in pain as Gavin and Shurri helped him to his feet.

J-U-M-P, Gavin signed with one hand.

Shurri's gaze flicked toward the river, then back at Gavin. She nodded.

"We're jumping!" she told Arthur.

Willef was a dead weight between them as they shuffled toward the cliff. He still clutched his stained machete in one hand. Gavin tried to pry it loose as they stumbled for the cliff, but the man held it with an iron grip.

He and Shurri positioned Willef at the edge and looked down through the rising mist at the white-slashed pool ten meters below.

"Have to push him," Shurri said through clenched teeth. "Arthur—"

He darted past her and leapt off the cliff.

Gavin looked back. The sky beast was in a full limping run, headed right for them. Gavin caught Shurri's eye and nodded. They gave Willef a hard push and he fell head-first off the cliff. Shurri grabbed Gavin's hand and they jumped after him.

A second later, Gavin hit the frigid pool on his side. Shurri's hand was ripped away as he tumbled in the current. His shoulder smacked a rock and he screamed bubbles.

He rolled out of the main deluge and surfaced, sucking down a lungful of air. The sky beast shrieked at him and pounded the cliff's edge with its claws as it paced, trying to find a path down into the chasm.

Gavin searched the pool but couldn't see the others. A cloud of bloody water swelled from below. He took a deep breath and dove down, grateful for his father's swimming lessons in the Casmin Sea.

Willef floated lifelessly against a smooth boulder. Gavin grabbed his wrist and pulled him to the surface. Blood seeped from his chest into the water.

Arthur and Shurri were on the far side of the pool opposite the waterfall, near the continuation of the river.

With a loud screech, the sky beast leapt from the cliff and dove into the center of the pool with a tremendous splash. It dove gracefully, a stream of silver bubbles trailing behind its body as it arced through the pool.

Gavin looked around frantically. A gleam of silver caught his eye near the rocky shore of the pool — Willef's machete.

He paddled for the shore, slowly pulling Willef behind him. The sky beast clung to an underwater boulder at the bottom of the pool, limbs splayed out as it looked up toward the surface at its prey.

Gavin shoved Willef onto a shore of large, smooth stones, then scrambled away, moving toward the machete.

"*Gavin!*" Shurri screamed.

He grabbed the blade as the sky beast burst from the water, jumping through the air to land on the shore in front of him.

Gavin froze. The beast opened its blunt beak and snapped it shut with a *CLACK*. Its wings fluttered, shedding water.

THUNK!

A rock hit the side of its body. Its head twitched sideways to look for the source of the assault as another rock thwacked its beak. Arthur and Shurri were on the shore, throwing baseball-sized stones.

The beast spread its wings in a display of aggression and opened its beak to shriek at them. Gavin jumped forward and drove the machete through the sky beast's throat until the tip came out the other side, dripping black. Then he twisted.

The sky beast spun in a fury, knocking Gavin off his feet and sending him back into the water. He popped his head above the surface, sputtering, as the sky beast collapsed on the shore. Its claws scrabbled over loose stones as it tried to stand. It rose on shaking limbs, then collapsed with a heavy thud. Its silver eyes dulled as it turned its head to look at Gavin — and then it was still.

Gavin paddled on his side to where Willef lay on the shore. He crawled from the icy water, body shivering, teeth chattering — half from the cold, half from the adrenaline.

Willef's wounded chest rose and fell with slow breaths. He stared up at the darkening sky. Gavin knelt down beside him.

Shurri and Arthur walked over and sat on the other side of Willef. He blinked, then seemed to notice their presence for the first time. Shurri leaned closer to inspect his wound, then quickly sat up, pressing the back of her hand to her mouth as she looked away. She took Willef's hand and squeezed it tightly. He squeezed back.

"I named the twin mountains," he wheezed. A little smile touched his pale lips. "No one done it yet, not even Tolbard. So I figured...why not?"

"What did you call them?" Arthur asked.

"Gretchen and Ursula." His eyes twinkled with a fond remembrance.

Shurri brushed a strand of hair from her face with a bloody hand. "Where are you from, Willef?"

"Someplace friendly," he said weakly. "Filled with...warm people."

Arthur frowned. "I didn't think such a place existed on Earth."

"You can always find it," Willef told him. "If you look."

He turned his head toward Gavin and drew a deep breath.

"Did your father tell you," he whispered in a wet, raspy voice, "what I did wrong on the Halcyon?"

"He said you made a mistake, and you couldn't forgive yourself."

Willef blinked slowly, then nodded. Dark blood welled in his chest wound.

"I led many people to their deaths, but I survived. Your father—" he closed his eyes against a wave of pain, then sighed. "Your father went the right way."

Gavin tried to sign the words, *My father isn't always—*

Willef grabbed Gavin's hand with surprising force. "No one is perfect. But being *practical* is what makes a survivor."

Gavin pulled his hand away and signed angrily, *If my father was practical, he would have killed the sky beast when he had the chance. Now look.* He shrugged hopelessly, gesturing to Willef's wounds.

"My good boy," said Willef with a shaky smile. "No one sees the future. You make your choices when you can, the best you can." He met the eyes of Shurri and Arthur. "All of you remember. This colony—"

He breathed in sharply and squeezed Gavin's hand painfully hard, then his body relaxed as he let out a long, quiet sigh — his final breath.

Shurri folded Willef's hands over his stomach and lay on her back, her movements robotic. Arthur lay down next to her, reaching for his sister's hand. Their fingers intertwined and held on fiercely. The first stars had begun to shine in the twilight. The twins stared up at them with wide eyes, too shocked to cry.

Gavin stumbled to his feet and stood next to the

dead sky beast, his clothes dripping. He peeled off his torn jacket and threw it against the stones on the shore with a wet slap. Looking up at the cliffs, he realized he and the others were trapped in the river valley.

He walked to Shurri and lay down next to her.

"What are we going to do?" she asked in a daze.

Gavin had no answer.

THE ENVOY

The *Celerity* set down in a field, its landing engines scorching moss from a scattering of silver-gray boulders. It had been surprisingly simple to find a suitable landing spot for the thirty-meter vessel. The area Jeff targeted based on previous scan data and his own intuition was comprised of rolling hills and sparse tree cover.

He walked down the ramp with Ayani at his side, breathing in the clean air — aromas of wet, peaty soil and the mineral tang of spring water. It had been a long time since he smelled anything so pure. The streets of Seattle had staled long ago.

Phobis burned bright in the vibrant blue sky. Jeff paused to shade his right eye and looked at the horizon. Twin mountains rose in the distance, wispy clouds occluding their peaks. To the west of the mountains was the Casmin Sea. From that distance, it appeared as a beaten sheet of silver.

Ayani walked past him carrying a government issue short rifle, a weapon she gripped with easy confidence. She wore a small backpack that fit snugly between her shoulder blades.

"Fresh water won't be a problem," she said, probing the soft ground at the bottom of the ramp with the toe of her boot. "Natural springs are abundant. I have enough rations for two days, and a homing beacon on the Celerity. We can go wherever you need."

Jeff stepped off the ramp. "We're a little far from the mountains, but—"

He froze when the soles of his boots hit the soft ground. White light exploded in his vision, blinding him. From far away, like an echo, he heard Ayani ask, "Are you alright?"

The initial overpowering flood of white dimmed enough to reveal a vast forest of solid-looking light beams rising from the ground in every direction. Some were as thick as a tree trunk and others as thin as a thread. They flowed upward in varying intensities, pulsing and shimmering — but they all had *substance*. Just above Jeff's head, they dissolved into nothingness. Small, glowing particles like drifting fireflies floated up from the faded edges of light.

"Do you see that?" he whispered. "The light..."

"I see the sunlight," Ayani replied, squinting up at the sky. "What else is there?"

Jeff heard a sound flowing through the light. It seemed to be infused in the beams, a kind of tinkling, crystalline song. He realized he was experiencing a visual and aural representation of Galena's living organisms. The moss, the trees, the microscopic bacteria — they all emanated their own crystal song, and they were all connected by it.

One pillar of light rose higher than all the rest — high enough to touch the sky. A grayish tint infused its glow, as if it were somehow tainted. It flickered like a dying flashlight. Jeff immediately realized the source of that beam was his destination.

Ayani grabbed him under the armpit and hauled him to his feet at the bottom of the ramp. Jeff looked down in confusion.

"I didn't realize I'd fallen," he said in a stupor. "The light hurts my eye."

"You're also crying, but I won't put that in my report."

Jeff wiped his wet cheek and looked at the glimmer on his palm. Tiny threads of light stuck out from the moisture like cactus spines.

"You were saying something about those mountains," Ayani reminded him.

"Right. We'll head in that direction. I feel something...something different than the Weaver...but I don't think it's on the surface. It's deeper."

"Are you sure you're okay? You dropped like a sack of bricks." She looked at him and gasped. "Your *eye.*"

"What is it?"

Jeff cautiously touched his closed eyelid, then studied his fingertips.

"Your iris is glowing white."

"That's new," he mumbled.

Jeff patted his pockets and found his tinted glasses. He put them on and the light beams rising from Galena's surface dimmed to the point of tolerability.

They walked in silence as they moved farther from the ship. Jeff hesitated near the first thick light beam he came to, then slowly moved his hand through it, feeling a slight warmth.

Ayani walked past him, shaking her head as if he

was crazy. To her, he was standing in an open field moving his hand around through empty space.

"You carry that gun like it's a part of your arm," he commented as he caught up to her.

"Why don't *you* have one?"

Jeff smiled. "I have you. I was told that's all I needed."

"I might fall into a chasm, or get eaten by a giant bird. Then what?"

"Just toss me the gun as it's happening. I brought it up because there's a gap in your file."

Ayani walked steadily onward, her eyes scanning the ground and seeking out the best path between boulders and protruding roots. They passed a copse of tall trees with smooth, ash-gray skin. A trio of thick branches crowned each trunk. The branches grew straight out from the trunk for several meters, then bent abruptly skyward, giving the treetops the appearance of massive talons.

"I was assigned to a special unit," she said at last. "I'm not surprised the files were purged. It's best if I don't talk about it. Long story short...yes, I'm very familiar with this weapon."

"Good enough for me," said Jeff.

They crossed a small stream and walked through a field of chest-high boulders.

"Not much life here," Ayani said. "Some smaller plant growth, and those trees. I haven't seen a single animal."

"They're here. A lot of them are below us."

"Burrowers?"

Jeff frowned, trying to translate the planet's sensory bombardment into words.

"Something about the trees," he told her. "They have roots that aren't roots. They're like...neurons stretching out to form some kind of continental web."

Ayani looked at him sideways. "Neurons?"

"There's a network of signals underground, all traveling along those roots."

He paused to look up at the top of a tree, its three branches clawing for the heavens.

"The trees are upside-down," he said, pointing. "Look. Those are taproots. The canopy is beneath us." He bounced gently on the soft, squishy soil. "I think most of the animals live down there, and I think these trees are all connected. They might even form the largest organism on this planet."

Ayani prodded the soil with the tip of her gun. "Is that what you felt on the ship? The presence of this superorganism?"

"No," said Jeff. "What I'm feeling now is...pleasant. Calm. It's hard to describe. A symphony of life. What I felt before was almost malignant. It was...darker. It didn't fit."

Ayani's eyebrows went up skeptically. "And you want to go find this thing that is not pleasant or calm?"

"I have to know what it is, and why I can sense it. It might be connected to the Weaver."

"Which means it *also* might be connected to you," said Ayani.

Jeff walked away from her, in the direction of the two mountains.

"I know how you got that scar," she called after him. "I know how you lost your eye."

"Remember what I told you about rumors," he

said over his shoulder.

Jeff self-consciously ran a light finger over the scar on his scalp. He started above his left eye and traced it back over his head in a straight line almost to the top of his neck. Images of the crash pulsed in his mind — fire and twisted metal. Screaming. *His* screaming.

"You crashed a dock shuttle into the hull of Shipyard 6," said Ayani as she caught up to him and matched his pace. "Now I know what's inside. You were trying to set the Weaver free."

Jeff knelt beside a shallow stream and splashed his face with cool water. He pinched some loose soil and rubbed it between his fingertips, studying it thoughtfully.

"I was trying to kill myself," he said as he stood up to meet her eyes. "And, yeah, maybe try to release the Weaver in the process."

"Why?" Ayani asked, genuinely confused. "You have a higher status than almost anyone in our sector. You can get fresh food, *real* food, any time you want. I get that you're grouchy about a so-called forced assignment, but most people would give everything to have that opportunity."

Jeff wiped his palms on his white shirt, leaving dirty smears. "The allure of status fades after the first hundred years," he told her. "And honestly, apples from the orbital farms aren't any better than the hydroponic stuff they grow on the surface."

"Why'd you do it?"

He sighed, thinking back over the past three hundred years to the days leading up to the crash. "I missed my family. I missed having friends. I looked into the future and saw more of the same. More longing, and more loneliness."

"But you have so much time to make friends, *and* a new family."

"Friends are flashes in the dark. My wife grew old with me. She lived every day with the knowledge that I was watching her die. She knew I'd have to deal with that pain as long as I lived. Nobody else needs to feel like that." He looked up at Phobis, not bothering to shield his eye. "Nihilism is impossible to avoid on a long enough time scale. There's a good reason humans don't live forever."

They walked in silence for a long time. The air cooled near a broad, flat stream. Ayani found a shallow crossing and led the way through the slow-moving water.

"What stopped you from trying again?" she asked.

Jeff cracked a half-grin. "You wouldn't be a very good therapist. I was under closer surveillance after that. They called it a 'no-knives' policy. After a while, the doctors said there was a chance that the Weaver's 'depression' or 'disrupted state of mind' was affecting my thoughts. I didn't consider it much at the time. I was too busy trying to learn how to see with one eye. After I healed, I started to focus more on the connection between us. Instead of resisting, I opened my mind during my visits, just to see if maybe it had been trying to reach me."

"What did you find?"

Jeff hesitated, then said, "A kindred soul. Years don't matter to the Weaver. The first thing it showed me was how to deal with the time…all that endless time. And it showed me...a lot more."

"Like what?"

"It showed me that my problems are insignificant in the grand scheme of things."

"That doesn't make them any easier for *you*."

"Easier to ignore, perhaps," he said. "How far are we from the ship?"

Ayani checked her glowing wristpad. "Four klicks."

He nodded and stopped next to a tree. "This should do it. Would you mind shooting the ground?"

"The...ground?" she repeated.

"In a half-circle, like this," said Jeff, sweeping his index finger in a broad arc over the soil.

Ayani hesitated, then Jeff nodded encouragement and gestured at the ground again.

She flicked off the rifle's safety. *CRAKCRAKCRAK!* Bright blue projectiles streaked from the nozzle with each pull of the trigger and thudded into the dirt.

The ground swelled up beneath their feet as if something was rising from below. Next to Jeff, the tree groaned and creaked. Its trunk vibrated. A hole opened in the ground between the impact point of the three slugs. Roots popped as they slinked away from the projectiles, moving like snakes through the soil.

"Ladies first," said Jeff with a grin, nodding at the hole.

"I'm not going in there!" Ayani shouted over the creaking tree.

Jeff peered down into the hole for a moment, then hopped over the edge and fell.

He landed on his feet in waist-deep water, sending a jolt up his legs and back. Ayani splashed down next to him a few seconds later. She came up sputtering and cursing, swiping wet strands of hair from her face. The bright beam of sunlight piercing down from above narrowed and disappeared as the hole in the ground sealed itself, plunging them into darkness.

Ayani flicked on a small flashlight and attached it to the barrel of her weapon, glaring sideways at Jeff.

"How did you know that would happen?" she growled.

"Just a hunch. This is the real Galena, down here."

Ayani played her light around the small underground cavern. Thick, wet roots hung from the ceiling. Several of them curled up slowly when the light found them.

They stood in a shallow river that flowed gently from one side of the cavern to the other. Walls of black, jagged stone gleamed in the light.

"Well," Ayani sighed. "We're down here. Now what?"

"Listen," said Jeff, shifting on his feet. "I should have said this up there, but I didn't. There's some truth to the rumors that my handlers don't stick around because I'm hard to work with. You caught me on a good month. The bigger issue is that I tend not to care as much about my own safety as they do theirs. The term 'reckless endangerment' comes up quite often in my debriefings."

"I jumped in the hole, didn't I?"

"You did," he nodded. "And now that we're down here, I realize I may have glossed over the danger of what we could be walking into. In other words, you should think about staying here."

Ayani searched his face in the same way she had when they first met — probing his seams to find out how he was put together.

“What are we walking into?” she asked.

“Nothing good,” he replied. “Nothing friendly.”

Ayani popped the magazine from her rifle, checked the rounds, and slapped it back in.

“Well,” she said, and racked a round into the chamber. “I have enough friends already.”

MERRITT

Merritt clicked on the electric lamp near the long work table inside his home. Chill night air poured in through the open door as Kellan stood in the entryway, admiring the inside of the corrugated metal dome. He walked over to the long table, his eyes sweeping over several of Merritt's unfinished repair projects.

Uda appeared in the doorway, but didn't enter the home.

Her eyes flicked to Kellan with more than a glint of distrust before finding Merritt's. "I'll say good night. Toma will be wondering where I am."

Merritt nodded.

Kellan turned to her with a wide grin. "Good night, Uda, and thank you."

She nodded quickly and walked away. Kellan sighed pleasantly and turned his attention back to the work table.

"I'm to understand Toma is her child?"

"That's right," Merritt replied as he crouched next to a small, dented electric heater. He plugged it in to a dirty power strip and the lamp next to his work table dimmed considerably. "One of a handful of children born since the crash." He pulled out a metal bowl filled with dark brown stew from a low cabinet and placed it atop the stove. "Food will be ready soon."

Kellan looked at the stove, an amused smile tugging at his lips. "It already smells great." He touched the corner of one of Henry Tolbard's paper maps, pulling it closer to him. "Tell me about your son's field trip."

Merritt stirred the stew absentmindedly while he looked into the shadows at the back of his home, thinking back to what Uda told him less than an hour ago.

Careful.

Behind him, Kellan chuckled. "Did you think I was going to drop shock troops into the colony and round up the farmers?"

Using a spoon crafted from *Halcyon* scrap metal, Merritt scooped stew into a white bowl carved from the fallen trunk of a Galena tree. Kellan took a long moment to admire both when they were placed in front of him on the table. Merritt filled a bowl for himself and pulled over a tall stool to sit on.

"I didn't know what to expect," he finally answered, blowing on the hot stew. "I still don't."

Kellan took a careful sip off his spoon and tested the flavor. "It's good, but salt would make it excellent."

"Haven't found any of that yet."

"I brought some. Are we allowed to talk business, just the two of us? Is there some kind of council?"

"No one person makes a major decision," said Merritt, "but we can still talk."

Kellan stirred his stew. "Let's bull through the technical stuff first then, shall we? Anyone in the colony who worked on board the Halcyon has no responsibility to any Earth government. Their contracts were with the employers who placed them on the starliner. Scientists like Dr. James and any surviving military personnel signed two year contracts, which they will have fulfilled four times over by now. I expect some of these folks will be wanting a ride home."

"Some, yes," Merritt said between bites.

Kellan set down his bowl of stew. "And those who signed up for the Farming Initiative have been accruing an annual crop debt against a joint government program...a program which suffered a significant financial loss when the Halcyon nose-dived into Galena."

Merritt set down his bowl of stew and wiped his mouth. "I imagine that must have cost a pretty penny. I also imagine it doesn't have an impact on the farmers' contracts as written."

"Not directly, no," Kellan admitted. "But it does put pressure on the ones whose bank accounts are intimately tied to this venture."

"Yours included?"

Kellan smiled without humor. "If I had that kind of money, I'd have been here years ago. However, as the primary architect behind this grand adventure, I have more than money on the line."

Merritt reached behind him and grabbed a jug and two dirty cups from a rickety shelf. He splashed some of Skip's homemade potato vodka into both cups and handed one to Kellan, who sniffed it curiously.

He licked his lips after draining the cup. "Will

wonders never cease?"

Merritt took a sip of his and set it aside. He spread his hands on the table in front of him and looked at Kellan. "How will your plans affect us?"

Kellan hesitated, then said, "I understand it must be very strange for me to show up out of the blue after you've survived eight years alone. I assure you no one back home forgot about the colony. Your government, like all the rest of them, moves slowly. Yet it still has a strong interest in seeing Galena become a second Earth. My job as liaison to the World Space Association is to facilitate that goal. That means supplies. Expansion. Growth, both economic...and population."

Merritt's eyes narrowed.

"Come now," Kellan said easily. "You're a smart man. There are scientists in the colony. Surely someone has done a population study."

Begrudgingly, Merritt nodded. There were too few colonists to create long-term, sustained growth.

"You need more people," Kellan continued. "Otherwise your grandchildren won't be able to find their mouths with their spoons. It won't be hard to convince people to come here after they learn it's Earth's soil keeping them sterile. On top of all that, you need a wee touch of civilization to jumpstart the progress."

Merritt grunted and drank the rest of his vodka. "Look how Earth ended up."

Kellan held up his hands placatingly. "Just a *wee* touch. There's a chance to start fresh here. Build it from the bottom-up, the right way. My ship only brought supplies. We start small. We build roads.

Proper houses. We make the place ready for a larger population. Then we worry about the rest."

"What about the crop debt? You're not hauling soyflower back to Earth in your shuttle."

"The percentages taken from the farmers were always meant to go right back into the community. Up until now, you just haven't had a community large enough to eat it all." He met Merritt's eyes. "But that doesn't mean the debt is satisfied. I want to be clear on something. This colony will grow, with or without the consent of the first colonists." He quickly held up his finger. "But that's not a threat. I didn't come all this way to offer threats. No one benefits from an antagonistic relationship." He put his hands on his chest. "Least of all the person who wants more out of the bargain. Instead, I came to offer an opportunity."

Merritt searched Kellan's face for a long moment. His eyes seemed earnest, almost pleading. "What kind of opportunity?"

Kellan smiled. "Can we take a walk?"

Merritt stuck his hands in the pockets of his padded utility pants as he stepped outside, following Kellan. His long-sleeved knit shirt was just enough to dull the cold bite of a gentle wind. Overhead, the twin nebulae reached across the dome of the sky, surrounded by countless stars.

Kellan stopped and drew a deep breath of unpolluted air.

"I realize I'm doing most of the talking," he confessed.

"What opportunity?"

Kellan walked unhurriedly westward, toward the heart of the colony. Merritt matched his stride as they passed a tall row of soyflower stalks illuminated by the moon, which was just starting to peek over the horizon.

"As usual," Kellan began, "when you're dealing with a voyage of this magnitude, funding can be tricky. Before Earth was mapped, explorers needed to secure patronage, usually through a wealthy sponsor. You and the other colonists would have been alone here many more years if I hadn't gone the same route."

"You borrowed money?"

"I traded. I told you, I favor opportunity." He peeled a green leaf from the stem of a soyflower stalk and sniffed it. "There is a fascinating array of wildlife on this planet. Fortunately, much of it is isolated from the colony by natural land formations. There's a mountain range to the southwest of particular interest."

"Of interest to whom?" Merritt asked. The path they were on led them past Uda's home. Merritt glanced in that direction. A warm light glowed from Toma's bedroom window.

Kellan scratched his neck, a gesture which struck Merritt as self-conscious.

"A group of passengers will be arriving on the next ship," he said. "Eleven or twelve months from now. Passengers who paid exorbitant sums for the chance to see alien wildlife. Turns out that off-world bragging rights can be extremely lucrative."

"You're bringing them on safari?" Merritt's incredulity was the only thing keeping him from laughing at the ridiculousness of the concept. "This isn't a game preserve."

"No, it isn't. I had to get creative. Funding through the proper channels dried up after news of the crash. Most of those in charge wanted to abandon the project. I know better."

"You'll die if you take anyone out there."

"Oh, I believe you. That's why I want you to guide us."

This time Merritt *did* laugh.

Kellan smiled good-naturedly. "Well, I was expecting either a laugh or a punch to the face. I'm glad it was the former."

Merritt shook his head as his laughter tapered off. "The answer is no. I have far too much to worry about here. I don't feel like dying for the sake of another man's vacation."

"Fair enough. I'll ask again when the time comes. What would you say to guiding me and a few others on something a little more small-scale? A two-day trip, perhaps. Out and back, just to get a feel for the land?"

"The answer is still no."

Kellan stopped and lightly touched Merritt's shoulder. "What if I wiped out your crop debt?"

Merritt set his jaw. "I'll work off my debt, just like everyone else."

Kellan looked up at the night sky and sighed. "Janos will be disappointed. I promised him a nice hike after the long voyage." The lights of the colony center shone between the trees ahead. "You have a medical center?"

"A small hospital, yes."

"May I see it?"

Merritt gestured onward. They walked in silence

to the colony center. Two small electric light globes hanging from poles cast warm light on the ground between the few modest structures. The square was empty of other colonists. Merritt led the way up the steps into the prefab hospital. An overhead lamp was on, but no one was inside.

Kellan looked around the room, past the patients' tables, his gaze landing on the living moss gestation tanks against the wall. He stepped close to one of the tanks and peered inside. A hand-sized patch of thick, red, wiry roots undulated in the center of the bubbling tank.

"Is this a native plant?" Kellan asked, looking back at Merritt with a smile.

"It's kind of a plant and an animal."

"And you grow it in tanks." Kellan stood up straight. "Why is that?"

"It heals. Soon after we arrived, my son was crushed under heavy crates. Leera James saved his life with the moss."

"You're farming it," Kellan whispered in admiration.

"It dies after it heals us. We make sure there's a steady population."

"Can it reverse death?"

Merritt's voice deepened. "No."

Kellan stood up straight and grinned impishly. "I can." He walked back to Merritt and leaned against a metal table, crossing his arms. "Funding from my eager hunters paid for my supplies and crew, but not my ship, the Renata. I needed more money. I looked at the facts. You will have a population problem, and I had a funding problem. I found a way to solve both."

Merritt felt himself growing more suspicious the longer the conversation dragged on. "What are you talking about?"

"Clone tourism. I tracked down ninety-nine rich people to pay me a lot of money to bring their DNA here, to Galena, and clone them. I have the equipment on my ship."

Merritt's brow furrowed. "They would exist in two places at once."

Kellan shrugged. "I'm no moral philosopher. If they want a backup of themselves on Galena in case Earth finally goes under, I'll make no judgment. And it's a fresh supply of colonists."

"They would be nothing more than blank slates."

Kellan wagged a finger. "You haven't heard of LifeScan. Wonderful new tech. Only been on the market about three years back home. Takes a deep scan of your brain, every molecule of it. Maps it and stores it. Memories are a part of that map. They're like stories written in your brain. You can read them if you have the right glasses. Well, we found the right glasses, and with it, found a way to duplicate consciousness. You didn't think we were going to grow a bunch of babies, did you? Full-grown adults will be popping out of those vats. Juice them up with their old memories, let 'em do some jumping jacks and they're good to go. Better, probably. No wear and tear on the old biological machine. Rich folks back home get a LifeScan every six months or so. It's all the rage. The LifeScan data is why we can't bring more DNA samples at a time. The samples themselves fit in a tiny tube. We could have brought millions of those. But the LifeScan data…that's another story. A hundred million terabytes of folded data per scan, stored as dense as we can manage, and each data drive *still* weighs two hundred kilos. Not so easy to transport on my small ship."

Merritt scratched the back of his neck, then crossed his arms. "This is an awful lot to take in. Making copies of people back on Earth?"

"It's an odd idea to digest," Kellan admitted. "Are you set on not taking me and a few of my men on a tour of the surrounding area?"

"I am."

Kellan reached into his pocket and pulled out a small glass vial. A strip of blue material, like thin plastic, was suspended within. He set the vial on the metal table next to him.

"I'll bring back your wife."

Merritt's arms slowly uncrossed as he stood up straighter, his eyes locked on the vial.

"That's her DNA," said Kellan quietly. "She was passenger number one-hundred."

"That's Emily?" Merritt asked, the words like gravel in his throat. "There were a hundred other people on that ship. How did you know to bring her?"

"Mr. Alder, do you know what your wife's job was?"

He shook his head numbly, still staring at the vial. "Something for the government. She couldn't talk about it. Something with plants."

"She was a very bright woman, and that's an understatement. Your wife's work is a major reason most of humanity didn't starve when the crops failed. I brought her DNA just in case I needed her expertise. But you're doing just fine on your own. And judging by the flavor of that vodka, she's already been helping you."

Heat slowly rose to Merritt's cheeks. "So now you'll use her DNA as a bribe?"

"As soon as I landed, I knew I wouldn't need to clone her. The colony is far enough along that it isn't justified. This is business, Mr. Alder. I need a local to help keep me and my men alive, or my venture will fall into the red."

"Why? What are you looking for?"

Kellan smiled. "More opportunity. What do you say? You guide my team, and I'll bring your wife back."

"It wouldn't be her if she wasn't scanned," Merritt said softly, once again staring at the vial. "Just a shell."

"Her senior government status allowed for one LifeScan in the event of a life-threatening illness. Emily's consciousness was duplicated shortly before she passed."

"I won't let you bring her back just so I can watch the cancer kill her again."

"The cancer has been wiped out on a molecular level. She will be better than new. What do you say? Take me and my men on a little field trip, steer us clear of the dangers. You get Emily back and I'll *still* wipe out your crop debt."

Merritt couldn't take his eyes off the vial. He thought about Gavin. What would he say if Merritt asked him? Would he want his mother back, no matter how it happened? The boy was only seven when she passed. Would he remember her? Would he be content to let her rest in peace?

He opened his mouth to answer Kellan, then

hesitated. He expected to turn down the offer. Instead, he heard himself say, “I’ll do it.”

WESTON

He walked through the tunnel alone, stopping occasionally to admire the view beyond the translucent tunnel walls. Sunlight filtered down to the sea floor, dancing over the dunes and flashing like sequins over the myriad car-sized holes that dotted the otherwise smooth sand. Weston lowered the sun visor of his helmet to cover his face shield and could barely see a thing. He slid it back up, shaking his head at the wonder of it all.

A sense of relief grew inside him the more distance he put between himself and the steep ramp down which his companions had tumbled. He hesitated for a few minutes at the top of the ramp, even after the others assured him they were unharmed. Something within Weston, some urge to not leave the civilians alone in an alien place had taken root.

But they're not alone, he thought as he trudged down the long tunnel. *Miles is with them, and he's as good a soldier as they come.*

That thought was the only reason he had allowed himself to walk away, back toward the rock-walled elevator which had delivered them to a deeper level of the underwater compound.

Weston had tried to puzzle out what type of life form would build such a place. Had it once been filled with water, the creatures swimming along the tunnels instead of walking them?

Would've saved them some time, he thought with a half-grin.

A sudden sensation of being watched tickled the back of his neck, and he turned around. His breath fogged briefly on the inside of his face shield. The tunnel was empty behind him.

Up ahead, the door leading back to the circular stone elevator awaited. It looked shiny at that distance, as if a thin film of water or oil flowed across its surface. Weston checked his wristpad: less than two hours of oxygen remaining. He could extend that with the spare tanks, but he wanted to save those for when the others came back, just in case. If he was feeling more confident once he got past the elevator door, he would take off his helmet.

The sensation of being watched intensified to the point of being a physical vibration in his bones. Weston realized it wasn't his imagination when the tunnel floor began to vibrate under his boots.

A loud, sonorous *hroooommmmm* filled his helmet. It sounded like the lowest note on a mountain-sized tuba.

Sand floated up slowly from the sea floor — the vibration wasn't isolated to the tunnel floor.

Weston's breaths came rapidly as a shadow blotted out the sunlight streaming down from the rough water's surface above. The silhouette of the massive whale-like creature approached from above. It was still near the surface, but descended quickly. Two oversized flippers on each side of its long body propelled the beast downward, toward the sea floor.

Looking at it slightly from the side, Weston realized the conical head was instead a jaw protrusion jutting from below the creature's mouth. The top of its body was mostly flat, all the way from the long slit of its mouth below its four eyes to the tip of its blunted, flukeless tail.

HROOOOOMMMMMM sounded the creature as it dived deeper, gaining speed. Weston screamed into the noise as the pressure of it thumped like pistons into his ear canals.

It didn't slow as it sped down to the sea floor. Instead, it rammed its jaw cone into the ground with a thunderous *BOOOOM*. The cone — easily half the length of the creature itself — disappeared up to its base near the creature's mouth in a plume of sand that engulfed the creature like a cloud.

The ground shook so hard from the impact that Weston tumbled sideways. He tripped over his own boots and fell on his side. As the impact echo and shaking subsided, he pushed himself to his feet with a groan.

The sand cloud began to clear enough to reveal the whale creature with its spear-like cone still embedded in the sea floor. Its massive flippers paddled slowly, keeping the beast facing downward. Its two larger black eyes seemed to be searching the ground near its cone.

Tentacles erupted from the sand beneath it. They snapped upward and latched onto the whale's head. Weston tried to count how many there were but lost track in the struggle.

The whale creature back-paddled, sliding its long cone from the ground. Impaled on the end of it was a nightmare octopus the size of a rhinoceros. Its mottled skin flashed different colors as its tentacles slid over the slick flesh of the whale. Two of them found its attacker's eyes and latched on.

The whale chomped down on the tentacled creature, its mouth crowded with squat, fat teeth.

Only five arms, Weston thought distantly as black blood swirled around the squid-like creature. *Five arms but the size of a tank. No wonder nobody swims here.*

The whale backed away from the sea floor even farther, then slammed back into the hole it had just created with its cone. Weston steadied himself against the tunnel wall as the impact rocked the floor. A spurt of black blood geysered from within the hole, and the grasping tentacles went limp.

Slowly, the whale creature ingested the dead squid. Weston turned away from the sight. He tried to cover his mouth but his glove bonked against his face shield. His trembling fingers found the slide-lock under his chin and he popped off his helmet in time to lose his breakfast on the tunnel floor.

He wiped his mouth, thinking about how he'd recently been lamenting the fact that he hadn't been able to swim as much as he used to back on Earth.

"I think I'll just find a nice lake," he said weakly. "Or a stream. Or a bowl of water."

The whale drifted lazily up toward the surface, its wide mouth chewing slowly, almost as an afterthought. A tentacle slithered out of its mouth and coiled around its jaw-cone. With a decisive chomp, the whale severed the tentacle and sucked it back into its mouth.

Weston stood up straight and swung his arms to get his blood flowing before continuing down the tunnel. His right arm smacked into the spare oxygen tanks dangling from his power pack. They clattered against the tunnel wall.

The sea floor just outside the tunnel exploded as if someone had stepped on a landmine. A blur of tentacles and silvery eyes the size of dinner plates swirled inside the cloud of floating sand. The eyes locked on to Weston and the creature shot toward the tunnel.

Weston shouted in surprise and collapsed to the floor as the creature attacked. It spread its tentacles wide and hit the tunnel with a loud *THUMP*. Its five thick tentacles slid over the tunnel walls, searching for a way inside. Its mouth opened and closed and its teeth tapped against the wall —

— the wall which groaned under pressure from the constricting tentacles.

Weston got to his feet and ran for the end of the tunnel. The creature stayed with him, sliding over the top of the tunnel and even outpacing him for the last stretch, as if guessing his destination with the hope of getting there first.

Its two silvery eyes glided over its body like spotlights, constantly moving so the creature could maneuver into any position while always watching its prey.

Weston slammed his fist against the indentation in the middle of the stone door at the end of the tunnel. A square piece of rock slowly slid inward.

Above him, the octopus squeaked over the tunnel wall. Small hooks on the sides of its tentacles tapped against the wall like fingernails.

"Where's a mutant whale when you need one?" he mumbled shakily as he reached into the square hollow and pushed a switch.

The door slid upward and the octopus immediately shot away from the wall. It zoomed along the outside of the tunnel in a blur, heading toward the ramp which descended toward the underwater compound.

Toward the others, Weston realized.

LEERA

Walking in front of Leera, Niku and Miles were enveloped by darkness as they left the underwater tunnel behind and stepped through the doorway of the looming structure of slate-colored stone.

The door slid shut behind Leera. Her helmet lamp flicked on in the black, sending a white beam onto a rough, dry stone floor. She looked upward, but her lamp wasn't strong enough to pierce the deep gloom overhead. Darkness swallowed the beam several meters up. Looking at it from the outside, she guessed the structure's height at around fifty meters, shaped like an egg with a pinched, conical top.

"Lot of wasted space," Niku commented, tilting his lamp up.

Miles swept the immediate area around them with his helmet light, revealing nothing but more empty stone floor.

"Not much for furniture, whoever they are," said Leera.

"Or *whatever* they are," Miles added. "I couldn't make out much detail, but I'd say there are at least a dozen other similar buildings in this complex."

"I saw several tunnels leading away from this one," said Niku. "There's no way we have time to map it all."

Miles checked his wristpad. "It's cutting it close,

even with the spare tanks. Let's say one-and-a-half hours."

"Unless we take off our helmets," Niku said.

Leera checked her own wristpad. The scrolling atmosphere monitor on the bottom of the glowing screen reported little difference from the air topside.

"A slightly elevated argon count than we're used to," she told them, "but not a dangerous amount."

"Pathogens?" Miles asked.

Leera tapped a button for a more detailed breakdown of the readings.

"Nothing the suit can detect," she reported.

"It wouldn't be calibrated for this environment," said Niku.

"Right then," said Miles. "Helmets off as a last resort."

He looked back and played his helmet lamp across the sealed door to get his bearings in the dark, then set off in the opposite direction. Niku walked behind him and Leera brought up the rear.

She swiped through the screens on her wristpad as she walked, pausing over an auto-mapping interface. After a tap, the screen pulsed several times and populated with a single line, broken in the middle by two thinner lines leading back the way she'd come. Leera looked behind her and realized the break was the door, the thicker line to either side was the wall, and the two thinner lines were the tunnel walls.

She slid a toggle on the screen to zoom out. The wall curved around to both sides from the entry door and met again on the other side of the building, where two more doors appeared as gaps in the wall line.

There was no indication of anything else in the

room.

Leera tapped a small button that looked like a wireframe cube. The flat, top-down view of the floor zoomed out farther and tilted as the image became three-dimensional. The screen now showed the structure from the outside, as if she were floating in the water twenty meters above and to the side of its peak. Sliding her finger on the screen, Leera could rotate her view around the building and zoom in and out, but she couldn't slide the view to other nearby structures.

Need to be inside them, she realized.

Leera tapped a button labeled *Automap* on her wristpad screen and it glowed green. She looked up just in time to bump into Niku's bulky power pack.

"Oh, sorry."

"Two doors," said Miles, sweeping his helmet lamp between them.

They were identical — slightly taller than Miles with rounded corners, made from the same smooth, dry stone as the walls and floor.

"Is there any way to check the atmosphere on the other side?" he asked.

Leera shook her head. "Not through this material. The automap shows a small section of tunnel just on the other side of each door."

"And past that?"

"Can't tell. Should we split up and try each one?" Miles and Niku turned back to look at her. She smiled in the dual beams of their helmet lamps. "Just kidding."

"Left is best," said Miles, stepping to that door and pushing the switch in its center. The door slid upward.

"Unless right is, you know, right," Niku countered.

Another underwater tunnel with invisible walls awaited them behind the door. It extended farther than they could see, its terminus swallowed by the surrounding dark waters.

"Hello, what's this?" Miles asked walking into the tunnel.

Four circular cutouts, several inches deep, were set in a square pattern in the stone floor by his boots. Each was as large as an elephant's footprint, and circular except for a small, sharp groove protruding from the back of each one.

Miles put his boots into two of them, spreading his stance wide to reach both. Leera and Niku each stood in one of the other two. They glanced at each other, beaming.

"We're moving," said Miles.

Leera looked down at the floor. She felt no motion, but the ocean floor beyond the invisible tunnel wall was indeed slipping slowly past. There was no other indication of movement — no machinery in the floor or track for the cutouts to follow. Looking back, it became apparent the four grooves they stood in were sliding along — and passing through — the stone tunnel floor as if it weren't a solid.

Niku laughed and Leera felt a warm tear run down her cheek.

"One, two, or four legs?" Niku asked.

Leera looked down again at the configuration of the cutouts.

"Four," she replied. "I don't know why, but I see whoever built this as being lower to the ground."

"They might have tall torsos," said Niku.

Leera noticed the ocean floor moving faster outside the tunnel.

"Lean forward," said Miles.

He was already leaning at a forward angle. Leera and Niku did the same, and the ocean floor outside became a blur as they were carried forward at incredible speed, somehow without feeling the friction or momentum.

"How is this possible?" Leera whispered.

"I have a feeling we'll be asking that question a lot," Niku replied.

"Ease up now," said Miles. "We're coming to the end."

They all stood up straight and the ocean floor outside slowed to a stop when they were a meter from another closed door at the end of the tunnel.

Leera stepped cautiously out of her groove and tested the ground. It was hard stone. Now that they had stopped, the cutouts seemed immovable — frozen into the stone floor. Even with a hard push, she couldn't make hers budge.

She checked her automap and saw the two thin tunnel wall lines extending back down the tunnel. To her surprise, the screen pulsed and began to sketch out the area beyond the door.

Miles gestured for Niku to do the honors that time. Niku did a little mock-bow and found the switch in the middle of the stone door. It slid upward silently, and they all drew in a deep breath.

They stepped into a massive dome. The waters

pushing down from above were held away by the same invisible material as the tunnel walls. Reaching higher than the stone structure through which they had entered the complex, the ceiling of the dome was closer to sunlight. It filtered through twenty meters of clear water to send dancing sunbeams across the dome floor and all that covered it.

"There's so much in here," said Leera in awe, stepping forward involuntarily.

Several enormous red coral structures rose from the foundation like pillars and twisted overhead as they reached for the ceiling. The stone floor was an expanse of gentle rises and slopes, as if to simulate the surface of the ocean on a calm day. Two five-meter dark pools of still water were visible from the entrance, placed near the center. Surrounding them were flat tables formed from the stone itself. The way they were arranged — in small, circular groups — made Leera wonder if they were more chairs than tables, meant for family or friend gatherings.

"Look," said Niku, pointing up.

An amorphous blob of water the size of a car floated high above their heads, drifting very slowly toward the far side of the room. Above it, many other blobs floated in other directions. Occasionally, the blobs would twitch in unison, as if rocks had been thrown into their surfaces.

Looking down at the wavy floor, Leera noticed holes larger than what a human could crawl through pitted the stone from wall to invisible wall. Her automap program couldn't penetrate them to see if they ran any deeper than half a meter.

"This seems like a hub," said Miles. "I count five

other doors."

"There are more," Niku added. "Watch where the water blobs hit the wall."

Leera craned her neck in her bulky suit to look upward. The nearest large water blob made gentle contact with the invisible wall and paused in its movement. A silver disc irised open from a pinpoint in the wall and became transparent. The water blob swelled noticeably, then shrank back to its original size. The silver iris reappeared and closed, and the water blob began to traverse its slow and steady path toward the far side of the dome.

"There's nothing inside," said Miles.

"Nothing we can see," Leera corrected.

He frowned up at the water blobs. "I don't like the sound of that."

Niku crouched down near a hole in the floor and peered inside, his helmet lamp illuminating the dark crawlspace.

"It's deep," he reported. "There's a drop-off a short ways ahead."

"Let's save that for another trip," said Miles. He checked his wristpad. "We should wrap it up here and head back. I don't want to leave Weston alone longer than we have to."

"How are we ever going to explore it all?" Niku muttered.

"I can take some air samples to analyze back at the colony," said Leera. "That will flag known and unknown pathogens. If it comes back clear, then we wouldn't have to wear helmets."

"We could leave them at the first tunnel and have the run of the place," said Miles, smiling. "I like it."

"You'd come back?" Leera asked.

"Are you kidding me? I wouldn't miss it. Besides, I'm no farmer. I need to look busy so people don't ask questions."

"What about those?" Niku asked, nodding toward the two calm water pools in the middle of the room.

They walked to them as a group, following the easy rise and fall of the wavy floor. Broken sunlight undulated over the stone and their suits.

Leera gazed down into the dark pool. Her identical reflection inside her space suit stared back — white hair above a tired face, out of which peered two curious eyes.

"I need a nap," said Niku as he looked down at his own reflection. His gloved fingertips touched his face shield.

Miles walked to the other pool and crouched down near its edge. He placed the side of his helmet against the floor to look at the pool from as low an angle as possible.

"I think there's a film covering both pools," he said.

"Well, don't touch it," Niku told him.

Miles reached out and poked a gloved fingertip into the water. The film covering the dark, still pool retreated from his fingertip like oily water from a drop of dish soap. He stood up quickly as the dark water cleared.

"It's not the ocean floor," he said, somewhat confused.

"What is it?" Leera asked, walking over.

"I don't know. A pit?"

She stood on the opposite side of the pool and

leaned over the edge to peer down. The walls of the pool extended deeper into the floor, creating a stone tunnel three meters in diameter and at least ten meters deep.

"I see something," Niku whispered.

Leera squinted deeper into the watery pit, but the floor was nearly lost in darkness.

"Not in there," said Niku. "Outside."

She followed his gaze beyond the wall of the transparent dome. The sand on the ocean floor was black and ridged like wind-swept dunes. Her eyes focused on movement near the tunnel leading back to the entry structure. Black sand churned up in a slow-motion cloud as something swam low to the ocean floor, heading toward the dome. The only aspect she could discern at such a distance was a misshapen, mottled mass.

"Another animal for your diary," Leera told Niku, trying to keep the worry out of her voice.

"Do you feel that?" said Miles, sounding just as uncertain.

"Harder to breathe," Niku replied. "Pressure on my chest." His eyes squeezed shut. "And in my head."

Leera felt it, too. As the creature swam closer, her chest tightened, reminding her of the two high-altitude climbs she'd done as a much younger woman. Accompanying the chest pressure was a high-pitched sound deep in her ear canal.

"It's moving fast, whatever it is," said Miles.

Niku groaned and pressed his hands to the sides of his helmet. "Weston is still back there," he said through clenched teeth.

Miles quickly tapped on his wristpad. "Wes, you

there?"

He breathed quickly as he waited for a reply. Leera cycled through his and Niku's suit medical readings. Both had elevated blood pressure and heartbeats. She checked her levels next — almost as high, and certainly higher than usual.

"Wes?!"

No response.

In a cloud of black sand like smoke, the creature reached the invisible dome wall. Five tentacles as thick as a person, and twice as long, fanned out to stop its forward motion. Each tentacle had two long, slender suckers on its underside, and its edges were lined with thin, bony hooks.

A black slit dominated the fleshy mass at the base of its five tentacles. The slit opened to reveal a circular mouth rimmed with dagger-like teeth, a muscular tongue lashing.

The creature sank to the ocean floor as gently as a snowflake and settled in a gauzy plume of fine black sand. The five tentacles aligned themselves to point in the same direction. A bulbous head ballooned up behind the tentacles like the driver of a five-horse chariot. Two dull mercury eyes the size of Leera's torso seemed to glide over its mottled, oily skin, pulsing against the wavering mass of its sac-like head.

Its tentacles began to slowly crawl over the ocean floor, parallel with the dome wall, pulling the head behind them as the creature's eyes peered inside. One tentacle touched the invisible dome wall and slid off.

"It can't get us in here, right?" Miles asked nervously.

"The doors aren't big enough," said Niku.

Leera looked over at the pool of clear water. She hurried over to it and fell to her hands and knees, shining her helmet lamp into its depths. A shadow hugged the wall near the floor.

"There might be an opening in the wall at the bottom," she said hollowly.

"Let's get out of here," Niku urged. "*Now.*"

He ran to her as fast as his suit would allow and helped her up by her shoulders. The pressure in her chest squeezed the breath from her lungs and she collapsed. Niku fell to his knees beside her, pounding his face shield as he groaned in pain.

The high-pitched ring in her ears moved deeper into her skull, becoming a physical pain that pushed against the backs of her eyes.

She screamed.

Then the pain vanished, leaving her briefly dizzy. She tumbled onto her side, breathing hard. Niku crawled on his hands and knees, gulping down the urge to retch. Behind him, ten meters away, Miles walked toward the invisible dome wall.

The creature had stopped its crawl. Both dull mercury eyes were locked on Miles. Its head sack pulsated as two encrusted siphons filtered water.

Miles was transfixed. He bumped into the dome wall and stood perfectly still, his arms hanging limp at his sides.

"Miles?" Leera said weakly.

Niku pushed himself up and hooked his arm under Leera's armpit, hauling her to her feet.

The creature's mottled skin turned bone white in a blink. A thick black line traveled over its flesh from the tips of its tentacles to the top of its bulbous head. When the black line reached the back of its head, it reappeared on the tips of its tentacles and passed over its body again like a shadow from something passing overhead.

"Cuttlefish," Niku whispered hoarsely. "Cuttlefish do that."

The line swept over the creature more quickly. A small cloud of black sand puffed up from beneath it, and the creature rose from the ocean floor.

"*Miles*," Leera called out forcefully. "We're *leaving!*"

Miles dropped to his knees as the creature rose higher above him. The black line pattern swept over the creature's white body so fast it appeared almost solid. Its large eyes slid to the top of its bulbous head, which began to deflate.

Faster than Leera could scream, the creature's skin flashed back to its mottled color and it rocketed away from the dome — a streak of movement in dark water.

It fanned out a short distance away and dropped to the floor. Its tentacles crawled madly across the black sand and pulled the creature down into an unseen hole. It disappeared from view, leaving only a cloud of sand behind.

"The tunnel!" Leera shouted. "The tunnel connects—"

The pain in her skull slammed back, dropping her to the floor. Niku screamed beside her. His breath came out in a strangled wheeze. This time it hit Miles, too. He curled up in a ball near the dome wall, clutching his chest.

Niku's scream turned into a growl of determination as he got one foot beneath him, then the other. He grabbed a fistful of Leera's space suit and dragged her over the stone floor. They crested one of the gentle stone waves and he lost his footing. They rolled down together in a ball of limbs.

"Miles..." Leera whispered when they came to a stop.

"You...*first!*" Niku grunted as he got back to his feet.

Leera pushed herself up and they stumbled up the next rise.

Her next breath never came. The air left her lungs but the pressure was too great to fill them again.

She looked at Niku, terror in her eyes, and could tell it was the same for him.

The door...the door was only steps away. She glanced back as she stumbled. The creature exploded from the clear pool of water — a mass of oily, pulsating mollusk flesh pulled behind five powerful tentacles.

The creature fell on Miles. Tentacles wrapped around his orange space suit and pulled him in, toward its mouth. Miles vanished into a writhing lump of wet flesh.

The attack had taken less than two seconds, and at the end, the pain in Leera's skull switched off like a light.

She swayed in place as the weight instantly left her chest, but she was unable to move. Like Miles, she was transfixed on the creature. Its body pulsed as it tightened into a protected ball around its prey.

Slowly, one dull mercury eye slid up from

underneath its body to stare at her.

Niku grabbed her from behind and pulled her through the open doorway. She fell back onto her power pack and scrambled backward as the door began to slide shut from above.

In a spray of blood, the creature erupted from its protective position and lurched for the door. Its five heavy tentacles pounded the stone floor as it half-crawled, half-glided toward Leera.

It leapt from the floor and spread its tentacles wide, the red teeth of its mouth fanning apart — and the door closed. There was a loud thump as it hit the stone barrier.

The stone portion of the doorway only covered a meter of the wall to either side before it became invisible. The tip of a tentacle appeared at the edge of the stone, probing the wall. A moment later, the bulk of the creature slid into view, its mercury eyes sliding slowly over the bulb of its head.

The creature used its suckers to climb up the wall, making a full arc over the door, before plopping back to the floor in a wet heap and sliding from view, dragging a wet trail of bloody slime.

Niku dropped to one knee beside Leera. She clawed for him in a blind panic, and he held her close as she sobbed.

GAVIN

The river widened half a mile from where Gavin, Shurri, and Arthur had left the bodies of Willef and the sky beast, until it nearly touched the cliff walls. Moonlight poured into the river canyon, turning the rushing water black and lighting the rounded stones that crowded both shores.

Gavin shivered in his wet short-sleeved shirt. The padding of his workpants was heavy with icy water he couldn't squeeze out. Even if he hadn't left his torn jacket behind, it wouldn't have helped him keep warm.

His soggy boots slid over smooth stones as he kept one shaking hand against the canyon wall for support. The other gripped Willef's machete, his knuckles white as bone. He had wrenched it from the neck of the sky beast and washed the creature's dark blood from the blade before setting out down the river shoreline.

Behind him, Shurri and Arthur followed silently. All conversation had died hours ago, not long after their third failed attempt to climb out of the canyon.

The river had thinned and widened as they tracked its path, only once touching the walls of the canyon on both sides, and then only for a few meters — distance enough to soak through clothes to bone once again.

Gavin clenched his jaw shut to stop it from chattering.

At the back of the line, Arthur slipped and fell. His hands shot out to stop his fall but they also slipped and the side of his head cracked against a large stone. He groaned weakly as Shurri knelt beside him and rolled him onto his back, into her lap. Blood, black in the moonlight to match the water, trickled from his scalp above his ear.

"That really hurt," he said quietly.

Shurri kissed his forehead and hugged him close. She looked over to Gavin.

He set the machete on a stone next to her and signed, *I'll scout ahead.*

She nodded and turned her attention back to her brother, humming softly.

Gavin watched them for a moment, then continued following the river downstream. He kept his palms pressed against the cold rock wall as he maneuvered around a small bend. Up ahead, the river widened until it rushed against both sides of the canyon. Unlike the last time, it showed no signs of thinning as it gurgled farther into the night.

Looking up, Gavin stared at the thin strip of stars visible from the canyon floor. A shadow moved along the top edge of the wall. Two small eyes glinted in the moonlight. Three more sets of eyes soon joined the first, moving slowly along the top of the canyon as they watched Gavin.

Rock bats, he thought.

One of the creatures dislodged a small stone. It tumbled down and plonked into the rushing river with a small, bright splash. A thin vine or root dangled from the top edge of the wall from where it had fallen. Gavin squeezed between two large boulders and walked as far as he could, to the point where the river swelled and cut off his path.

He leaned out over the water and grabbed hold of the vine. After wrapping the end of it around his hand three times, he gave it a solid tug. The vine snapped halfway up and came coiling down on his head. He swiped it off violently, then kicked the rock wall, screaming internally.

The wall near his boots cracked under the impact.

Gavin knelt down and pushed against the crack. The wall was brittle there, crumbling away like hard-packed dirt. Thin roots criss-crossed just under the surface. Gavin grabbed a handful of them and pulled. Thinner taproots snapped as the longer roots popped free of the rock, creating a hole the size of Gavin's head in the canyon wall.

He widened the hole by hitting the edges with the heels of his palms. When it was wide enough to squeeze his shoulders through, Gavin stuck his head inside the void. It was pitch-dark, but the space had a cavernous feel to it — empty and large. The air was stale and warm, with a slight odor of fungus. He whistled sharply and the sound traveled, echoing down an unseen passage to his right. Gavin squinted in the darkness, unsure if he could see faint light glowing from that direction, or if his eyes were playing tricks on him.

"What are you smiling about?" Shurri asked him after he clamored back over slick rocks. Arthur had his head in her lap and seemed to be sleeping.

How is he? Gavin signed.

"It wasn't a bad cut," Shurri replied, gently wiping a lock of hair from her brother's forehead.

Gavin waited for her to look up before signing, *The good news is I may have found a way out of the canyon.*

Her eyes narrowed. "And the bad?"

He picked up Willef's machete and tucked the blade under his arm so he could sign, *We have to go underground.*

"You mean where your dad almost got eaten by a cave worm?"

We're not near the mountains, Gavin signed. *No one has seen it outside of that region. We can't stay here.*

Arthur needs to rest, she signed back.

"No I don't," he said, one eye cocked open.

Shurri sighed. "Well, *I* do."

Better someplace dry than out here, Gavin signed.

He led the slippery way to the hole he'd opened in the canyon wall. Arthur and Shurri shared a skeptical glance as Gavin crawled inside, clutching the machete.

Shurri climbed in next. She brushed dirt from her hands and swiped a lock of straw-colored hair from her face, smudging her cheek. By the dim moonlight coming from the opening, Gavin could tell she was shaking. Arthur grunted as he climbed on all fours into the cavern.

"We had lights in our backpacks," he said as he stood up. He wiped his hands on his thermal shirt, smearing mud.

Gavin pointed off to their right. An almost

imperceptible glow was indeed illuminating some deeper section of the underground space. He took Shurri's hand and put it on his shoulder, then nodded at Arthur, who put his hand on his sister's shoulder. Together, they walked deeper into the cavern.

The large room they had crawled into from the riverbank remained cloaked in darkness, but a wide tunnel became visible ahead, lit faintly by a distant source. The rock and dirt walls were rough and craggy, and the tunnel took many sharp turns as the trio walked under hanging roots and dripping water. The ground underfoot was angled upward and was wet with gritty mud. Gavin assumed they were following a wash passage for water runoff, or perhaps the fading vestige of an underwater tributary.

"This is a natural tunnel," Shurri whispered from behind.

Gavin smiled, impressed — but not surprised — that she'd made the connection. *Cave worms makes smooth walls,* he signed quickly.

"Our mom wants us to go back to Earth," she added, sounding embarrassed. "She says Galena is making Arthur too independent."

Gavin stopped suddenly and looked over his shoulder at her.

What made you think of that? he signed.

She shrugged. "Just wondering if it's worse there, or here."

There.

"Even with cave worms?"

Why did she let you come out here if she wants you to go back on the ship? he signed.

"I think she's worried about the visitors. Aren't

you curious about them?"

Not really, Gavin replied. *I'm staying.*

She offered him a shy smile. "I'm staying, too."

"Staying in this cave *permanently,* if we don't get out of here," Arthur reminded them from the back of the line.

Shurri rolled her eyes and nudged Gavin forward.

Blue light grew stronger after the tunnel straightened out and rose sharply, painting the rough walls with a strong, almost neon fluorescence. At the top of the rise, the tunnel opened suddenly into a dome-shaped cavern. The walls of the underground dome were covered in vibrantly glowing blue living moss. Much like the red living moss on the surface, they came in rectangles of various widths and lengths. Like patches of sod several inches thick, they lined the cavern walls, most of them unmoving. Several of them crawled slowly across the walls and over each other. Whenever one patch of moss touched another, a wave of darker blue light would ripple across both specimens, as if they were both the surface of a single pond and someone had dipped their finger into the water.

The very peak of the dome was twenty meters off the floor. A hole two meters wide at the peak allowed moonlight to pour down into the cavern. The cone of moonlight illuminated a small mountain of hex crabs on the floor.

Shurri tightened her grip on Gavin's shoulder. They waited in the painful silence, but the crabs didn't move. The machete glinted with neon blue light as Gavin quietly walked toward the crabs. Each flat, hexagonal shell was wider than a large dinner plate.

He tapped one of them with the tip of his machete and it cracked like dried wax.

"Dead," said Arthur. "All of them?"

Gavin walked in a wide circle around the mound, looking more closely at the crabs near the top of the pile. Their pale shells were translucent, allowing the cone of moonlight to set them aglow.

"They all have holes in their shells," whispered Shurri. "Look."

Gavin crouched down at the bottom of the mound and scooted one of the empty shells away from the rest. A dozen hollow, jointed legs curled over the creature's belly. Gavin flipped it over and some of the legs crackled as they broke apart. A star-shaped hole had been punched into the top of the shell. He inspected several other dead hex crabs and found the same type of hole.

"What is this?" Arthur asked.

I think it's a trap, Gavin signed as he stood. He looked at the hole in the ceiling. *The crabs fall in and something eats them.*

"Or maybe it drops them in after it eats them?" Shurri asked.

Maybe, Gavin signed, smiling unconvincingly.

"*Those* tunnels have smooth walls," she said, pointing to the far side of the cavern.

Two tunnels branched off from the dome-shaped room, plunging into darkness. Unlike the constantly-changing shape of the entry tunnel, those two had uniformly smooth rock walls, as if polished over time by the passage of a large creature.

"We can't climb on the crabs," said Shurri. "They'll crumble."

"Do you hear that?" Arthur hissed.

Gavin did. A soft electric hum throbbed from somewhere nearby, like a low-grade current coursing through a power cable.

Shurri pointed at a mound of dirt against the wall in a dark section of the cavern. The three of them hurried over to it. Gavin tapped it with the tip of the machete and there was a metallic clank. He shared a quick glance with Shurri, who swiped at the dirt mound to reveal a glowing green square beneath a cracked plastic cover.

Gavin pushed off more dirt to reveal a coffin-shaped capsule nearly three-meters long.

"It's an escape pod from the Halcyon," Shurri said.

A small info screen above the green square showed a heart rate and blood pressure.

Arthur's jaw dropped open in disbelief. "Someone's still inside!"

Gavin ran his palm over the surface of the escape pod. Star-shaped dents covered nearly every square inch. Whatever ate the crabs had wanted to get in.

Shurri flipped open the plastic cover and pushed the green button. It blinked, awaiting a second confirmation. Gavin grabbed Shurri's wrist to warn her to wait. In truth, he didn't know why he hesitated. She pulled her hand away and pressed the button a second time.

There was a loud hiss of escaping air as the lid of the pod cracked open. Gavin and Arthur strained to push the heavy lid aside while Shurri used the machete handle to chip at the hardened blue impact foam which filled the inside of the escape pod. After a strong swing, it cracked apart like broken rock.

The three of them ripped out chunks of hard foam and tossed them aside, revealing the sleeping form of a male passenger, perhaps thirty years old, wearing a neoprene body suit. Nose tubes carrying oxygen and a transparent face mask supplying the bare minimum of nutrients had kept him alive for eight years since the crash. His matted hair had grown to his shoulders and his beard was a tangle of black knots.

"How long could you live in one of these things?" asked Arthur, studying the pod's info screen.

"A long time, I guess," Shurri whispered.

A distant scrabbling noise like bone on rock turned all three of their heads toward one of the dark tunnels. Gavin stood slowly and walked over to the nearest tunnel entrance, rolling the soles of his boots heel-to-toe to soften his footfalls.

A slight breeze coming from the void moved through his jaw-length hair. He walked over to the second tunnel and held his breath. From deep within, something slid along the smooth walls, moving closer.

At that exact moment, the occupant of the escape pod bolted upright. He ripped out his nose tubes and yanked off his face mask, then screamed at the top of his lungs. The noise emanating from the gaunt, bearded face was shockingly loud, and Arthur and Shurri stepped back in surprise. Gavin ran over and slapped him in the face, but the man only took a deep breath and screamed louder, his body shaking. Absolute terror filled his wide eyes — eyes that were stuck on some old horror.

Rocks ground against each other in the darkness of the second tunnel and something climbed over them.

Gavin grabbed Shurri and Arthur by the arm and pulled them toward the first tunnel. Shurri jerked away and went back to the escape pod. She slapped the man in the face again and he blinked. His screaming faded to a gurgle and he seemed to notice her for the first time.

"Come with us!" she hissed, pulling on his wrist.

He sat in the pod, dazed.

Shurri gave up and ran back to join Gavin and Arthur. They hurried down the first tunnel, a cool breeze turning icy the farther they ran. Gavin looked back and saw the spindly silhouette of the escape pod passenger stumbling after them, rubbing his numb legs. Apparently, he had come to his senses in time to follow.

The light in the tunnel faded quickly as they moved farther away from the glowing blue moss. In the enveloping shadows, Gavin motioned for Shurri and Arthur to keep going. Before they could pull him with them, he doubled back and ran for the cavern.

The escape pod passenger tripped and fell as Gavin reached him. The man's limbs were probably dancing with pins and needles. His face was a grimacing mask of pain when Gavin lightly patted his cheek. The man opened his eyes and saw Gavin, who jerked a thumb toward the dark end of the tunnel.

A loud rumbling noise emanated from the cavern. The floor under Gavin's feet vibrated. The cave worm exploded from the other tunnel in a shower of rocks. It barreled through the mound of dead crabs, crushing their shells, and slammed into the opposite wall.

Gavin grabbed two fistfuls of the passenger's clinging neoprene body suit and yanked him to his feet. He caught a glimpse of the cave worm, easily ten meters long and two meters in diameter, coiling against the wall of the cavern like a taut spring, crushing and smearing the blue moss against the rocks in streaks of electric cobalt. The glowing blue material coated the slimy skin of the worm in glistening stripes.

Hard black spikes as long and thick as Gavin's arms protruded from its pale flesh from end to end, scraping the rock wall like thick fingernails.

The creature's mouth turned toward Gavin. Inside a circle of razored teeth, the tip of its snake-like tongue peeled open like a blooming flower in the shape of a star. The circle of teeth snapped shut like a cigar cutter, sending a *CRACK* echoing down the tunnel louder than a gunshot.

Gavin ran, dragging the escape pod passenger behind him.

CRACK went the creature's jaws. It sprang from the cavern wall and launched itself down the tunnel, blotting out all the light.

"GAVIN!" Shurri shrieked from somewhere up ahead in the darkness. "GAVIN, IN HERE!"

His boots thudded on the smooth floor as he ran. The passenger stumbled behind him, wheezing as his unused legs strained to make the proper motions.

The worm drew closer, scraping the rock walls with its spikes.

CRACK!

It was right behind him.

The tunnel suddenly ended and Gavin slid to a stop on a steep cliff over a void. The passenger rammed into him and Gavin felt himself falling over the edge. Hands grabbed his arms and pulled him and the passenger to the side as the head of the worm burst from the tunnel, glowing blue from the blood of the moss.

Shurri and Arthur shoved Gavin onto a narrow ledge beside them that overlooked a wide hole. Dark water rushed past below. Gavin pressed his back to the wet rock wall next to the others as they shuffled sideways along the ledge, away from the tunnel. Cold spray from the powerful underground river drifted up and soaked him all over again.

The worm turned its head in their direction, bathing them in neon blue light. Its circular jaws rotated slowly in its deep mouth, glistening razored teeth catching the light. The head stretched toward them casually, the worm sensing its prey had nowhere to flee.

The ledge beneath its bulk cracked and broke away in a crumble of rock, splashing into the river below. The cave worm retreated back into the tunnel just enough to avoid falling into the river. It slithered backward, into the shadows, and waited.

In the faint blue light glowing from the skin of the beast, Gavin could barely make out the details of his surroundings. He and the others were in a natural hollow, wider and taller than the walls of the underground tunnels. The ceiling reached a tapered point a few meters overhead. Wet rock jutted from the walls, glistening in the dim light peeking past the waiting form of the cave worm.

The only way out was back the way they'd come.

Gavin looked down at the river.

Unless... he thought.

Shurri's hand found his in the darkness. "Digested by a cave worm or drowned in an underground river," she said loudly over the rushing water. "Willef said to make your choices the best you can, right?"

She jumped. Gavin reached for her and lost his footing. His boots slipped off the ledge and he plunged headlong into the void.

MERRITT

Henry Tolbard returned to the colony sometime before dawn. He went straight to Merritt's home and roused him from a fitful sleep. Merritt had spent his broken slumber wide-eyed between snatched dreams of his family. Whether they were of Gavin or his deceased wife, Emily, the dreams were filled with dread.

"The families who wished to go to the mountain cave are safe," Henry told him as he sat on a stool near the long work table. The older man sighed with great relief as he relaxed his body.

Merritt sat on his hammock and studied the adventurer. Henry's clothes were filthy and his white beard looked almost gray, but his smile was wide and proud. He carried a hard, twisted walking stick of grayish wood.

"Are those roots?" Merritt asked.

"Branches." Henry held up the stick and examined the polished knot at the top. "Found it near the cave. Remarkable, isn't it?"

Merritt's knees popped as he stood. His body felt overused and under-rested.

"Everyone happy?" he asked as he shuffled to the pot of bitterbell tea waiting for him on the stove.

"Pah!" Henry laughed. "Hardly. But they

understand."

Merritt flicked on the burner and rubbed sleep from his eyes with his knuckles. "I hate to say it, but it may seem like I was being overly paranoid."

"No such thing," Henry chided. "Not in this place. What if the people on the ship had been an invading force, perhaps from a hostile nation on Earth? Everyone would be dead instead of safe in that cave."

"Yes, well. I'm sure I won't hear the end of it when they get back and find out about our new friends."

"They are comfortable and alive," Henry told him with a shrug. "What more does anyone need?"

Merritt poured boiling bitterbell tea into a metal cup and passed it handle-first to Henry. He knew the older man didn't use bittersweet syrup. Merritt added a healthy dose of it to his own cup and took a quick sip.

Henry readjusted himself on his stool. "Speaking of our friends, what have you learned?"

"A fake-nice bureaucrat promises the impossible in exchange for compliance."

Henry studied him a long moment. "He said that?"

Merritt shrugged. "Not in so many words. The implication drips from every sentence."

Henry took a deep breath and let it out slowly. "Felt good to be *out there* again, you know? In the wild." He took a sip of his tea. "If things go south with the bureaucrat, maybe we should all move to the cave."

Merritt paused in the process of pulling on a fresh shirt and looked at him quickly. Henry winked, betraying his joke.

"He wants to expand," Merritt said. "Aggressively. Says nothing will change for us."

"...for now," Henry added.

"That's the feeling I got." He took another sip of tea, weighing his next question carefully. Henry was a giving man, but he clammed up tight regarding one specific subject. "Was it like this in the early days on the moon? With Avalon and Haven?"

Henry was silent for a time.

"Like what?" he asked at last.

"Idealistic. We have a vision for our colony, but someone with means and political pull on Earth has a different view."

Henry's eyes focused on a distant memory, and he shook his head, no. "It was always my wife's grand vision. I tell people I just went along for the ride, and it's true. We had the money and the right friends to hold true to our idealism. And now humanity has two shining Camelots on Earth's moon...all because my wife dreamt it so." He set down his cup, rested his weathered hands atop the knot of his walking stick, and met Merritt's eye. "I will tell you one thing, though...something I learned from experience. Idealism or no, you don't build a colony on a new world by giving the workers an equal seat at the negotiating table."

Shortly after sunrise and a quick washing-up, Merritt and Henry walked through the colony, full packs on their backs, greeting the early risers. During the main harvest season, most farmers were out from just before dawn until an hour before lunch. In the winter, many didn't show their faces until late morning.

"It won't warm up much today," Henry commented as they left the farms behind and entered the forest of sparse, ash-gray trunks.

"How do you know?" Merritt asked.

"Old men always know."

Henry's walking stick pushed down into the soft, wet soil as he walked, darkening the lightwood tip. Merritt had made it clear that Henry could stay at the colony. Kellan hadn't mentioned bringing anyone else along. Henry waved him off. When Merritt persisted, Henry stopped him with a stern glare that brooked no argument.

In truth, Merritt was happy for the company. There was too much secrecy about current events, and he was relieved to share some of the burden with another.

He stopped at the edge of the clearing where Kellan's shuttle had first landed. Henry stood next to him, leaning against his walking stick.

"My, my," he said softly, scratching his beard. "They *have* been busy."

Half a dozen polygonal prefab buildings were arranged in a loose circle around the center of the clearing. Surrounding them like an outer barrier were stacks upon stacks of large storage containers. Beyond the barrier, at the edge of the clearing, was a grouping of low canvas tents and a latrine.

There was no sign of the supply shuttle. Merritt knew through Skip and his watchful eyes that the shuttle had been making non-stop trips to the orbiting ship since Kellan and his crew arrived.

"You brought a friend," said Kellan from behind.

Merritt and Henry turned to find the short, red-haired man breathing from exertion, smiling at them. He wore a dark green military BDU and black combat boots. He smoothed down his small red mustache and swiped sweat from his pale forehead.

"I'm sorry to say, Mr. Tolbard, but this offer was for Mr. Alder only."

"The more the merrier," said Henry coldly, nodding toward the wilderness. "Especially out there."

Kellan put his fists on his hips and studied the older man. "Not in this case, I'm afraid. 'A small complement travels lightly.'"

Henry bristled. "You're quoting me from my own book?"

Kellan smiled without warmth. "I thought you'd be happy someone read it."

Henry's eyes glinted steel as he looked from Kellan to Merritt, who nodded his regret at the situation.

After tapping the end of his walking stick angrily into the ground, Henry turned away and said, "I think I'll go look in on Uda and Toma."

Merritt was taken aback. "They're still at the farm?"

Henry waved over his shoulder as he slowly walked back in the direction of the colony. "Couldn't drag her away."

Kellan crossed his arms and watched Henry thoughtfully. "I was shocked to read his name on the Halcyon manifest," he confided. "I thought he had died at Avalon decades ago, and then surely in the crash. He may have told you he left a farewell letter to his grandchildren before the Halcyon left Sunrise

Station. No? It's quite emotional for such a stolid fellow. Although, if I'm being honest, it read more like a suicide note. I think he fully intended to die on that voyage."

Merritt met Kellan's eye, then slowly looked away. "Fate and irony seem to be close cousins."

Kellan laughed. "Precisely. Very good." He quickly looked Merritt over from head to toe, as if seeing him in a different light. "It was smart of you, by the way, sending some of the colonists away. I would have done the same. You never know who's really inside the orbiting ship, do you?"

Merritt looked at him again.

"Oh, come now," Kellan soothed, pointing skyward. "We can see everything from up there. Don't worry, your people are perfectly safe. In fact, if anything attacks..." He paused to claw half-mockingly at the air like an animal. "...we have precise ground-targeting munitions that would eliminate the threat."

Kellan smiled and stared right at Merritt, seemingly daring him to ask the next obvious question: *Can those munitions be turned against the colony?*

Merritt let the unspoken threat pass, and Kellan sighed. After another glance up at the gleaming jewel of his ship in the upper atmosphere, he said, "I'll get my gear," and left Merritt standing alone.

Kellan took the steps up to the nearest prefab structure two at a time, leaving the door open behind him. A moment later, a hulking bald man in black tactical armor ducked through the doorway. His heavy boots thumped on the metal stairs as he surveyed the small camp. He saw Merritt and frowned before turning away to talk to a man taking inventory of the storage crate contents.

"Mr. Alder!" Kellan called from within the prefab building. "You'll want to see this."

Merritt kept his eye on the oversized bald man as he walked up the stairs. The man stared right back, eyes as cold and hard as the mineral from which Galena took its name.

The inside of the prefab structure was more spacious than expected from the outside. Rows of bunks lined the back wall, but only three showed signs of being used. The rest of the single room was given over to more storage crates and a small folding table near the door.

"Not much to look at," Kellan admitted as Merritt walked to the table. "The permanent housing units will be a little more grand. Come and look." He waved Merritt over to a storage crate.

He lifted the lid slowly. Liquid-like smoke spilled out over the edge of the storage crate. Inside was a bulky machine with several different sections resting in a swirling cloud of viscous smoke. The top and bottom were blocks of different-sized coils. Merritt guessed them to be cooling units. The middle of the intricate device was a storage system of some kind. It was shaped like a cube and glowed with a faint green light. Beyond the frosted glass were rows upon rows of fingernail-sized black squares.

Kellan tapped the number 1-0-0 into a small keypad next to the glowing green cube. A dull red light pulsed behind one of the small black squares.

"That's your wife," said Kellan. "That's Emily."

Merritt bent down closer to the device. He

swallowed hard, then stood up straight.

"Part of me wished you were lying," he said.

"I'm not lying. That's the reference chip for Emily's LifeScan. Three of these crates hold her scanned data. Put all that together with the vial of DNA I showed you and the incubation tanks that are arriving before the end of the month, and it will be like she never left. Look here," he added, redirecting Merritt's attention to the folding table. A sprawling paper blueprint was rolled out, held down by fist-sized chunks of mineral lead sulfide native to the planet. "Road infrastructure for the expansion," Kellan explained. His finger traced a line from one side of the paper to the other. "Just one small example of what I see this place becoming. My settlement to yours. One colony. What do you think?"

Merritt studied the blueprints, the analytical portion of his mind temporarily blocking out thoughts of seeing Emily again. "I think you're going to need a lot more people to make this happen."

"That won't be a problem. When I tell my superiors what we've found here, there will be no request I can make that won't be approved."

Merritt hesitated, then asked, "What have you found?"

"It's what we *will* find," Kellan corrected himself. He rolled up the blueprints and puffed out his chest. "It's what you're going to *help* me find, and I think we'd better get started."

THE ENVOY

Beneath the soft soil of Galena's surface was a maze of tunnels that seemed to run for kilometers in every direction. Jeff and Ayani departed his ship, the *Celerity*, more than two hours ago, and had been traveling underground most of that time. Just when he thought they were coming to a dead end, another tunnel opening would reveal itself in the darkness off to one side, yawning like a shadowy mouth as the light from Ayani's rifle drew closer.

Branches from the upside-down trees sprouted through cracks in the ceiling, sometimes blocking their passage in a thick net. Ayani had swung her long knife at the first of these obstructions and a vine had shot out and wrapped around her wrist. She methodically disentangled her forearm, grunting and sweating from the effort. Afterward, they pushed between the branches, parting them like rigid curtains, instead of trying to cut through them.

Ayani looked back at Jeff from time to time. At first he thought she was checking to make sure he hadn't fallen into a crevasse, but he could tell there was something odd in her lingering gaze.

"Your pupil is still glowing," she confessed when asked why she kept looking back. "The light is faint, like it's far away."

Jeff could still see the beams of light emanating

from every living thing on Galena. Down there, in the tunnels, thin walls of multicolored light extended from every branch and vine; every spot of moss. Small pools on the uneven floor shone with a uniform luminescence after water droplets teeming with microscopic organisms fell from above.

"Does it disturb you?" Jeff asked. No light shone upon his palm when he waved his hand close to his eye.

"It's…alien," said Ayani. "Speaking of which, do you think these tunnels are natural?"

Despite his brooding thoughts, he welcomed the chance for conversation. They had been walking in silence for nearly half an hour as they attempted to follow the direction Jeff thought they should go.

"They could have been made by lava or water…or something else."

"Something else," Ayani mumbled to herself. She glanced back briefly, then looked away. "I know why you feel the way you do about Kellan," she said.

Jeff watched his boots as he walked, splashing into shallow puddles that swirled with purple and green aurorae. A sheet of light blocking their path split down the middle as Ayani forced her way through a thick blockade of branches. Jeff's white Envoy uniform was streaked with green muck when he emerged on the other side.

"Is that another one of the rumors floating around the academy?" he asked, having heard a few of the more outlandish stories himself. "Did he lock me up for disobeying orders or chain me to the outside of a shuttle to see if I could really die?"

"Trager told me about Farah."

Jeff was silent for a long time.

"Why would he do that?" he murmured, the rock walls amplifying his words.

"He said it was so I knew what I was walking into. What you might...do."

"Trager told me not to 'do' anything. He made it clear that Kellan was an afterthought...which he had already been to me for years. Until now."

"You aren't known for your strict adherence to the rules," Ayani reminded him.

"I've left all that in the past," he said, ducking under a low branch dripping with water. "The only thing left for me is the future, and too much of it."

Ayani shined her light over the wet walls. "Do you think whatever took out the first colony made these tunnels?"

"No one really knows what destroyed the first colony."

"The new colonists might. We could ask them."

Jeff stopped and looked up at the ceiling, absentmindedly studying rays of faint light visible only to him leaking through a spiderweb of cracks in the stone.

"No one knows except me," he clarified. "Kellan killed them. He sent them here without telling them the dangers."

"Even *he* couldn't have known everything about this planet," said Ayani, stopping and turning back.

"He knew enough to recognize it wasn't safe for a colony."

"Others have survived here eight years."

Jeff's voice was low, and his right eye gazed at something far away, as he said, "I pushed everyone away for more than three centuries after I lost my wife. Her name was Kate." He paused a long moment before continuing. "There were people I considered acquaintances, and those who were slightly more familiar acquaintances." He picked at a loose rock and it tumbled to the ground. "One day, despite my best efforts, Farah and I became friends. It simply...worked. I knew what would happen if she got close, if I grew to love her even a fraction as much as I loved Kate." He looked down, shaking his head as he remembered. "Nineteen years we were friends. It was a different love than I had for Kate, but it was still love. Just as strong. I told her not to come here. I was—"

He choked on the words and swallowed hard.

"I was a fool," he finished.

"No," Ayani said simply.

Jeff cleared his throat and stood up straight, snapping out of his dark reverie. His glowing pupil met Ayani's eyes. She looked away for a split second, then held his gaze.

"I was in the room when the top brass debriefed him after the first colony vanished twelve years ago," Jeff continued. "This was before they made the whole incident disappear, as if Farah and the others never existed. Do you know she's not even in the public database? All of her records were purged." He snapped his fingers. "A ghost that only I remember. Kellan admitted there was a possibility of migrating organisms on Galena. He said he'd been told there was only a slim chance they would pass through the exact spot he ordered the colonists to land. Months away, of course. Plenty of time to relocate should the need arise." Jeff smiled sadly. "That's how he put it in his preliminary report. *Should the need arise*."

"But he never told the colonists," Ayani realized.

Jeff sniffed and wiped his nose. "Communication between probes on both sides of the Rip proved trickier than expected. They had to physically cross back to send a burst, and they weren't built to handle more than a few trips. Too much radiation. Kellan claimed he sent a hard-coded warning in one of the probes, but there's no record of it."

Ayani studied him a long moment, arching an eyebrow. "That's a Starliner full of heavy baggage. Are you *sure* you left all of it in the past?"

"That, and a lot more," he told her, gesturing down the tunnel.

She started walking again, and he followed. The tunnel narrowed and they crouched low before emerging into a small, dark cavern. Five black openings in the cavern wall awaited their choosing.

"Are we lost?" Ayani asked.

Jeff stared at each of the tunnel entrances in turn. He pointed at the jagged black hole on the right. "That one," he said. "It's the only one with light inside."

"It's pitch black!"

He shrugged. "I guess we're doing the whole trust thing."

An inhuman shriek echoed to them from deep within one of the other tunnels. Ayani tightened her grip on the rifle as her feet slid apart in a bracing stance. Her eyes flicked over to Jeff, and he nodded toward the center tunnel. She slicked back her brown hair — black in the darkness and wet from the constant water dripping from the ceiling — and blinked hard to clear it from her wide eyes.

A crumbling sound of rock grinding against rock rushed toward them as a burst of rank air blasted their faces from the darkness. Ayani's mouth twisted in disgust and Jeff nearly choked on the acrid fumes that made his eye water.

"It's big," Ayani said evenly, aiming down the barrel of her rifle.

She popped off a round, the sound deafening in the rocky cavern. The muzzle flash illuminated the mouth of the tunnel...and a mouth within. Shiny teeth as long as swords swirled in a circular maw as the giant worm twisted. Spittle flew as it shrieked again, a thick, lashing tongue vibrating from the noise.

Jeff ran into the right-most tunnel, Ayani close on his heels. He could see a purple light up ahead, but he couldn't be sure if it was natural or if he was seeing the life-light of Galena's organisms.

Ayani's rifle barked twice, flashing the rough tunnel walls and blinding Jeff. He stumbled forward in the fading afterglow and snagged the toe of his boot on a protruding branch. He went down hard, with barely enough time to shield his face with his hands before his knuckles cracked painfully against the rock floor instead of his nose and teeth.

Ayani had been running backward. Her heels hit his boots and she fell on him, shouting curses.

The creature shrieked, and Jeff couldn't help but cover his ears to block out the sharp pain assaulting his ear drums. A chemical stench flooded past in a gust of humid wind, and he could *hear* the clacking of the thing's teeth through his covered ears.

He looked back. The worm filled the tunnel from

wall to wall, twisting like a corkscrew as it rushed toward them. Ayani shoved against Jeff so she could stand up, then she fired three more rounds. The worm didn't so much as slow down.

She mumbled under her breath as she dropped her rifle, and Jeff realized she was taunting the creature, daring it quietly to come closer.

She was getting her wish. The mouth opened wider as it drew closer until it seemed the worm's long teeth grew from the walls of the tunnel itself.

Ayani dug in one of her side pockets and yanked something out. She slapped it between her palms and slammed it against the wall…where it stuck, a small red light pulsing from within. She grabbed Jeff under his arms and pulled him deeper into the tunnel as a web of red lasers spit out from the device, forming a barrier.

The worm hit it full speed — and went right through it.

Ayani gave Jeff a shove and fell back on her hands and heels, scrambling away from the creature as Jeff army-crawled over the jagged ground.

With a squelching moan, the worm slowed and sagged. Seams opened along its body where the lasers had cut. Green muck seeped from its wounds and splattered hissing into steaming puddles.

Jeff and Ayani panted on the floor, staring at the monstrosity.

"You dropped your gun," he told her.

"Oh?" she replied between breaths. "I didn't see. Since you know where it is…"

He closed his eye and nodded. "Okay, sure. No problem. I can tell you where you'll find it."

She threw back her head and laughed. Then she offered her hand and helped him, groaning, to his feet. They surveyed the steaming ruin of the cave worm.

Ayani slapped Jeff's shoulder, startling him.

"Welcome to Galena," she said with a smile.

MERRITT

Kellan had indeed planned to travel with a light complement. Merritt led the way through the sparse forest on the outskirts of the colony's border, while Kellan and his hulking bald friend, Janos, followed behind.

Merritt had been expecting a vast array of specialists, experts, and other various overqualified remora. Instead, Kellan had impressed upon him the importance of speed.

Toward that end, Merritt had brought only a light pack and his stunner staff. He didn't bother to stop and explain all the little details about Galena's flora. Kellan could learn from someone else about how the sprawling tree canopies were underground or how one could make a passably tolerable toothpaste from the pulpy root of a dry, stiff-leafed plant they called wildweed.

Kellan wore a wristpad over his long, dark green left shirt sleeve. He checked it constantly, apparently drawing his bearings from his orbiting ship to guide Merritt in the direction toward which Merritt should be guiding them — if it were any sort of real ranging expedition instead of an attempt to get to the finish line as quickly as possible.

"She's called the Renata," Kellan said, walking faster to catch up to Merritt. "My ship."

Behind them, Janos marched in silence, as he had been doing since they left camp. He carried an automatic rifle on a strap over his shoulder and wore a constant scowl.

"I'm sure she's very nice."

After a moment of walking in silence, Kellan said, "I thought it was winter."

"Some days feel more like it than others."

Kellan stared at him for a long moment, then said, "You don't seem to ask too many questions, Mr. Alder."

"I do if I think I'll get an honest answer."

"You don't think I'm being honest?"

"I don't think you're here for any of the reasons you've mentioned."

Kellan smiled ruefully and nodded, then checked his wristpad. After getting an apparently satisfactory reading, he focused on the ground in front of him. Above, Phobis beamed brightly in a blue sky.

"I am truly here to bring this colony to fruition," Kellan told him. "I have no ulterior motive. That being said, opportunities have arisen along the way that I would be foolish to ignore. We are currently in pursuit of one of those opportunities."

Merritt shifted his stunner staff to his other shoulder. "I'm not blind to opportunities either, Mr. McEwan, but I also have other priorities."

"Your family and your fellow colonists," Kellan agreed, nodding. "I understand. If any of them could guarantee me the fortune I need to make this colony a reality, I'd be talking to them instead of out here in this glorious nature."

Merritt had noticed Kellan's reverence for his

surroundings, despite their small group moving at a rapid clip. His face would take on a look of childlike wonder as he gazed at a distant mountain or pressed his palm to the cold surface of a lead sulfide boulder. For all his mystery, Merritt was inclined to take the man at his word with regard to his plans for the colony.

"No one expected space expansion to cost enough to bankrupt every Earth government a thousand times over," Kellan went on. "With asteroid mining and the seemingly bottomless pit of resources on Mars, funding never should have dried up. But then Earth's crops began to wither. Money was funneled elsewhere. Long-term viability of the colony is dependent on a profitable resource, preferably a renewable one."

"That's why we're farming," said Merritt.

"Food is necessary, but that's just grease for the wheels here on Galena. Let Earth deal with their own food problem."

"You're talking about a mineral resource. Something you can sell on Earth."

Kellan looked at him cryptically. "Perhaps." His wristpad beeped and he swiped the screen. "Janos," he said abruptly.

He touched Merritt's shoulder to stop him. Janos nodded at his boss and trudged ahead.

"Ten meters, right in front of you," Kellan called at the man's broad back, consulting his wristpad.

"What is this?" Merritt asked.

"This is it," Kellan answered, grinning.

"We're only three miles from the colony."

"Yet you've never been here, have you?"

"No. Henry hasn't mapped this part of the forest yet."

Kellan chuckled. "What was it you said about fate and irony?"

Merritt ordered a quick break near a trickling stream so they could refill their canteens. He slowly pulled off his left boot as he sat beside the stream, wincing from the blister on the ball of his foot. He had stepped in a puddle almost as soon as they'd set out and his sock was soaked through. Merritt peeled it off and slapped it against the rock he was sitting on. Phobis was still high in the sky, baking the back of his neck. Despite the cooler season and a steady breeze, the rays of Phobis seemed to hold a heat lamp directly to the skin of anyone passing through the open fields outside the colony. Since the colonists had used up the last of the sunscreen shortly after the crash, they relied on high collars and floppy hats to keep their necks from glowing red.

Earlier, Kellan had demanded a rest after he'd caught a glimpse of a sky beast high overhead. He'd stared at it long after it became a tiny speck in the distance, doing a poor job of hiding his unease. Everyone had phobias, thought Merritt as he banged the sand from his shoe on the side of a rock. Perhaps Kellan's was being carried away by a giant raptor as dinner for itself or its offspring.

Kellan sat with his back to a tree, drinking water from his canteen he had just filled in the stream. He had a look of contentment on his face as he observed his surroundings. His companion, Janos, busied himself by stalking the tree perimeter, scowling at the landscape. Merritt chewed on a piece of soy jerky he had been saving for such an occasion.

"Can I tell you about the future?" Kellan asked as he stared up at the top of a tree. "The future of this colony?"

Merritt took a swig from his own canteen and wiped his mouth. "I'm all ears."

Kellan took a moment to gather his thoughts, drew a deep breath, and began.

"It starts off small, of course. You and the other colonists have already laid the groundwork for the next step. In the beginning, I never expected it to grow beyond the few farms providing sustenance for the colonists working them. The architects of this colony project, myself included, envisioned it as a proof of concept."

"You wanted something on record you could point to as successful to raise funding for other projects," said Merritt.

"Other colony projects, yes," replied Kellan, nodding. "Imagine how many other worlds are out there like this. Imagine how many rips there are that we haven't found."

"I don't have time to imagine it. I have enough to deal with as it is."

"That's true. Guiding a colony to its full potential is no small task."

"All I do is make sure people have food on their tables and that they don't get eaten by alien crabs."

Kellan smiled. "And if we're measuring by all the yardsticks that matter, you've been successful. Mostly. Yet I think we can do more. I don't just see farmland anymore. I see sprawling cities. I see skyways connecting them across the continents. I see a new Earth untainted by the politics and strife of our home. Imagine a place where children can walk the streets without fear of being taken."

"We already have that here," Merritt told him.

"So does every small village still clinging to antiquated ideologies," Kellan laughed. "What I see is a worldwide network of thriving metropolises, richer in technology, science, and *safety* than all the cities on Earth combined."

Merritt twisted his wet sock to drain the water. "You should talk to Henry Tolbard about how long it actually takes to build a city on a new world. Apply that to a global project and it's safe to assume your grandchildren's grandchildren might walk the streets."

"I'm just here to get it started," said Kellan. "I fully expect to pass the torch to my successor. But my job is the hardest, because I have to lay the foundation. And if the foundation is weak, then the whole structure crumbles."

Merritt sighed as he pulled the wet sock back over his blistered foot. "Sounds like quite the burden you've saddled yourself with." His foot squished back into his boot as he slipped it inside.

A loud *THWACK* broke the ensuing silence. Merritt sprang to his feet and heard it again. It was coming from the other side of the tree Kellan was leaning against. Kellan stood up and followed Merritt as they tracked the source of the noise.

THWACK!

Janos stood in a wide stance and yanked his machete from the flesh of the tree. Spongy gray material crumbled from a ragged hole. He raise the machete for another swing, a determined look on his face.

"I wouldn't do that," Merritt warned.

Janos ignored him and hacked faster.

"Tell him to stop!" Merritt yelled.

Kellan looked up at the branches far above. "It's just a tree."

"No, it isn't," Merritt growled, lunging for the machete.

Janos put a large hand on his chest and shoved hard. Merritt stumbled backward. His boot heel hit a stone in the stream and he fell on his side in the water.

Ropey vines erupted from the ground at the base of the tree, flagellating like the tentacles of a crazed monster. One of them wrapped around Janos's ankle and yanked his foot down under the ground up to his shin. The soft ground gave way easily as the canopy underneath shifted.

Kellan lurched forward and grabbed Janos under the arm as he was yanked down into the ground up to his waist. A look of pure horror replaced anger as the large man realized what was happening. He cried out for help as more vines slithered around his limbs, spreading them apart as if he were on a torture rack.

Kellan fell on his stomach beside Janos, who was now buried up to his neck. Fresh, thick vines emerged from the dirt and coiled around Kellan's torso.

"Merritt!" he screamed in a shrill falsetto.

Merritt was already on his feet, digging through his backpack. His clothes were soaked from his splash in the stream, and water dripped from his hair into his eyes, blurring his vision of the pack contents. He swept away the water, then found what he was looking for: a small metal canister the size of a hand grenade.

Janos vanished beneath the ground with a sudden jerk. Kellan looked as if he were lying on a bed of quicksand. The vines wrapped around his rib cage slowly pulled him down. The hole over where Janos had disappeared was already sealing itself.

Merritt slapped the top of the canister twice to prime it, then twisted a gear-shaped dial at the top. He dropped it into the hole after Janos and closed his eyes. There was a flash of piercing white light and a blast of heat. Janos screamed. Kellan would have, but one of the vines wrapped itself around his throat and slithered into his mouth.

After the flash dimmed, Merritt plunged his arms into the soil, clawing past dead, writhing branches until he got a handful of Janos's shirt. Inch by inch, he helped the giant of a man crawl out of the pit.

He glanced sideways at Kellan, who was flopping around on the ground like a fish as he struggled to unwrap the thick vine from around his throat. It spasmed and twitched as he peeled it off his skin and yanked it from his mouth. Kellan spat blood on the ground and rolled onto his back, his eyes bulging as he sucked in air through a pinched windpipe.

When Janos was halfway out of the hole, he shoved Merritt away and climbed the rest of the way out himself.

"You're welcome," Merritt sneered as he climbed slowly to his feet.

Janos stomped away, slapping dirt from his clothing.

"What was that?" Kellan asked in between ragged breaths.

Merritt brushed wet soil from his clothes. "The trees are connected to the underground canopy," he explained. "Neither of those things like it when someone hacks at them with a machete."

"You've seen this reaction before?"

"Several times. Usually it's a small ground quake. When we first got here, we tried to cut down a tree in the forest near the colony. We had barely scratched the surface of it when all the other trees started creaking and leaning toward the man holding the ax."

Kellan pushed himself up onto his elbows. "Did you say leaning?" He collapsed back to the ground, his arms spread wide as he stared at the sky. "Incredible."

"What was he trying to do?" Merritt asked, nodding toward Janos.

Kellan shook his head weakly. "Who knows? He just likes to hit things with his machete."

Merritt knelt down on the ground next to his pack and began to put back everything that had tumbled out during his hasty search for the canister.

"Have you seen enough yet? Ready to go back to the colony?"

Kellan propped himself back up on his elbows and squinted at Merritt. His throat was already turning purple.

"What was that canister? Some kind of flash bomb?"

"The underground canopy doesn't like excessive heat, especially in concentrated bursts," Merritt explained.

Four years ago, Willef had come back from a scavenging mission with a crate of magnesium flares. Merritt and some other farmers had been clearing new fields for planting, a process which involved laborious hours digging out the deep roots of several varieties of surface brush. Tough, sinewy roots from the bulbs of bladeweed and the net-like growths of chokevine sought out thick branches of the underground tree canopy, sometimes burrowing as deep as five meters, to leech moisture. Severing the parasitic plant roots near the surface only caused new growth to sprout from below.

Merritt had dug a deep hole one day — all the way down to the canopy — and dropped three magnesium flares, burning like white stars, among the roots.

Bladeweed and chokevine withered in a flash, but the canopy branches shrank away from the heat like snakes, a thick oil oozing from their skin to protect from the flares. The ground rumbled and Merritt had lost his footing, slipping down into the hole. Three slender canopy branches, supple as leather whips, wrapped around his ankles and dragged him deeper. He called for help, but he was alone.

Merritt was shin-deep in the ground at the bottom of the hole and sinking fast when his groping hand closed around one of the flares. He shoved it into the soil against a branch wrapped around his ankle, screaming as his flesh peeled away — along with the branch.

The wound had burned and itched for weeks as it healed.

Gavin was the one who recognized the benefit of having a controlled device that could disperse an area of the underground canopy. If the crab sticks ever failed, the farmers could use targeted underground detonations to divert the migration around the colony.

Why don't we move the colony? Gavin signed to him one day.

Merritt explained that they hadn't yet found an area on their continent large enough for all the farms that wasn't crowded with lead sulfide boulders just below the surface. There had been talk of relocating the houses away from the underground canopy and commuting to the fields every day for work. Regardless, the crabs would arrive on schedule every other year and devour the second harvest unless the colonists set up the crab sticks, and if they had to set up the sticks anyway, then, well...

"My son figured out how to combine a heat flare with the signal pulse that we use to divert hex crabs around the colony borders," Merritt told Kellan. "The crabs only travel where there's canopy directly under the soil. The pulse makes the canopy retreat deeper underground."

"Your son figured that out?" Kellan asked.

Merritt couldn't stop his pride from slipping out, and he smiled. "He'll be a better engineer than I ever was."

Kellan got to his feet and gently probed the purple bruise on his neck.

"Remind me to thank him when we get back to the colony."

"Just keep your bodyguard from attacking

everything he sees with his machete, and our chances of actually *making* it back to the colony improve significantly," said Merritt.

"You hear that, Janos?!" Kellan shouted at the back of his friend standing a good distance away. "Keep your sharp objects to yourself!"

Janos offered a rude gesture over his shoulder in response, and Kellan chuckled.

"You see? It's settled. Shall we get moving?"

Merritt shouldered his pack and wriggled the toes inside of his wet sock. With a heavy sigh, he left the moderate shade of the small group of trees and set out across the open field.

GAVIN

Gavin fell through a void toward the sound of rushing water, expecting his skull to be dashed against a rock. He plunged into dark, icy water and the frigid river stabbed his skin like daggers.

His hands cracked against sharp stones as he tried to hold on. Gavin pulled them toward his chest and they went numb. He tumbled in a curled-up ball until he could guess which way was up, then kicked hard. His head popped out of the torrent long enough to draw a deep breath.

The underwater river passage was pitch black.

He turned downstream and a low-hanging rock struck the top of his scalp. His skull bounced off it and he knew he'd been cut deep. Keeping one hand pressed to the gash, he curled up into a ball again and tumbled down the river, snatching quick breaths when he could.

The walls of the rocky passage glinted with light. Gavin oriented himself to face downstream again and saw a bright circle ahead — daylight!

His shins struck an underwater boulder and he silently screamed a stream of silver bubbles as the current tumbled him like a rag doll.

Gasping for air above the tumultuous surface, he saw that he was being carried toward a thin pillar connecting the floor of the tunnel to the ceiling. The tunnel forked beyond the pillar, moving toward the light on the right side and into darkness on the left.

Gavin stroked powerfully to the right, fighting against the strong current. He barely cleared the pillar in time, rushing past it in a spurt of white foam, only to be yanked behind it in a swirling eddy. His head cracked against the rocky pillar and his vision exploded with white light. He went limp in the water, then slowly brought a numb hand to his bleeding scalp. The current yanked him out of the eddy and pushed him toward the left fork of the river.

Blinking in the darkness, Gavin could only see dim light shining off the wet, jagged rock walls as he was taken away from the tunnel exit. The current grew stronger and he was pulled underwater. The river roared in his ears. He struck a wide, smooth rock and slipped over it — and fell down through the air, tumbling in a waterfall.

Frigid water enveloped him as he plunged into a black pool, leaving a stream of purple bubbles guiding the way back to the surface.

Purple? Gavin thought distantly as he swam madly after the bubbles.

His head burst above the surface and he sucked down thick, humid air. The damp, mineral scent of wet soil and cave lichen overpowered the metallic taste of his own blood — he had bitten his tongue at some point in the river.

Gavin wiped water from his eyes. They adjusted slowly in a dim purple light which illuminated a small underground cavern. He swam away from the short waterfall and found the edge of the pool. With great effort, he hauled his numb body from the water and flopped onto his back.

He touched a hand to his head and it came back covered in blood. His shirt was in tatters. Bloody slashes covered his chest and stomach, black in the dim cave light.

Next to the waterfall, a pile of broken rocks created a kind of staircase that disappeared into darkness — a remnant of an old cave-in.

Gavin exhaled sharply as he crawled to his feet. He could see better in the cavern as his eyes became more accustomed to the dim purple light. Thick roots hung suspended from the black rock ceiling, connected to each other by mossy vines that dripped water down to the pool below.

Limping to the rock pile at the base of the passage, he found himself instinctively signing Shurri's name, as if trying to call out for her. He shook his head in frustration and collapsed against a rock.

Craning his neck to look higher, he saw a razor-thin sliver of sunlight far above.

Gavin smiled, and his head throbbed painfully as a result. He looked down at the lacerations on his chest, then up at the jagged rocks he needed to climb.

He sank down, hissing out a tight stream of air from his numb lips.

There was no way he could make enough noise for anyone on the surface to hear him. Even if he banged rocks together, the roar of the river would drown him out.

Gavin closed his eyes against a wave of dizziness. When he opened them again, he noticed the small opening through which the purple light was leaking into the cavern. After another glance up the rocky passage, Gavin pushed himself up from the ground and limped away.

His left ankle had been twisted. Every step sent a red-hot streak up the left side of that shin, causing him to pull his weight off it prematurely.

The hairs on the back of his neck stood up, and Gavin froze. A strange kind of electricity filled the air, inaudible but somehow tangible, vibrating his bones. Without seeing the source, he knew it was coming from beyond the opening ahead of him.

The vibration intensified and Gavin's vision flicked to black. He had the sensation of falling, even though he could feel the ground beneath his feet. A vision of the colony approached quickly from a distance, as if he were approaching it through a dark tunnel. It slammed into existence around him and he found himself standing in the colony center —

— only things were different. There were no farmers. Soldiers roamed the area, heavy rifles strapped to their backs. A man walked past Gavin. His father! Gavin reached out for him but his hand fell through empty air.

That's when he noticed the chains around his father's wrists and ankles. His hair was shoulder-length and hadn't been washed in weeks. Dirt smears covered most of his face. Fresh scars covered the rest.

Gavin was yanked sideways in the vision and sped over fields of soyflower stalks, slamming to a stop next to a row of machines he didn't recognize. They belched black smoke into the sky and pumped thick sludge into a ravine. Farmers Gavin recognized stirred the sludge with long poles. All of them were chained.

Shurri was there.

Her clothes were torn and stained. The skin of her wrists and ankles had been rubbed raw. There was no life in her eyes as she numbly prodded the black sludge with her pole.

In the vision, Gavin looked up at the sky. A dozen ships hovered in the low atmosphere. A salvo of missiles erupted from the side of one, drew gray streaks of smoke across the sky, and impacted just outside the colony, shaking the ground. None of the chained farmers paid the ensuing mushroom cloud any mind.

Suddenly he was back in the waterfall cavern, clutching his chest and gasping for air. The burnt tar stench of the black sludge lingered in the air.

Gavin slowed his breathing and forced himself to relax. He couldn't explain what he'd just experienced, but he knew it couldn't be real. He hadn't been gone from the colony long enough for it to happen.

After debating the situation for a long moment, he continued on, ducking through the low passage leading away from the waterfall.

A narrow tunnel, naturally carved out by a previous offshoot of the river, rose slightly and curved until Gavin could no longer see the waterfall cavern.

The tunnel ended.

Gavin stepped out into a cathedral of rock and crystal. The vaulted ceiling thirty meters high was a field of dragon's teeth — long stalactites dripping with chalky minerals glistened in the purple light.

There were levels to the cathedral — platforms of varying heights, some surrounded by mineral formations which functioned as natural walls. Most of the walls had large openings like windows where the minerals from the ceiling had only just started to meet the rocky protrusions from below.

Purple light shined from crystal formations embedded in the rock. The crystals pulsed like beating hearts, and black fibrous tendrils moved behind their faceted surfaces.

Gavin was not alone in the cathedral.

Twenty meters away from him, on a central platform wider than all the others, was an organism unlike any other he'd seen on Galena.

There was a symmetry to the creatures on the surface. That symmetry afforded them a kind of practical beauty. Even the sky beast could be admired for its efficiency, ugly as it first appeared.

The creature on the platform in that underground cavern was a pulsating sac the size of the a drop shuttle, only without form. It looked like the misshapen lung of a giant beast.

Its black skin was translucent in places. Dense braids of vibrating filaments brushed against the skin from inside as the sac shivered and twitched. Black, fibrous webbing like muscle tissue stretched over the rest of its surface, congealing in large mounds at its base to keep it from rolling off the platform.

This tissue formed into ropes that stretched upward from the organism to connect it to the walls of the cavern like a cancerous tumor that sends out tendrils to embed itself deeper into a human host.

It was the organism that was electrifying the air, causing Gavin's bones to vibrate.

As strange a sight as it was, Gavin was somehow

more perplexed by the presence of a man and a woman he didn't recognize standing near the organism, looking up at it and talking quietly to each other.

Gavin took a step backward. His throbbing left ankle struck a rock and he fell on his backside with a wet thud.

The man and the woman stopped talking and turned toward him. The man was older, with graying black hair and a patch over his left eye. The pupil of his right eye glowed with a dim white light. The woman was younger, with long brown hair and a dangerous-looking rifle.

"Hello there," she called, her voice like a lifeline in the underground cavern. "Don't be afraid."

"He might be dangerous, Ayani," said the man jokingly. "Protect me."

"He's a kid!"

"Are you saying you weren't a threat to anyone at his age?"

"Kid, are you dangerous?" she said loudly.

He shook his head and got back to his feet, approaching warily, casting constant glances up at the alien organism. A stench like gasoline overpowered his senses as he approached, making his eyes water.

Despite the casual nature of their conversation, the woman still watched him closely and kept a firm grip on her weapon.

"I was just telling Ayani it looks like a Portuguese man o' war," said the man, addressing Gavin. He clasped his hands behind his back as he studied the creature, then looked at Gavin as if expecting a response.

What's a man of war? Gavin signed without realizing he might not be understood.

"A siphonophore," the man elaborated.

You know sign language? Gavin asked with his hands.

"I know many languages. A Portuguese man o' war looks like a jellyfish. Long stinging tentacles dangling from a translucent sac. A predator," he added, looking back at the creature. "Or rather, a group of predators. Of course, this is the biggest one I've ever seen."

"It's not a jellyfish," said the woman, Ayani. "And it's not listed in your file that you know how to sign."

The man shrugged. "That's because I never told anyone."

Ayani turned to Gavin. "Who are you?"

Gavin signed his name and told them he was from the colony. Ayani's expressive eyebrows rose as she looked at her companion.

"What are you doing down here, Gavin?" he asked.

His hands were a blur as he explained the circumstances which had delivered him to the cathedral cavern. The older man kept his eye locked on Gavin's, but still managed to translate the more salient parts of the story to Ayani. The light in his pupil seemed to glow a little brighter as he listened. Wetness shone on the naked scar that carved a straight line through his scalp.

"You've been through a lot," he said, somewhat sadly. "My name is Jeff." He nodded toward the creature. "What's your first impression?"

It feels like it doesn't belong, Gavin signed. *On this planet, I mean. Who are you? Why are you down here?*

Jeff didn't seem to notice him. His eye was closed and he stepped closer to the fluttering organism.

"Hey, now," Ayani warned.

"It wants to show me," he said in a low voice, reaching for a translucent patch of black membrane.

Just before his fingers touched the creature, he sucked in a quick breath and yanked his hand away, shaking it like he'd touched a hot stove.

"No..." he said under his breath. Tears welled in his right eye and he stumbled backward.

"Jeff, what is it?" Ayani asked.

He sat down on the wet ground and slowly pulled his legs to his chest, slowly shaking his head. His eye was wide and focused on another time.

"This is what killed the Weavers," he said. "It destroyed their planet. What is it doing down here?"

"You mean its *species* killed the Weavers?" asked Ayani.

"No. I mean *this*. It's the only one."

Ayani looked at the creature as she stepped away from it, her mouth curled in disgust.

What's a Weaver? Gavin signed into the silence.

"Another alien species," said Jeff.

Gavin studied the pulsing organism that dominated the palatial cavern like some tainted centerpiece swollen to grotesque proportions, following the tendon-like ropes connecting it to the slick walls.

A single organism that destroyed an entire species...

He shuddered to think it had been under the

surface the entire time the colonists were on Galena.

Why does it stay down here? he signed. *Why not destroy this planet, too?*

Jeff pointed to a nearby section of the wall. Gavin walked over, frowning when he realized something was moving across it. Thick, ropey branches from the underground canopy system crawled over cracked black rock. As soon as they emerged from the broken stone, they were singed as if by fire. Their outer layers peeled back, crusting black and withering the exposed flesh beneath. The burnt branches snapped off and new growth immediately slithered from the rock.

"The canopy system created a shield around this cavern," said Jeff. "I can see it in the light. It's the only thing holding this organism at bay."

"Then why doesn't it at least kill us?" Ayani asked.

"It wants to use us," Jeff replied. "It's hoping we'll help it escape. We can't let that happen."

It showed me something, too, Gavin signed.

Jeff stood up slowly, suspicion in his eye.

I saw the colony, Gavin signed. *Only it was worse. We were slaves.*

"Listen to me," said Jeff, stepping toward him. "This organism has a dark purpose inside. You can't trust anything it shows you."

How can you know? signed Gavin.

Jeff's hands moved in response as he signed, *Kid, I know a lot.*

But maybe we can use it to stop what I saw! Gavin signed emphatically.

"No!" Jeff shouted. Then, more gently, he added,

"No. It doesn't work like that. We have to quarantine this thing until I can figure out how to kill it. That means nobody comes down here. It's dormant now, trapped by the canopy, but if it ever wakes up..."

Ayani patted her rifle. "I have this."

"Unless you have a hundred thousand bullets," Jeff said, "we wouldn't stand a chance if it decides we're a threat." He turned to Gavin. "I'm trusting you to not tell anyone about this."

Gavin stared at him. *Who are you?* he signed.

Jeff sighed wearily and looked at the creature. "I'm the one responsible for keeping this thing away from Earth, and from you and the other colonists."

I need to get back to my friends, Gavin signed. *Come with me to the colony and talk to my dad.*

Ayani perked up, but Jeff shook his head.

"Not yet. I need the scanning equipment on my ship, and I have to send a message to Earth." He realized Gavin was still staring at him. "But we'll go to the colony soon. I promise."

Gavin nodded and smiled at Ayani. He cast one last, long look at the alien creature tethered by fibrous tendrils to the cathedral walls, then limped back through the rocky passage to the bottom of the jumble of rocks which, hopefully, was his path to the surface.

He took a deep breath and began to climb.

MERRITT

Janos stopped abruptly and yelled, "Here!"

He stood next to a thin stream which spilled from a raised spring. Meter-wide patches of living moss crawled slowly across the moist ground nearby. A short distance from the spring, a black arch rose from the loose soil and met the ground again four meters away. The material of the arch was so black it seemed to suck in the light around it. Merritt had a hard time discerning its edges. A broken piece of another arch lay half-buried in the soil.

At the base of a tree next to the arch was a lead sulfide tombstone. On it were etched the initials *NB*. Beneath the initials was a crude etching of the Sol solar system, with a scratch of an arrow pointing toward the third planet.

NB was here, thought Merritt.

Kellan fell to his knees in front of the tombstone.

"So it *is* true," he whispered, running his hand over the rough surface.

Merritt stepped closer to the arch and realized he'd misjudged its size. Its sides were just beyond the reach of his outstretched fingertips, and the black arch was slightly wider than his own body.

Janos walked to the arch and struck it with the bottom of his rifle. It didn't make a sound.

"It's a circle, not an arch," said Kellan, rising to his

feet. He looked down at the broken piece half-buried in the loose soil. "Or it used to be. They called it a torus."

"Who is N.B.?" asked Merritt. "Someone from the first colony?"

"Noah Bell," Kellan replied absentmindedly. He stood next to Janos, stroking the outer surface of the arch with a distant look in his eyes. "Remarkable."

"Who is Noah Bell?"

"The man who founded Diamond Aerospace."

Merritt frowned at the incongruent information. "He built the orbital shipyards?"

"His company did," said Kellan, "but he had...moved on...by then. Rumor had it that he and another man, Commander Tag Riley, visited an unknown alien world almost four hundred years ago. Looks like it was Galena. Riley came home to Earth, but Noah never returned."

"How did they visit Galena so long ago? That was before the Rip."

Kellan grinned and patted the side of the arch.

"So you weren't looking for his grave," said Merritt.

"Not his grave. The torus. It's evidence of a series of encounters that has been completely wiped from public memory. An artifact left behind by an extraterrestrial species. A machine capable of transporting objects and people across vast gulfs of space...and so much more." He looked up at the sky, then back to Merritt. "You're not going to Earth again, are you, Mr. Alder?"

"This is my home now."

Kellan stared at him intently.

"Diamond Aerospace built six of those orbital shipyards on government contract," he told Merritt. "You know what they look like, right? Giant eggs in space, squashed a little bit in the middle. Five of them have been producing ships for almost three hundred years. But the sixth...the sixth was never intended to be a shipyard. It's home to a very special visitor." Kellan nodded toward the black arch. "This torus and many more like it brought their creator back from extinction. They were programmed to recreate the exact conditions of its birth. Four hundred years ago, the creature we now call the Weaver emerged from Earth's ocean and entered a low orbit around Venus. That's not the end of the story, but the end result is that we captured the Weaver that built this torus and have been studying the creature for more than three centuries. Nearly every modern medical and technological advancement has sprung from the research undertaken at that orbital facility. GravGens, stasis pods...even Rip travel."

"How can you derive hard tech from an organism?" asked Merritt.

"We have a translator. He's an envoy between our two species who can sometimes elucidate the inner musings of the Weaver."

The muscles of Merritt's jaw worked as he digested so much information.

"You're hoping to find a tech gold mine here, with the torus."

Kellan scratched his temple and raised his eyebrows. "Well, I certainly have my fingers crossed. The equipment to properly analyze an object of this size is still more than a year away...but it will come on one of the next trips. And there's also another wee mystery I need to solve."

"Which is?"

"I mentioned a man named Riley," said Kellan. "He and another crewman were on a mission to Titan when they encountered a torus. Neither of them made it back to Earth. They died on that mission. Yet, days later, they both washed up on a beach in Florida, right as rain. *Righter* than rain, actually. Their old scars were gone. No sunspots on their skin. Teeth like new. They had been reborn, but with all of their memories intact...and short of severe physical trauma, they could not die again. I believe a torus was involved. Events which followed shortly after made it clear they were deposited back on Earth by one of these rings. That's classified, by the way. I'd appreciate it if you didn't go spreading it around."

"Who would believe me?" Merritt asked flatly.

"Good point."

"Why didn't you tell us about the first colony?"

"Ah, yes. I thought that might come up." Kellan rubbed the back of his neck and Janos looked bored. "I am sorry I didn't tell you, or anyone else. Truly. I was bound by my superiors to keep it quiet. Let me ask you, would the knowledge of what happened to those settlers have stopped you from coming?"

Merritt chewed on the question a long moment. "No."

Kellan nodded. "I suspected as much. And that's the right answer. It's best forgotten, in my opinion. A group of people found paradise, and then paradise ate them alive." He shuddered.

"A warning would have been nice."

"Boss," Janos interjected. "It's time."

Kellan glanced down at his wristpad. "So it is."

"Time for what?" Merritt asked as both men walked away from him.

They didn't seem to be in as much of a hurry now that they'd located the alien artifact. Kellan was all smiles and jokes, and Merritt noticed Janos's seemingly perpetual frown turn nearly into a straight line. He trailed behind them as they walked up a low hill smeared with thick, ropey ground cover and numerous basketball-sized lead sulfide rocks. Kellan stopped at the top of the hill and shielded his eyes from the glare of Phobis as he craned his neck to look up.

His ship, the *Renata,* glinted with reflected sunlight high above.

"Do you know much about the Rip, Merritt?" he asked. He waited for an answer, and received none, before continuing. "Scientists found matching energy anomalies in our own solar system and this one. We had to blow up Ceres to trigger the opening on our side of the wormhole, but this side was already open. Do you know what that means?"

"Someone had already opened it."

"Correct." He looked down from the sky and took a satisfied breath as he admired the landscape. "I don't know if you realize how lucky you are," he added. After a pause, he asked, "Where was I?"

"Someone opened the Rip," Janos said, a slight Eastern European accent touching his words.

"Ah, yes. Thank you. Someone opened it on this side, but not on ours. This indicates they knew what the Rip was for, but lacked the means to get to our solar system."

"Or they haven't arrived yet," said Merritt.

"Quite right. I suppose time will tell." He flashed a quick smile, then checked his wristpad and looked up at his ship. "It took a lot of thinking, Merritt, to puzzle this one out. Here was a species that knew what to do with an energy signature that could open a wormhole. Was this their first attempt to do so, as detonating Ceres was for us? Or had they done it before?"

Merritt's gaze wandered the landscape as he worked through the questions. His brow relaxed when he landed on a possible answer.

"More Rips," he said at last.

"Top marks!" shouted Kellan with glee. "I'm particularly proud of this next bit. Concentrate now, because this is no small leap to make." His stance widened and he spoke with his hands, gesturing along with his descriptions. "Over here is Galena," he said, making a fist. He held up his other fist an arm's length away. "Over here is Earth. And over here…" he moved one fist slightly. "…is Venus. Do you remember what I said happened near Venus?"

"The alien creature went there after leaving Earth."

Kellan nodded. "And it left behind trace amounts of a very bizarre energy signal. It was like a trail of broad-spectrum cosmic noise that took our forebears quite a while to detect. Fortunately for them, this energy signal doesn't dissipate. It hasn't yet, even after four hundred years." He glanced at Janos. "How are we doing on time?"

"Soon," Janos answered.

"The U.S. Government keeps a detailed report of the alien creature's energy signal," Kellan continued, addressing Merritt. "I called in some heavy favors and made a copy of that data. After I analyzed it, do you know what I found?"

Merritt shook his head, no.

"It was identical to the energy signature that created the Rip! At some point in the past, the alien creature or one of its kin traveled between Galena's system and our own. It punctured spacetime and left behind two doorways, only we couldn't see them with the naked eye. It takes an awful lot of science and the detonation of a large mass, like Ceres, to activate the Rip for human travel. Otherwise it would have been just like any other patch of dead space."

"What are we doing out here, Kellan?"

The short man smiled proudly. "I found another one."

"Another Rip? Where?"

Kellan pointed to the sky. At that moment, the gleam of his ship in the atmosphere separated into two distinct gleams and moved quickly apart.

Merritt watched the gleams in confusion. "What about the colonists?"

"The Renata is still perfectly capable of transporting people to Earth through the Rip, even without its cargo hold."

"What about the radiation? It takes heavy shielding to survive Rip travel."

"It's a smaller Rip," Kellan told him. "I didn't choose the location. It's simply where the creature traveled once before. Projections show the atmosphere will absorb the excess radiation."

Merritt became more heated the more he spoke. "What about gravity? It's not like putting a satellite in orbit. It's a cosmic anomaly."

"I would never endanger the colony," said Kellan, watching the sky. "It's perfectly safe. Having a Rip this close would cut out two months of travel time, which looks very attractive to those who balance the scales when it comes to such a large project. Ease of transport and whatever tech I can divine from that torus will mean a never-ending supply of everything this colony needs to flourish. This is the answer."

Merritt looked between Kellan and the gleams in the sky, his fists opening and closing in agitation. One of the gleams vanished higher into the atmosphere.

"Put a stop to it," he said firmly.

Kellan's gaze dropped casually from the blue sky. "No."

Merritt marched toward him, reaching for his wristpad. Janos's bulky mass stepped in his path and shoved him back. Merritt's boot heel caught on a ropey vine and he fell onto his back.

Kellan stepped from behind Janos and looked down at Merritt with something like pity. "Change is hard," he said. "You had to change everything about your life when you came here. I admire that. And I'm sorry that you'll have to change again. Progress is both a creator and a destroyer. I'll keep my promise. Your people will be happy. But you need to be with me, not against me. Big things are coming for the colony."

"Hypermass objects in position," Janos reported, glancing down at his own wristpad.

Kellan kept his eyes on Merritt's as he said,

"Detonate."

A distant orange firework appeared high in the sky and froze in mid-bloom. A split-second later, the bloom contracted to a pinpoint. A silvery bubble swelled from the pinpoint to match the apparent size of Galena's moon as it appeared in the night sky. A low rumble shook the ground and the bubble flattened to a thin line in a microsecond as if smashed from top and bottom. At the same time, a smaller bubble swelled in the center of the flat line and burst. The entire sky flashed white and the light seared Merritt's eyes. He howled in pain and surprise and turned away, shielding his face.

The ground lurched sideways, sending all three men tumbling to the ground. A sound like thunder coursed through the lower atmosphere. A nearby tree trunk cracked down the middle with the sound of a gunshot and exploded outward as if hit by cannon fire. Several other trees did the same, peppering Merritt, Kellan, and Janos with jagged chunks of spongy wood.

"Safe?" Merritt screamed over the steady rumble of thunder. "*SAFE?!*"

He pushed himself to his feet and stumbled sideways as the ground shook back and forth, sending hard vibrations up his legs. The overexposed white light in the sky leeched color from the ground and trees, leaving Merritt's surroundings sharply contrasted in monochrome.

He ran in the direction of the colony, not caring to look back for Kellan and Janos.

GAVIN

He reached the top of the rocky passage, fresh scrapes and bruises covering his legs and arms. Rushing water roared just ahead in the darkness as he hauled himself onto a flat boulder. He was on the edge of the underground river, just beyond the fork that had previously sent him away from the exit. A circle of sunlight shone brightly farther downstream.

Gavin laughed silently, mostly from exhaustion, and began to scoot on all fours across the rock, angling for the wall. There was a narrow ledge he would be able to cling to on his way out. He reached for it and his hand slipped out from under him, sending him plunging head-first into the river.

He struck a pillar in the middle of the dark tunnel as he was swept downstream and bent backward around it, the full force of the river pushing on his stomach. Icy water slammed up his nostrils, choking him.

Gavin rolled over onto his stomach against the pillar and slid off it inch by inch, scraping his skin against its jagged surface. He managed to slip away and was immediately thrust downstream, into sunlight.

The river exited a squat cave mouth and slowed as it widened to touch shores of small, smooth stones. There were no cliff walls at that section of the river.

The stones gave way to Galena's rich soil, which rose gradually away from both shores.

Gavin tumbled lazily in the water until he could drag himself onto the nearest bank, where he used the last of his strength to roll over onto his back in the bright sunlight. Frigid water still rushed over his lower legs, but he could no longer feel them.

Hard shivers racked his body as warmth slowly returned, bringing with it a million dancing needles of pain. The stones beneath him clacked together as he shook.

Footsteps approached quickly, but he couldn't make his head turn to look.

Shurri knelt beside him, staring at the cuts on his chest and stomach. Her hair was matted with blood, and one arm hung limp at her side as she gently touched Gavin's cheek.

"I was wondering if you were coming back," she said gently.

Behind her, the bearded man they'd found in the stasis pod stood with his arms crossed over his stomach, half-bent over and shivering. Dark hair hung down past his shoulders in wet curls. His lips were purple and his teeth chattered loudly.

Shurri helped Gavin scoot higher up the bank until his feet were out of the water.

Arthur? he signed weakly.

Shurri nodded farther down river. Gavin searched the bank until he saw her brother on his back, eyes closed. His white knit shirt was dyed red.

"He's alive," she told Gavin, her voice shaking. "For now."

Gavin's hand moved slowly to spell out, *M-O-S-S.*

Shurri pushed back a lock of wet hair from Gavin's forehead. Tears filled her eyes and she whispered, "You know my mother doesn't want us believing in that voodoo magic."

Gavin cracked a half-smile as warmth surged through his veins. He propped himself up on his elbows, then rolled to his side and, with Shurri's help, stood up on shaking legs.

She gingerly touched the edge of his scalp wound. "It's a deep one," she said, sucking in air through her teeth. "I think I can see your skull."

What's it look like? he signed.

"Like bone, dummy," she chided.

Gavin studied the river.

He signed, *I think this is the same river that flows to the hydroelectric dam.*

Shurri's gaze followed the flow of water. "That means we could follow it all the way back to the colony."

Hopefully, Gavin added.

She supported him as they walked over to Arthur. The escape pod passenger fell into step beside them.

"I'm Ahmed," he said, his voice quivering from the cold. "Thank you."

Gavin blinked slowly and nodded.

Ahmed suddenly sat down and hugged his knees to his chest. He buried his head between them and sobbed between waves of shivers.

Gavin and Shurri shared a sympathetic glance as they knelt down beside Arthur. His breath came in quick, rapid snatches. His torn shirt was red from a deep hand-length wound on the right side of his torso. Gavin gently reached under Arthur's back and felt a matching wound on the other side. A slight depression on the left side of his ribcage indicated where the bones had been crushed upon impact with a boulder in the cavern.

Have to carry him, Gavin signed.

"Why don't we bring the moss back here?" Shurri asked.

He smiled and nodded — a much better idea. He stood up and Shurri put her palms on the only uninjured part of his chest.

"I'll go. You rest. I can carry two patches by myself."

Reluctantly, Gavin agreed.

Shurri kissed him quickly on the lips and walked up the embankment, away from the river and toward a line of trees. Gavin painfully lowered himself onto the stony shore next to Ahmed, who wiped his nose and looked up with bloodshot eyes. Gavin stared at Arthur.

"What moss?" Ahmed asked.

Gavin tapped his throat and shook his head.

Ahmed nodded quickly and looked away, overtaken by that brief flash of embarrassment Gavin was used to seeing in others when they realized his disability.

Then Ahmed smiled weakly. "Yes or no, then?"

Gavin nodded.

"Was I…was I in the pod for a long time?"

Gavin nodded again. At the same time he hinged his closed fist up and down, indicating a head nod. *Yes.*

"How many days?"

Gavin shook his head and made a stretching motion with his fingers, then held up eight of them.

"Eight weeks?" Ahmed whispered.

Gavin shook his head again.

"Months?

No, signed Gavin, snapping his thumb and first two fingers together.

"*Years?!*" Ahmed croaked. He swallowed hard. "Were you searching for me? Is that why you were in the cave?"

No.

"Are there other survivors?"

Yes.

"Is there a man...a man named Christian and a woman named Adrienne?"

Gavin hesitated, then signed, *No.*

Ahmed looked quickly down at the ground, then gave a small nod, as if he'd been expecting that answer. He sniffed loudly and blinked.

"What a way to wake up," he said, his eyes growing wide. "I worked in the administrative office on the ship. I was in bed on the Halcyon when...when the alarms went off. I thought I'd wake up on the surface a few hours later with everyone else."

At least you didn't end up in the ocean, Gavin signed.

Ahmed shook his head in confusion. "I'm sorry, I...don't understand."

They sat in silence until Shurri called to them from out of sight. Gavin tapped Ahmed's shoulder and waved in that direction. He nodded understanding and got up to find her.

The pair of them returned a moment later, each

carrying a wide, sod-like patch of red moss. Shurri carried hers upside-down so the millions of tiny bug-legs on the bottom wouldn't touch her skin. They waggled lazily in the open air, searching for the ground.

Ahmed carried his right-side up, grimacing against the crawling sensation as the little legs picked at the sleeves of his neoprene suit.

Shurri immediately brought hers to her brother and laid it over his injured torso. The living moss turned slowly in place until it oriented itself long-ways to cover his neck down to his knees. Then it settled down and went still. The red color on its mossy back dulled to the color of rust.

Ahmed seemed to understand and brought his patch to Gavin, who eased himself onto his back. As Ahmed knelt beside him and held out the living moss, the ground seemed to bounce up from below. An earthquake coursed beneath them, rattling the stone on the shore.

"What is that?" Ahmed said sharply, dropping the moss. "Is that the worm?"

The sky exploded in a flash of white light. Shurri screamed and covered her eyes with her good arm. Gavin turned away from the light and scrambled to his feet, his left ankle throbbing from when he'd twisted it in the cavern.

A tree near Shurri split in two with a loud crack and she screamed again.

The white light faded and Gavin looked up. A large purple-green smear had appeared in the sky.

A Rip.

Surrounding clouds that had been pushed out in

a wide ring crept back toward the Rip, bleeding across the sky like spilled ink toward a drain.

Gavin locked eyes with Shurri. She looked as lost as he felt.

"Meteors!" shouted Ahmed.

A trio of bright orange streaks appeared in the sky. The three were soon joined by a dozen more, then a dozen more again.

"Debris," said Shurri.

"From what?!"

Gavin stumbled toward Shurri, tapping Ahmed on the shoulder as he passed. He gestured for help with Arthur, then signed, *Cave,* to Shurri. Gavin picked up Arthur's feet while Shurri and Ahmed each grabbed an arm. The rectangular carpet of living moss hung like a sodden towel over his body.

They struggled to carry Arthur the short distance back to the cave mouth. The stones shifted constantly underfoot as the ground vibrated. Shurri only had the use of one arm. The other was pinned to her side at an awkward angle. She said she hadn't wanted more moss to die just because her shoulder was bruised.

"Is it safe to go back in there?!" Ahmed yelled over the thunderous noise and rattle of stones. "What if it collapses?"

As if in response, a sharp whistle grew louder and the first of the orange streaks made landfall. The chunk of debris at its head slammed into the ground, soil and boulders violently erupting in all directions.

"To the cave!" Ahmed shouted.

They reached the low overhang as smaller bits of debris struck the ground outside the entrance. The shrill whistle of their rapid descent peaked abruptly and ended with the deep *THOOMMM* and shake of a heavy ground impact.

Some plummeted into the river, sending up gouts of water. Broken rock shrapnel sliced through the air.

A larger debris chunk hit the ground above the cave mouth, cracking the rocks overhead. Pebbles and fist-sized stones rained down on their backs as they shielded Arthur and the living moss.

Shurri looked at Gavin helplessly. She shook in his vision as the ground vibration intensified. The loud *CRACK* of exploding trees punctuated the air between debris hitting the ground.

A chunk landed right outside the cave, sluicing a wave of water over Gavin and the others. He sputtered and wiped Arthur's face, making sure he was still breathing.

The whistling stopped, and so did the impacts. A slight tremor shook the ground, but nowhere near the earthquake that struck after the white flash.

Hesitantly, Gavin emerged from the cave mouth to look at the sky. The Rip had pulled in all the nearby clouds, leaving no white. Orange firework bursts seemed frozen in time like blooming flowers.

A stronger tremor rocked the ground, and Gavin grabbed the cave wall for support. When it ebbed to a low-grade vibration, he turned back toward Arthur, then Shurri.

The colony, he signed.

"I'm staying with my brother," Shurri told him. "You go."

Gavin looked at Ahmed, who held his knees to his chest and rocked forward and backward, eyes wide and unseeing. Shurri shook her head, then grimaced from pain as she cradled her injured arm.

I'll bring help, Gavin signed. *I promise*.

He crawled up the low embankment on all fours, not trusting his shaking legs and injured ankle on the stones near the shore. When he made it to the soft ground closer to the forest at the edge of the river, he stood up and limped along the tree line, following the river downstream — toward the colony.

MERRITT

His boots pounded the soil as the world shook around him. He ran through the forest toward the colony as flaming debris rained from the sky, exploding through trees and slamming into the ground.

There was no shelter that far from the colony. Even there, the best place for cover was probably one of the hard-shelled prefab buildings. At a sprint, Merritt was still too far away.

Kellan and Janos ran behind him, puffing to keep up. Merritt threw a glance over his shoulder in between debris strikes to check if they were following. Kellan being able to run for so long didn't surprise him, but the big man, Janos, had barely broken a sweat. His thick arms pumped rhythmically as he barreled ahead, eyes focused past Merritt. As Merritt had done with his stunner staff, Janos had tossed his weapon aside shortly after he started running.

"The equipment!" Kellan shouted. "The cloning equipment!"

Emily, thought Merritt.

There was little chance of one of Kellan's storage crates surviving a direct impact from a debris strike, even if it was inside a prefab.

His thighs burned painfully, but his legs kept

churning. He had planned to run straight back to the colony, but anyone there was likely already indoors.

He adjusted his course slightly, angling for Kellan's encampment. His path brought him to a section of the river without a bridge. Merritt jumped into it from the shore, landing in waist-deep water. A chunk of flaming debris struck the water meters away. Water and knives of rock exploded upward, sending him flying sideways downstream. He hit shallow water on his shoulder and felt something snap inside him.

Multiple lacerations down the other side of his body bled freely.

A deep rumble coursed through the ground, splitting it open just past the shoreline. A fissure cracked open in the ground, zig-zagging like a lightning bolt. The two sides snapped apart as if a taut rope had been cut, the abyss between them swallowing boulders and trees.

Merritt clawed his way to shore as the earthquake lessened to a low vibration. He flipped onto his back and panted shallowly, sure that he had broken a rib.

That's when he heard the screaming.

He held his breath and waited. Kellan screamed his name, but it sounded like it was coming from below.

With a pained groan, Merritt climbed to his feet and shuffled along the chasm which had opened near-instantly in Galena's crust. The far side was five meters away in most places and followed a zigzagging path through the forest.

Merritt couldn't see the bottom.

He found Kellan clinging to the edge of the fissure, his body dangling over the void. Kellan had managed to grab hold of a thick underground canopy branch that had been exposed when the chasm formed. He gripped it with one white-knuckled hand. His other arm was missing below the elbow.

"Merritt! Merritt!" he cried in a mad panic.

His body thumped against the crumbling wall of the chasm as his legs kicked uselessly beneath him. A meter below him, Janos clung to the cliff wall. He had apparently plunged his hands into the soft dirt up to his elbows closer to the ledge, then had slid down to where he now hung, straining with all his might to keep his arms in the wall.

Merritt dove to the ground near the chasm and grabbed Kellan's wrist. He felt the pull of a torn muscle in his chest and shouted in pain.

"*Up up up!*" Kellan screamed.

Merritt gritted his teeth and slowly crawled back from the ledge, hauling Kellan up inch by painful inch. A dull knife stabbed deep between two of his ribs with every small movement.

The only positive was that the debris seemed to have stopped falling.

"Hey!" Kellan shouted. "Let go of me!"

Merritt was pulled back toward the ledge, still gripping Kellan's wrist. He slid easily on the loose soil. His head peeked over the chasm and his arm hung down into it, his grip now the only thing stopping Kellan from falling into the abyss.

Janos had climbed high enough to grab Kellan's ankle. Dirt and blood smeared his bald head. He glared up at Merritt with animal determination, his muscles twitching under his shredded black combat armor.

Kellan kicked uselessly at Janos's hand with his other boot.

Merritt's eyes squeezed shut and he screamed as the combined weight of both men stretched his shoulder almost out of its socket.

Another snap in his chest as a rib gave out.

His grip loosened and Kellan's hand slipped down into Merritt's.

Then he felt someone next to him in the dirt, and more hands grabbing onto Kellan's arm.

Merritt opened his eyes to see his son beside him. Gavin strained to hold on. Blood covered half his face and his shirt was a shredded red rag.

Below them, Janos climbed higher, using Kellan's body as a rope ladder.

"We'll both fall!" Kellan yelled at him.

Janos ignored him. He grabbed onto Kellan's neck and hauled himself higher.

Merritt and Gavin slid farther out over the edge. Merritt's injured chest pushed directly on the rocky ledge.

"I can't..." he wheezed, his jaws locked tightly together.

Janos reached for Merritt's arm. He grabbed it just above the elbow, then planted the toes of his boots against Kellan's lower back so he could stand.

Merritt's stomach went over the edge as Janos reached up for Gavin.

Gavin let go of Kellan's arm with one hand and scooped up soil. Janos looked at him and Gavin threw it in the man's eyes. Janos roared and swiped at his face. Kellan's shirt ripped down the back and Janos fell free, disappearing into the darkness below. His scream followed him down, eventually growing so faint it could no longer be heard.

Gavin struggled to hold onto Kellan's sweaty arm as Merritt wiggled backward until he was no longer dangling over the ledge.

Together, they strained to pull Kellan up out of the fissure and onto solid ground. He rolled onto his back and began to sob, covering his eyes with his remaining hand. The stump of his left arm bled freely into the dark soil.

Gavin crawled over to his father, who lay facedown, breathing quickly and shallowly. Merritt lifted his head and met Gavin's eye. He raised a shaky hand to his son's face.

"What took you so long?" he wheezed.

Gavin wiped his nose and his eyes, silently crying and laughing at the same time.

LEERA

Leera and Niku were silent as they rode the tunnel transit system away from the dome. With a detached sense of dull interest, she had figured out they only needed to be standing in all four cutouts in the stone floor to get the track moving. Once underway, they stood side by side, each one in a single cutout, leaning against each other for support.

Leera's breath fluttered in her chest. Her throat was still raw from all the screaming and sobbing. Neither she nor Niku leaned forward very far on the return journey to make the transit system move faster. Her exhaustion ran bone-deep, and her mind could barely handle the current pace of ground movement outside the tunnel. They had plenty of air in their tanks to reach Weston and get back to the surface at their current speed.

Occasionally, the image of the sea creature bursting from the pool and landing atop Miles would flash into her mind. She would squeeze her eyes shut against it, and more tears would flow. Niku was always there to hold her tighter, and she took a small amount of comfort seeing that his cheeks had not remained completely dry.

The climb up the long slope they had slid down earlier was the most difficult part of their return journey. They paused frequently to sit with their legs pointed down the slope. Niku wondered aloud why the transit system didn't come all the way to the end of the tunnels, but Leera couldn't answer.

On one of their rest breaks, the floor beneath them rumbled. The water touching the invisible walls of the tunnel shivered. Leera and Niku shared an uneasy glance.

"Earthquake?" he asked.

"I don't think so."

Later, Weston greeted them with a huge smile when the doors to the circular stone room slid apart. Above him, the invisible ceiling let in the small amount of light filtering down through the water under a blue sky.

"Why weren't you answering on comms?" he asked quickly. "You'll never guess what I saw! This big squid tried to grab me in the tunnel, but it couldn't get inside!"

His smile dropped when he saw Leera's and Niku's faces.

"What is it?" he asked, looking behind them. "What happened? Where's Miles?"

Niku relayed the events inside the dome while Leera walked unsteadily toward the central stone pillar, the muscles in her thighs spasming from exhaustion. She leaned her back against the pillar and sank down to the floor.

After Niku finished his story, Weston turned to look at her with a mixture of fear and anger.

"We don't have the air to go back for him," he said.

Leera shook her head. "He's gone, Weston. Even if we went back."

Weston swallowed and stared at nothing. "He was my best friend," he said simply.

"He saved our lives," Leera told him, her voice cracking with emotion. She left it unsaid that the creature's interest in Miles had allowed her and Niku to escape.

Weston set his jaw and nodded. Leera hated seeing his boyish face go hard. Yes, he was a soldier. He'd likely experienced his share of loss. It seemed different, at least to her, to lose someone after being stranded together on another world for eight years.

"Well," he said, taking a deep breath, "we won't need our spare tanks if we leave now. Are you ready?"

"Ready," said Niku.

Leera nodded again.

"I found this," Weston told them.

He pushed his palm to the wall next to the door and depressed a rectangular block of stone. It clicked into place.

"You can stop the doors from closing automatically if this is pushed." He pressed it again to make it flush with the wall and the doors slid shut. "I was more excited about it earlier."

A square of blue light glowed to life on the pillar above Leera's head. Weston walked to it and pushed on it with his palm. Leera kept her gaze on the invisible ceiling as it became opaque and turned back into smooth rock. With a slight bounce of movement, the circular room ascended.

Now that they knew how to operate the doors, the trip back to the surface was a simple matter of going through the motions. They made it to shore under the bright light of yellow Phobis without incident, and Leera was as grateful as she'd ever been to remove her helmet and breathe the chill salty air beside the Casmin Sea.

She didn't care about the cold. She sat on the sand, helmet resting beside her, and stared at the black surface of the choppy water, her breath puffing out in slow plumes. In the distance, four-story-tall triangular walls of water stretched toward the sky, their blue-gray surfaces slashed by white — sentinels of the seas and oceans of Galena.

There were many opportunities for tears over the next few hours, but she had none left. The empty space for Miles's suit in the hand cart, his unclaimed gear back at the camp site, and the long walk back to the colony struck her the hardest.

Colonists had died on Galena before — many had died. For several years after the crash, she and the nurses had battled a bacterial infection among the colonists. The bacteria entered the body through small scratches and incubated for several months before launching a full-blown attack on the body. The long incubation time meant that no patient could remember getting scratched in the first place, especially since cuts and bruises were a normal part of everyday life on the new planet.

She lost half a dozen colonists before she traced the cause to a kind of bladeweed that liked to crowd out soyflower fields if given the chance. Now, at the start of every season, Merritt and the other farmers combed their fields, pulling up any adolescent pre-bacterial bladeweed bulbs they found.

As she walked through the sparse woods back toward the colony beside Niku and Weston, who each had a hand on the supply cart, it soothed her to think of her science, even though it carried a morbid undertone. Yes, she had lost six colonists — but no doubt had saved countless others by solving such a diabolical problem as was posed by the overzealous bladeweed.

Her family was never far from the front of her thoughts. Leera found herself musing about going back to Earth at long last. She had no energy for high hopes. If the ship in orbit had indeed come to offer a trip back, she would take it. If it had come for another purpose, then she would keep working.

Oddly — or perhaps appropriately — she found it easier to think about Miles the farther she got from the underwater city. A faint smile tugged at her lips as she remembered the years after the crash. He had always been an eager friend, willing to help not just her, but the community. His formation and leadership of the ranger program had saved many a colonist from spiraling down a darker, isolated path.

"It hypnotized him," Niku said, his deep voice loud in the stillness. "The same way cuttlefish do with crabs. They imitate reflections of broken water using chromatophores in their skin. I always thought it was...alien."

"Galena has trees, like Earth...only not the same," Leera said. "Whales, too, but different."

Weston grunted agreement. "You got that right."

"Any two biological systems will have organisms that need to survive in similar ways. They'll just adapt differently."

"I can't see the need for something to adapt into that squid monster," said Weston.

"More of an octopus," Niku muttered.

"It's very likely we've never seen its primary prey," Leera told Weston. "There's always a reason animals are the way they are. In nature, function always follows."

"I don't need to see its prey," Weston declared. "I'm never going back in the water." He paused a long moment, then asked, "Do you...do you think the squid thing is *them?* The ones that built the city?"

"No," Leera replied with certainty. "I think Miles inadvertently called it when he broke the film over the pool." She thought about Weston's own encounter with the creature. "Or it was a horrible coincidence that it was nearby when it sensed the film break."

"You think a covering so thin could keep that monster out?" Weston asked.

"Maybe it cloaked the pool entrance," Niku mused. "If the beast hunts by smell, such a film could smother any odors beyond, essentially rendering them invisible."

Weston raised his hands in confusion. "Then why even have the pool?! When would you *ever* use it if one of those things came crawling through every time?"

"You would use it if you ate them," Leera said thoughtfully, thinking back to the stone tables surrounding the two pools. Perhaps they weren't dining or picnic tables. Perhaps they were used to clean and butcher the tentacled creatures after they were lured through the pit entrance.

"Hey, look," said Weston.

He stopped and stared at the sky. The purple-green outline of a Rip was barely visible in the harsh noon light.

Niku shaded his eyes from the glare. "Is that real, or am I seeing things?"

"Looks real to me," Leera answered. "But I don't know what it means."

"Maybe it has something to do with the earthquake we felt in the tunnel."

The trees thinned out as the eastern farms of the colony came into view. The nearest farm was a low building with small, circular windows, surrounded by a healthy crop of soyflower.

"I thought we were angling for Merritt's place," said Weston.

Niku grinned and picked up his pace. "We're not far off. Besides, this is better."

He cupped a hand to his mouth and let out a loud bird call as he and the others approached the farm house. The front door creaked open shortly after and Uda ran outside, tugging on a jacket over her white coverall.

"Ha*ha!*" Niku shouted as his arms swallowed her smaller frame in a bear hug. "Told you I'd come back! Has Toma been asking for me?"

"He's forgotten all about you," Uda teased, winking. She grew serious when she realized someone was missing. Her eyes found Leera's, searching, and Leera dropped her gaze, her breath shuddering. "Right then," said Uda with a quick nod. "More on that later. Let's get you all inside where it's warm."

She herded Niku toward the house and hooked an arm in Weston's to guide him. With a glance back over her shoulder, she added, "Leera will want to be rested up for her shuttle ride tomorrow. It's a long way home."

Leera's next step became a stumble and she sank to her knees in the soft soil. Unable to speak, she looked at Uda for confirmation, terrified to believe her. Uda's eyes welled with tears as she smiled and nodded it was true: the orbiting ship would be going back to Earth, and it was taking on passengers.

Leera put her hands to her face and slowly doubled forward until her forehead touched the cold soil.

It turned out she had more tears, after all.

THE ENVOY

Jeff leaned back in the pilot seat and rubbed his jaw. The curved viewscreen in the *Celerity*'s cockpit showed two side-by-side graphs, each one overlaid with a dozen different biometric outputs. One displayed every available bit of data recorded from the Weaver in Shipyard 6 near Earth — subsonic audio emissions, a multitude of heat signatures, and various as-of-yet unidentified energy spectra. The other graph displayed the information Jeff had gleaned by using the ship's equipment to scan the underground creature on Galena.

The *Celerity*'s computer was telling him there was a sixty-five percent overlap.

He tapped on the control panel and cleared away extraneous data and other known readings which weren't shared between the two organisms. The remaining temperature clusters, signal pattern groupings, and energy output diagrams would have overlapped enough for any evolutionary biologist to claim the two species shared a primordial origin, if they weren't modern cousins outright.

Jeff thought back to his time in the "cathedral" cavern with Ayani. There had indeed been flashes of familiarity — moments where he'd felt like he was in Shipyard 6 with the Weaver instead of beneath the surface of a planet halfway across the galaxy. He could always sense an underlying electricity when he was in the presence of the Weaver. It was the same here on Galena — yet *this* sensation was tainted by a malevolence threaded into its very fabric.

He needed no more proof beyond what he could "see" with his remaining eye. The life-light that had revealed itself to him on Galena as solid, multicolored beams rising toward the sky showcased a vibrant ecology of thriving organisms.

Yet the poisoned emanations from the cathedral creature were marked by a shadow he'd not seen elsewhere since he'd arrived.

That shadow had wholly consumed the light beams in the cavern shortly after Gavin left to return to his colony and the walls began to shake.

Earthquake, Jeff thought instantly before seeing the truth — before *feeling* it.

The canopy network of Galena was crying out as fiery metal daggers fell from the sky, slicing through soil and root and branch. Its cries shook the land.

Inside the cathedral, jagged stalactites plummeted from the ceiling and smashed to pieces. Glowing purple crystals embedded in the rock shattered and blinked out, plunging the cavern into darkness. Ayani grabbed Jeff by the shoulders and flung him to the quaking ground, covering his body with her own.

He would later learn that Kellan had detonated the main section of his ship in the atmosphere, stupidly — but not surprisingly, given his history — subjecting the lands around the colony to meteors of flaming debris.

A dim light bloomed inside the creature,

silhouetting clumps of internal filaments as they hypnotically waved back and forth through viscous fluid, indifferent to the chaos. A deep, pulsing womb sound filled the chamber, drowning out the clatter of crumbling rock.

Rank stench billowed from mounds of glistening black tissue surrounding the base of the creature on the platform, gagging both Jeff and Ayani.

In the smothering gloom at the heart of the cavern, Jeff couldn't view the organism in its entirety as it hung suspended by its own thick tendrils. Darkness swallowed its membraned body near the ceiling, tricking his mind into thinking the creature had no end.

Its body sac fluttered like a stuttering heart, and one of the tendrils holding it to the wall snapped, the sound loud as a gunshot in the rock-walled chamber.

Stone screamed as the creature twisted its bulk on its broad pedestal. A flood of animosity bombarded Jeff's senses as it began to fully awaken, and he cried out in unison with the suffering canopy—

—just as the walls stopped shaking and the cracked purple crystals slowly illuminated to full brightness, bathing the cavern in rich swaths of violet. The rumbling faded, and fresh canopy branches slunk out of gaps in the rock walls to reform their shield, ashen flesh charring instantly.

The alien creature sagged on its platform, squelching into the folds of black tissue, and the shadowy life-light that had swallowed the cavern was diluted and lightened by a multitude of colors that — to Jeff's eye — erupted from the creature's body like solid beams.

Kellan had triggered the detonation to open a second Rip, Jeff realized when he and Ayani reached the surface. The wormhole burned bright and purple-green in the daytime sky. Even Kellan wouldn't be dumb enough to blow up the moon, so he must have used hypermass—

"I thought you'd be asleep," Ayani said from behind the pilot seat of the *Celerity*, startling him out of his remembrance.

He glanced back over his shoulder and greeted her with a half-grin as she stood close.

"I don't do much of that these days," he admitted.

Ayani spent a long moment looking at the graphs on the viewscreen. "Are they related?"

Jeff nodded.

Ayani sighed and leaned against the inner hull. "I take it you're not ready to go back home."

"You miss Seattle?" he asked.

"Now that you mention it...not really."

He offered a consoling smile. "Trager would send us right back here anyway once he saw the data. He and his buddies will never be finished studying the Weaver. That thing in the cavern beneath us would barrel straight for Shipyard 6 and peel it open like soft fruit to get at what's inside."

"What *is* inside?"

"I don't know. Nutrients, maybe? Some kind of power source? Maybe it simply hates."

"How do you know it will go straight for the Weaver?"

Jeff's eye unfocused as he remembered what he'd seen in the cathedral...what the creature had revealed about its own past.

"It showed me," he said.

He told Ayani about his vision of the Weaver's dying homeworld. Myriad lava plumes erupted from a landscape of fissures in the rocky surface. Mountains collapsed as the ground opened.

The sky was a black cloud, choking out sunlight.

In the midst of the chaos, two creatures spun through the air, slowly drifting lower. The Weaver was a craggy mass of rock-like flesh as large as a skyscraper with two tapered ends. The creature Jeff had recently encountered in the cathedral cavern was a translucent black sac half-enclosed with fibrous muscle tissue.

The Weaver had become entwined by the long, ropey black tendrils of its attacker. They burned chasms into the Weaver's smoking flesh.

The Weaver made no sound. A red pool shaped somewhat like a round mouth opened wider as it plummeted in slow motion toward a vast lake of lava below. Its attacker tightened its grip. Tendrils sank deeper until they met in the middle, spilling the segmented Weaver in several directions.

The tendril creature hovered in mid-air, shuddering with delight or some unknowable emotion, then drifted across the riven surface, searching for more prey.

"They're enemies," Jeff said, slowly emerging from the memory.

Ayani rubbed her eyes tiredly. "Trager would probably want to study it, too."

"I have no doubt...and I can't let that happen."

"What's your plan?"

"You mean *our* plan," he said, smiling. "You're here to protect me, right?"

"Don't push your luck."

"You pushed me down in the cavern when the debris was falling."

"That was instinct."

"And a good one. Thank you."

Ayani looked away briefly, uncomfortable with the compliment.

Jeff continued. "We need to figure out a way to kill it without also killing the canopy organism underground."

"I thought you said the canopy was the only thing keeping it locked up down there."

Jeff nodded. "They're still connected somehow. I'm worried if we yank out the tumor, the rest of the body will die, too. The canopy covers most of the land on Galena. Accidentally killing it would mean killing everything else."

Ayani frowned thoughtfully. "Do you really think one organism could have that much of an impact?"

"It wiped out a highly advanced species, one capable of constructing resurrection machines and tampering with the fabric of space. I don't want to think about the harm it would cause if it got back to Earth."

"Well," said Ayani, pushing herself from the wall. She gripped Jeff's shoulder and gave it a rough squeeze. "We'll need some supplies from town if we plan on staying a while. Eventually."

She walked out of the cockpit, leaving Jeff to bubble in a stew of a million thoughts.

Ayani was right, of course. They couldn't remain

isolated forever, and Jeff had questions — for one person in particular. He pulled up a probe map of the continent and began his search for the colony.

MERRITT

The hospital was a crowded place in the days following the creation of the new Rip. Merritt was one of many patients who needed medical attention. He slowly opened his eyes and stared at the bright ceiling. His body felt steamrolled. After saving Kellan from the fissure, he'd been barely conscious when his son helped him stumble through the hospital door. All of the beds were occupied by those in critical condition. Leera bandaged his chest and gave him a low cot near the wall while a rectangular patch of living moss slipped him into a gentle coma and healed his wounds. The living moss wouldn't physically stitch bones together, but it would align them for faster recovery.

Merritt turned in the cot, wincing at the dull soreness in his chest, and set his bare feet on the cold floor. Shurri stood near one of the other beds, looking down at her brother. His chest rose and fell gently. The dried-out husks of three square patches of moss were on the floor next to his bed.

"How's he doing?" Merritt asked.

"He's definitely been better," Shurri replied without looking away from her brother. Her pockets were stuffed with used tissues and her eyes were red.

"Gavin says he's stronger than he looks."

She smiled slowly. "He's really good at giving

himself half-compliments."

Merritt groaned as he got to his feet and shuffled over to stand beside her. He squeezed Shurri's shoulder and said, "He meant it."

She nodded and her bottom lip quivered. Merritt sensed she would burst into tears if she said anything, so he left her to her thoughts and walked toward the back of the prefab hospital. Leera was in the process of quietly instructing Uda how to refill the living moss incubation tanks after the moss was gone.

"How are you feeling?" she asked as Merritt approached.

"Like I was smashed between two boulders…but still better than I felt when I got here. Thank you."

"Well, progress is progress, no matter how painful," Leera said with a smile.

"What are you still doing here?" he asked. "Did you miss the shuttle?"

"The shuttle never *stops* running," said Uda. "They are bringing so much…"

"I decided to stick around a few extra days to help out," Leera explained. "The Renata isn't going anywhere until Kellan is up and walking again."

She nodded to a back corner of the room, where a long metal table had been pushed aside to make room for a coffin-like tank with white walls and a clear plexi lid. Inside, Kellan was suspended in a pink gel. Little square patches of living moss crawled slowly over the open stump of his left forearm. Wormlike flagella probed the wound from small pores on the sides of the moss.

"Is he in hypergel?" asked Merritt.

Leera nodded. "It has strong antibacterial

properties, and it keeps him in a deep sleep while I see what the moss can handle."

"You never miss the chance for an experiment."

She shrugged. "Well, I've found out the moss is immune to the sleeping narcotic in hypergel. Kellan's wound seems to be healing faster than a simple stitch job."

"Think they'll grow back his arm?"

"Now that *would* surprise me."

"Why go up to the Renata so soon? It still has a few months left of rad shedding in orbit."

Leera rubbed her tired eyes and blinked. "Kellan's people told me he wanted to go on a survey mission to the far side of Galena. I signed up. Besides, there are doctors in Kellan's crew that will be here for the bumps and scrapes, and Uda and Shurri are learning more every day."

Uda smiled.

"I figured you'd want to explore the city you found," said Merritt.

She drew a sharp breath. "It's just that...Miles..." Uda squeezed her arm. She sniffed and nodded, then flashed an embarrassed smile. "I can't go back down there. Not so soon, anyway."

"I'm going to check the beds," said Uda, excusing herself.

After she walked to the front of the hospital, Leera said to Merritt, "She's been a real blessing, especially with the colonists who went to the cave."

"They came back?" Merritt asked, surprised.

"Henry brought them back yesterday. Most only had minor injuries, but a few were struck by a rockslide in the cave when the earthquakes hit.

Everyone's alive, so there's that."

Merritt pulled her in for a long hug. She sniffed into his sore chest.

"We're going to miss you," he said quietly.

They separated and she looked up at him, smiling. "Likewise. But I'm finally going home."

The air was cool and crisp outside. Late afternoon light created long shadows across the common area at the center of the colony. Gavin and Shurri sat on two cross-sections of a tree made into short stools near a freshly-dug bonfire pit.

"Mind if I borrow him for a minute?" Merritt asked as he shambled over.

I'll find you, Gavin signed to Shurri as he stood.

She nodded and smiled at Merritt, then walked back into the hospital.

"Let's walk this way," said Merritt, pointing toward the first tree he saw. He waited until the pair of them passed beyond it before continuing. "If you hadn't come along when you did, either Kellan or I would be dead. Or both."

Would that be a bad thing? Gavin signed. *If Kellan died? Ahmed knows him. Says he can't be trusted.*

"Who's Ahmed?"

Found him in a worm cave. He was still in a stasis pod from the crash.

Merritt's eyebrows rose in surprise. "Eight years in a pod? I guess we have a lot more to talk about than I thought." He groaned and pressed a hand to his sore hip. "But to answer your question, yes. It would have been bad if he died."

Why? Gavin signed. *He wants to change our home.*

"Of course he does. There's good money in it. It

might not seem it to you, son, but this colony is fragile. We're better off dealing with the devil we know than the one we don't."

As long as you know him, Gavin signed in concession.

Merritt wrapped his arm around his son's shoulder. "We'll see. I heard a certain someone killed the sky beast. I should be safe, right?"

Gavin shrugged out from beneath his father's arm.

Willef would still be alive if we had killed the sky beast when we had the chance, he signed angrily.

Merritt's gaze sank to the ground as he thought fondly of his friend. "Willef wouldn't have killed it, either," he said. "We only hunt if it's necessary."

Gavin's hands moving in a flurry. *Taking out a possible threat IS necessary. I won't let it happen again.*

Merritt smiled sadly as he watched his son from the corner of his eye.

"Is that why you threw dirt in Janos's face?"

Gavin was quick with his answer. *I did it because he would have killed you.*

"Are you okay, son?" Merritt asked softly. For a moment, the shadow of fear passed over Gavin's face and his chin quivered. He looked ten years younger, like the small boy Merritt used to comfort when the guilt of a transgression overwhelmed his emotions.

Then Gavin swallowed hard, and signed, *I will be.*

"I'm glad you're here with me," Merritt told him. Then he signed, *You did the right thing.* He hated having to gloss over another man's death, especially a death for which his son was responsible. Janos would likely haunt Gavin for the rest of his years...yet he had saved his father's life. Merritt held out his arms for a hug.

Gavin spent a long moment deciding to accept the compliment, then he let his father hug him tightly.

Merritt kept his hands on Gavin's shoulders as they separated.

"See? I even walked away from the colony in case we hugged. I remember your little diatribe on not embarrassing you in front of your friends."

Gavin grinned and fake-shoved his father away. *That was six years ago!* he signed. *I'm going back to Shurri.*

Merritt waved as his son limped toward the colony, favoring his right leg more than usual. He looked up at the sky and squinted at the hazy outline of the new Rip. He didn't have the opportunity to ask Kellan where the other side of the wormhole led. How close to Earth had Kellan opened the door?

He took his time walking back to the colony. It felt good to be out of the hospital cot, despite the ache in his bones.

When he reached the common area, Skip was waiting, twirling his wispy goatee.

"Heard you walked off that way," he said. "Came to check on ya."

"Well, what do you think?"

Skip looked him up and down. "I sure wouldn't buy you at auction."

Merritt laughed harder than he had in a long time. He slapped his old friend on the shoulder and they walked beside each other through the common area. It looked like any other day. A few colonists lounged on the dry mossy ground near the cafeteria, while others carried baskets of freshly-pulled carrots or potatoes for their daily trade.

"How's Janey settling in?" Merritt asked.

"Already queen of the roost," Skip replied. "Got me out in the field twice as long as before she got here."

"You were hardly in the field before."

"Yeah, but it's still too much."

"The kids will help."

His arms rose and fell in exasperation."They're lazier'n me!"

Merritt chuckled. "They won't be for long. Not here."

Skip nudged Merritt's arm with his elbow and pointed over to where Gavin sat with Shurri. They huddled close together, laughing and staring into each other's eyes.

"Good to see some things are back to normal," Skip said.

There was a loud thump from behind the hospital building. Several members of Kellan's crew were stacking dozens of storage crates. Merritt thought of what Kellan had promised him — to use her DNA and LifeScan data to bring his wife back to life.

"Some are back to normal," Merritt agreed. "And some are still changing."

Skip grinned and draped his arm over Merritt's shoulder. "Ain't that just the way it goes?"

THE ENVOY

Cold darkness enveloped Jeff as he stepped into the prefabricated hospital building. He left behind the organic silence of the sleeping colony for the soft sounds of medicine: thick liquid bubbling gently inside illuminated tanks at the back of the room, each one crawling with various-sized patches of healing moss; buzzes and clicks from a rack of monitoring equipment next to a patient's bed; the low, steady hum of a stasis tank which glowed pink from the hypergel within.

A beam of moonlight stabbed the darkness from a high window, illuminating a work table stacked high with soiled bed sheets. Jeff liked the moon here on Galena. It was twice as large as Earth's in the night sky, and was unmarred by the progress of humans. Even with the naked eye, one could see the great scars of the luxury cities Haven and Avalon on the surface of Earth's moon. Galena's moon boasted only craters, and a vast, dark canyon that cut across the face along the equator.

Jeff could see only three patients in the gloom. Two slept on padded cots, intravenous lines inserted into the veins of their hands. The third patient was suspended in thick gel within the stasis tank.

No guard had been posted on the hospital door. Jeff stood just inside the entrance, shrouded by night and shadow, struck by a sudden melancholy...a longing for the way things should be. Such a simple thing, to be able to leave a door open without fear of looters or predators. The fact that you could only served to highlight yet another difference between the two human worlds — yet on Earth, there was a different breed of predator, one far more cunning than the beasts of Galena.

The colonists did post perimeter lookouts, though slipping past them had taken little more than a halfhearted effort on Jeff's part. A loose ring of pulsing crab sticks kept the migrating omnivores at bay, and the other potential animal threats were being managed. Cave worms never came to the surface, and one of the sky beasts — if not the *only* one — had been slain by Merritt's son, Gavin.

Jeff wasn't quite ready to reveal himself to the colonists yet, but Ayani had walked among them twice in as many days, deftly sidestepping their more direct questions while asking some of her own. The flaming debris shower from Kellan's destroyed ship had been a freak accident, sparking curiosity instead of lingering fear. For the most part, the colonists felt safe, Ayani told him. Jeff understood that safety often gave way to complacency, and he'd been right. He merely had to wait for a lookout to yawn greatly and study the night sky before slipping past at a distance.

Walking slowly through the dark hospital, his gaze drifted over surgery tools, sterilization stations, and crates of other medical supplies. The colonists had done well for themselves, despite their situation. Jeff would speak to them, learn more about their perils and their victories — but not yet. Something else weighed heavily on his mind — a looming threat too great to ignore.

Pink light washed over his face and body as he stood looking down on the coffin-like stasis tank. Kellan McEwan was suspended behind a transparent plexi lid, unconscious. He was curled in a loose fetal position, wearing a skin-tight neoprene body suit. A black tube connected his face mask to a neat row of air tanks secured to the inner wall of the tank. His left arm had been severed at mid-forearm, and a thick scar sealed the wound in a precise line. Clean work, Jeff thought. The colony would miss Dr. Leera James after she was gone, he was sure. Doubtless they would need her medical skills more than ever in the coming months with whatever Kellan had planned.

Maybe I can do something about that, Jeff thought.

He tapped the tank's control panel and white condensed air *hisssssed* from a row of vents near the floor. The tank lid hinged open, releasing a stinging aroma of rubbing alcohol and iodine. Jeff waited a long moment, but Kellan didn't stir. He reached into the thick pink hypergel and yanked off the man's face mask.

Kellan's eyes bolted open and his body contracted as if he'd been shocked. He grabbed the top lip of the tank with his remaining arm and pulled himself up out of the gel, gagging. Thick glops of it matted down his short hair and clung to his small mustache. He spat a mouthful back into the tank and sucked in his first full breath as he rubbed gel from his eyes with his hand. His left stump waggled uselessly, mimicking the motions of his right arm. He glanced down at it and froze. The tank hummed quietly.

"It doesn't hurt," he whispered to himself, his voice raspy after his time in the tank.

"It will," Jeff assured him. He sat on the edge of a metal table and crossed his arms.

Kellan's eyes found Jeff in the dark, seeing him for the first time. Recognition flashed across his face, and then resignation. "I was wondering who they'd send. Does Trager want me brought back dead or alive?"

"I don't know if you matter enough for either," said Jeff.

Kellan tried to stand but Jeff put a firm hand on his shoulder and pushed him back down. With a heavy sigh, Kellan settled back against the wall of the tank, squishing in the gel.

"You saw the new Rip?" he asked.

"Hard to miss."

Jeff had admired its alien beauty as he walked through the woods, toward the colony. Amorphous twin nebulae adorned the night sky to the west, but they now shared the firmament with a new arrival. The Rip Kellan had opened appeared as a black eye ringed with purple and green aurorae, glowing brightly amongst the ancient stars.

"Where's the other end?" asked Jeff.

Kellan allowed a small grin. "Wouldn't Trager like to know? It will shave off a healthy chunk of travel time. People will be able to zip back and forth between Earth as if this was another moon city."

"That will never happen," said Jeff.

"And why is that?"

"There's something in the ground."

Kellan snorted amusement. "Cave worms?

Hardly a threat to a few trigger-happy grunts."

"How much hypermass is still on your ship?" Jeff asked.

Kellan laughed, his throat dry and cracking. "The worms aren't *that* dangerous," he said. "Certainly not worth blowing up half the continent to clear them out."

"There's something else," Jeff said quietly. "Something deeper."

Kellan's laughter faltered as he warily met Jeff's eye. The faint light shining deep within Jeff's pupil seemed to unnerve him. He swallowed hard, and grimaced from the pain.

"Yes, well. That's not my problem. Whatever it is, I'm sure you'll figure out how to handle it. You are the Envoy, after all."

He stood up, the gel squelching around his legs. Jeff grabbed his throat and shoved him back down into the pink goop, submerging his head. He waited a long moment while Kellan tried to twist out of his grasp, the stump of his left arm making small circles in the goop. The gel's high viscosity made it impossible to move quickly.

Jeff released him and Kellan emerged, sputtering and coughing. After he rubbed the pink gel from his eyes a second time, he looked at Jeff more carefully than he had before.

"I need your help, and you need mine," Jeff explained. "If you ignore me, I'll make sure that no more shipments will make it to Galena. No supplies, no reinforcements. When I find the other end of the new Rip, I'll post sentry ships on both sides so no one can get through. Your dream dies."

"You don't have that authority."

"You know I do. My mandate is the safeguarding of Earth and its people." *And, most importantly, the Weaver,* he added silently. "Do you think Trager and the people pulling his strings would deny me a few warships if I told them what I found on Galena?"

He waited while the puzzle pieces shifted in Kellan's mind, watching the man's face as he tried to fit them all together.

"What did you find?" Kellan asked at last.

"Something that needs to be destroyed."

"Tell me." Kellan's face was alive with curiosity.

Jeff dealt him the greatest insult he could think of when he said, "Never."

Kellan clenched his jaw, his nostrils flaring in anger. Finally, he took a breath and collected himself, a wry smile playing across his lips.

"Why not go to Trager instead of me? You said yourself you could get anything you needed from him." He clicked his tongue and smiled. "Ahhh...unless they wouldn't *want* it destroyed. They'd want to keep it." He shook his head. "What a tangled web you weave. And what do *I* get?"

"You get to keep breathing."

Kellan went still. "You're bluffing."

Jeff placed his hand firmly on Kellan's shoulder and shoved down, sinking the man into the gel again.

"Alright!" Kellan gasped in a panic. He pushed Jeff's hand away. "Alright. But I used all the hypermass to open the Rip."

"Bring it to me on the next shipment," Jeff told him. *While I figure out another way to kill it,* he thought.

Kellan smirked. His eyes glinted with some secret knowledge as he held out a slimy hand dripping with pink gel to shake on it, but Jeff ignored it. He walked to the door, apologizing to the spirit of his deceased wife and to the colonists he'd never met for turning their fates over to a man he neither liked nor trusted.

Is there another way? he wondered. *Have I doomed them all? Who will the government send in Kellan's place?*

Of *course* they would send someone, he knew. Now that a closer Rip had opened, the logistical nightmare of steady supply had become a mere headache.

Ayani would probably tell him that entrusting the colony to a new overseer was a kinder fate than ignoring the alien creature in its underground cathedral. It would do a lot worse to them than Kellan or some other like-minded cancer ever could if it escaped.

Yet, Jeff had been alive a lot longer than she had, and few things scared him more than a person who had a mind to govern others.

Shake hands with one devil to keep the other at bay, he thought grimly as he stepped out under the stars. The new Rip shimmered in the night sky. He stared at it a long time, contemplating going back into the hospital and holding Kellan under the gel until he stopped moving.

For Farah, he thought, his heart aching deeply from her absence.

The urge passed, and Jeff blended into the forest shadows as he walked back to his ship.

EPILOGUE

Moonlight beamed into the open mouth of the river cave, dancing off the white foam of rushing water. Gavin squatted at the river's edge, checking to make sure he wasn't being followed. There had been a wedding celebration that night. Most of the colonists stayed up too late and drank too much of Skip's homemade vodka, including his father. Gavin had been able to slip out of their home without disturbing his heavy sleep.

The beam of his flashlight flicked on and swiped across the inner mouth of the cave. Black rock glistened and dripped. Gavin located the dark hollow along the right edge and entered the cave.

There was no sandy shore to follow, just a rock ledge barely wide enough for the toes of Gavin's boots. He pocketed his flashlight and pressed his stomach to the slick rocks as he shuffled deeper into the cave. Icy water splashed his back, soaking through his jacket.

His foot slipped off the ledge and his cheek cracked against the wall. Gavin scraped the rock as he slid down, his foot splashing into the rushing river. He managed to grab hold of a protruding rock before he could fall back into the water.

Gavin licked the inside of his cheek and tasted blood.

That's going to be fun to explain, he thought as he regained his footing.

His left hand found a void. He scrambled around the corner of the opening and tripped. Fortunately for his face, he managed to get his hands up in time to break his fall before he tumbled down the descending passage.

Shaking from the cold, he made his slow way down the dark tunnel, using the broken rocks from an ancient cave-in as a staircase. At the bottom of the descending passage, water cascaded down from an opening near the ceiling and plunged into a black pool.

He continued on, leaving the waterfall cavern behind and entering the smooth connecting tunnel which led to the cathedral. Purple light from large, faceted crystals embedded in the rock walls painted his dripping clothes as he emerged into the massive vaulted chamber.

On the central platform, the creature waited — a malignant tumor in the otherwise beautiful cavern.

Purple light shone through a translucent black membrane, sheathed in fibrous tissue like a half-grown lung. The giant sac pulsed and shuddered. A constant thrumming drone filled the cavern.

Blood pumping, Gavin thought, remembering when Leera let him listen to the sound of his own heartbeat with her stethoscope.

He swallowed hard and approached the central platform. The creature went still, and a silence fell over the cavern — heavy and deliberate.

Beyond the black translucent sac, clutches of thin translucent filaments caressed the inside of the membrane, dancing in viscous fluid.

Gavin felt a strong urge to place his palm against the membrane.

Is it true? he signed, wondering if the creature could see his motions. *What you showed me before, is it true?*

He hadn't been able to forget the nightmare vision that had flooded his mind the first time he visited the cathedral. The colonists were in chains, subjugated by an occupying military presence.

And Shurri...Shurri had looked like a ghost.

There was no answer from the creature. Thick tangles of filaments undulated behind its membrane.

Gavin climbed up on the slippery platform to stand ankle-deep in a reeking mound of wet, black fibrous tissue. He put his open palm against the warm membrane and closed his eyes.

Show me the future of this colony, he silently told the creature.

...and it did.

BOOK THREE is available for purchase here:

https://mybook.to/galena

<u>More Books by Samuel Best:</u>

The INFINITE SKY Universe

Titan Chronicles

Mission One
Deep Black
Last Contact

Galena Chronicles

Another World
Third Colony
Galena

Pantheon

Forthcoming

You can find more info on the author's website
https://sam-best.com

About the Author

Born in Cape Canaveral, Florida, Samuel grew up a mile from the gates of Kennedy Space Center. His grandmother built space shuttles, his father designed scientific equipment that flew on them, and Samuel watched the launches from his rattling front porch, dreaming of the stars.

His best-selling novel Mission One, a near-future first contact odyssey, is the book that launched his career as a science fiction writer.

He recently spent three years traveling the world with his wife. They welcomed their son near the end of that journey and are now spending their days exploring the United States while Samuel works on his next book.

Printed in Great Britain
by Amazon

37172399R00172